Joseph Alonzo Stuart

My Roving Life - A Diary of Travels and Adventures by Sea and

Land...

Volume II

Joseph Alonzo Stuart

My Roving Life - A Diary of Travels and Adventures by Sea and Land...
Volume II

ISBN/EAN: 9783337231798

Printed in Europe, USA, Canada, Australia, Japan

Cover: Foto ©Raphael Reischuk / pixelio.de

More available books at **www.hansebooks.com**

MY ROVING LIFE.

---o---

A DIARY OF

TRAVELS AND ADVENTURES BY SEA AND LAND,

DURING PEACE AND WAR.

---o---

BY JOSEPH A. STUART.

ILLUSTRATED BY PHOTOGRAPHS OF ORIGINAL SKETCHES
AND OF PLACES VISITED.

VOLUME II.

IN THE U. S. NAVY THROUGH THE REBELLION
AND AFTER.

AUBURN, CAL.

1895.

To my Children and Theirs This Account of

MY ROVING LIFE

Is Dedicated.

JOSEPH A. STUART.

PREFACE.

This account of the roving portion of my life is the result of a desire on the part of each of my children to possess a copy of my diaries kept during my wanderings. When I concluded at the age of sixty-six years to put my diary into type I thought I would preface it with a few pages of my ancestral record. That record, after three years of search, filled nearly two-hundred pages, which I put into a separate work on " *The Duncan Stuart Family; Our Branch and Its Connections.*" In that I gave a short account of other portions of my life, reserving to these volumes an account of my roamings. The typography and press-work have been my own work (except the press-work of the half-tones, as my little 4x6 press had not the requisite strength for a half-tone impression.) Now that the work is finished I am past seventy years old, and I trust that the typography will meet lenient criticism from the reader on that score. Trusting that my mistakes in life may be avoided by my descendants I present this record to them with my love.

JOSEPH A. STUART.

Auburn, California, February 14, 1896.

VOLUME II.

MY ROVING LIFE.

————o————

BY JOSEPH A. STUART.

——o——

CHAPTER I.

Dracut, Mass., Thursday, Aug. 25, 1864. I can stand it no longer. Abraham Lincoln has called for 500,000 more men, and the bounties are now extended to seamen also. Anne has repeatedly said she would be willing to have me go into the navy whenever bounties were offered to seamen. That has at last been done and I now feel that I can do my duty to my Country without entailing absolute suffering on those dependent upon me. At a special town-meeting held last week to devise means for filling her quota of 41 men without drafting I offered to start the list of volunteers on an assurance of a full bounty of $1000 and State Aid to my family of $12 a month, and was accepted.

U. S. S. Ohio, Charlestown, Mass., Aug. 27, 1864. I am to-day on board my old ship, the *Ohio*, as an Ordinary Seaman for three years. My outfit for uniform, mattress and blankets, amounting to $83 is charged against my wages of $16 per month, out of which 20 cents per month is also to come for a hospital and pension fund. The bounties were understood to be $300 from the United States, $325 from the State, and the Town was to make up the rest. The $375 which the Town was to furnish was deposited with the ship's Paymaster to my credit during my examination for enlistment, but after signing papers to serve in the regular navy I find that the State of Massachusetts discriminates against her seafaring sons in the way of bounty, allowing reports to be circulated in the newspapers without contradiction that the same bounty of $325 offered to soldiers on her quota would be paid to those entering the regular navy on her quota. Three-years-men could obtain vouchers for only $100 instead of $325 notwithstanding the State receives the same credit for a seaman as for a soldier. Another unjust and impolitic discrimination is practised by the United States in the fact that a green hand entering the army is paid $16 *and clothes*, while a sailor having had at least three years of sea training to obtain a rating of ordinary seaman has to give nearly a year's war service in order to work out of debt to the Government for outfit and the year's clothing. This discrimination is accentuated by comparing the case of the green hand entering the navy at the nominal rate of $14, (less 20 cents hospital fee.) The United States cannot expect the service to be popular with native born seamen under such treatment. We are all greatly incensed, and if again free neither State nor Nation would get our services.

Tuesday, Sept. 6, 1864. I am drafted for the West Gulf Squadron under Farragut. We expect to go on board the *Connecticut* tomorrow for passage. We have nearly 3000 "recruits" on board besides the regular ship's company.— Thieving and robbery are rife on board and we are glad we are so soon to get into a sea-going vessel. I had sent $365 of my town and $100 first installment of Government bounty home by Dracut's agent, reserving only $5 for my own use after paying out the rest for some incidental expenses. I succeeded in keeping that till last night. It was missing this morning with my postage stamps and gold pen. The ship's galley had become unequal to the demands upon it and is being replaced by another of special size. In the meantime we are forced to subsist on hardbread and water or patronize the cake stands. Tired of this prison fare I bought a pot of hot coffee yesterday and was spotted as to where I kept my money. They cleaned me out.

Wednesday, Sept. 7, 1864. The *Connecticut* took 100 men from us to fill her complement yesterday and we thought we were rid of that number, but the *Massasoit* hauled into the dry dock and sent her whole crew of 220 men aboard us. We had already received 100 men by a tug from Portland and Portsmouth early in the morning and were feeling quite crowded. Our draft was to have gone on board the *Connecticut* to-day, but on getting up steam a leak was found in her boilers requiring patching and we are detained on board.

Thursday, Sept. 8. Our drafts of recruits for the Atlantic and two Gulf Squadrons were sent on board the *Connecticut* early in the forenoon and we sailed at 3 P. M. Last evening during muster I met with quite an accident. After answering to my name and walking forward, but before we were piped down, a drunken fellow at target firing managed to put an air-gun point into my right ear, felling me to the deck. I was helped below to the sick-bay, where the man in charge stopped the bleeding, gave me a dose of salts and told me to report again at 9 A. M. At that time our drafts were being mustered on the quarter deck with our bags and hammocks for transfer to the *Connecticut* and I was too anxious to get out of a ship where I could be robbed and shot with impunity to care to remain and preferred to wait until I got on board a sea-going vessel before going to a doctor.

Sunday, Sept. 11. It is so warm that I find three flannels uncomfortable during the day. A large steamer hove in sight heading across our bows and created quite an excitement till near enough to show her colors, when she proved to be a Yankee cruiser. We exchanged numbers with her and dipped ensigns in salute, she then wore round and returned to her cruising ground. At 5 P. M. we met a gunboat on her way north. A shark has been following us, keeping close under our counter. The sea is rough and the wind is still ahead.

Monday, Sept. 12, 1864. At midnight last night we were treated to a sudden, heavy shower. The ship's company sleep below, but the recruits spread their bedding upon the quarter deck and hurricane deck under awnings, occupying the whole space except narrow strips from the officers' hatch to the hurricane deck and to the pilot-house. I lashed up my hammock and lay down upon it on a prostrate ladder till the decks were dried off, then opened out and slept till the call of "All Hands!" "Up all hammocks!" warned us to stow *our* hammocks in a huge pile 'chock aft' under guard. Hammocks of the crew were stowed in the hammock-nettings upon each side of the ship, but everything connected with the recruits was kept separate as much as possible. This forenoon a school of porpoise and one of flying-fish played about our bows. The wind, which has been ahead until now, is nearly abeam and we have all sail set. The crew were exercised at quarters handling the 'big guns', and they are big compared with those we had twenty years ago. I thought I knew the drill but found the commands radically different and greatly simplified, though I could have taken any place at a broadside smoothbore if an occasion required it. The exercise did not seem much like play, the beads of sweat on the brows of the gun's crew showing there was work in it.

Tuesday, Sept. 13. Hilton Head light hove in sight at 1 A. M. and at daylight we steamed in and came to an anchor just inside the *New Hampshire*, of seventyfour guns, at Port Royal, S. C. anchorage at 8:30 A. M. We sent 175 men on loard that ship at once for the South Atlantic Squadron.

Wednesday, Sept 14, 1864. The *Pawnee* came in from Charlestown yesterday and is coaling up to go to sea again. A collier came alongside us last night and we were set at work by squadrons carrying coal in baskets, our squadron having the mid watch.

Thursday, Sept. 15. We run up our anchor by the deck tackles with the full force of 600 men and left Port Royal at 10 A. M. A monitor in tow of a black gunboat came in as we were going out. We had the usual allowance of canned fresh beef boiled at dinner with maggots and weevils in the hardbread; fresh meat again at supper, preserved alive in the bread. We cooked to suit ourselves in or over our pots of hot tea. In the latter case there was considerable loss of weight, the fresh meat deserting rather than be treated to a vapor bath. One would suppose that sailors risking life and limb in the service of their country might be satisfied without meat three times a day, but our good uncle does things up brown and through his contractors furnishes meat as a part of the bread ration. (Probably from some returned long-voyage vessel and worked in by some contractor.)

Friday, Sept. 16. The sea is almost as smooth as glass. In the afternoon the crew exercised at the guns again. One half their number are green hands just from the *Ohio*, but are getting initiated in the mysteries and miseries of exercise with these masses of iron weighing 4 1-2 tons without the carriage, going through the various evolutions of running in, loading, running out, and firing some 75 to 80 times during the hour usually allotted to a drill at quarters. This is done "upon the jump," and as they leave their quarters at "beat the retreat" there is some wiping of brows and a few growls

from the old hands at the long continuance of the fun. It
was necessary however that the new hands should become as
perfect as they, and we recruits enjoyed watching them.—
We were especially amused when one fellow in his eagerness
to man the train tackle stumbled over the handspike and the
Officer of the Division orderd " Man wounded in the leg ! "
"Apply your tourniquet and take him below to have that
lubberly leg amputated ;" "Stop vent and sponge !" "Take
him down head first–do you want that leg to bleed to death?"
"Load !" The exercise went on without interruption and the
three men soon returned with the lubberly leg cured and took
their places again.

Saturday, Sept. 17, 1854. At 6 A. M. two sail east of us
are steering north under a press of steam, the foremost one
emitting dense clouds of black smoke, while the other's light
blue stream was perceptib'y gaining, promising prize money
for her crew. Blockade running is getting to be too risky
for profit to the runner, the "running" is too often from our
cruisers. Land, or trees rather, about five miles west of us
shows that the carrier of the blood-red flag needed only a few
hours more of darkness to have made his venture a success.
On examining my clothing yesterday I found vermin. To
get rid of them I washed out my flannels and gave them all
a thorough roasting against the smokestack before daylight.
When we get into our own ships we will all get a thorough
purification and the persistent breeders will get detected by
their messmates, reported to the officers, shaved, scrubbed
severely with soap and sand, and then made to do the dirty
work of the ship for a month, keeping at the same time in
condition fit for inspection at 9 A. M. quarters. This takes
out of them all laziness; for they have to exert themselves
from the time hammocks are piped up to do this extra work
and get their own "bright-work" ready for inspection. The

forenoon was quite hot, with a leading wind, but before noon it had become squally with rain, giving some discomfort to us in our crowded and exposed condition. A small schooner is making in toward the land which is five miles distant and appears to be in a hurry to get there by the way she carries sail during the squalls. We are up with Cape Florida. At night the officer of the deck brought me a tarpaulin to cover my hammock.

Sunday, Sept. 18, 1864. We made Key West light at 1 A. M., Sandy Key light soon after, and anchored off Key West at 6 A. M. While entering we enjoyed looking down through the clear water and watching the motions of the fish at the bottom. The channels between the ridges of coral are distinctly traceable by the contrast in color of the water under the sun's rays, but only a person familiar with the locality could tell which channel led to the goal. The pilot tells us that the *Magnolia* brought in the *Matagorda* last night as a prize with 850 bales of cotton on board. None of the East Gulf Squadron being here we got under weigh at 11 A. M. We saw a propeller outside steaming to the westward and could have overhauled her, but our orders are to not deviate from our course while the drafts are on board. I think we went in her direction as long as we dared, for the Tortugas were in sight when our course was changed to the north.

Tuesday Sept. 20. We anchored at Tampa Bay at 9 A. M. The steamers inside all came down to the mouth of the bay where we anchored and received their quotas. One of the four was an old ferry boat. At 5 P. M. we up anchor with a rush as our next port was to be Mobile Bay.

Wednesday, Sept. 21. It is cooler this morning. At 11 o'clock the shipping in Mobile Bay was in sight and we fired a gun and hoisted our number to announce our name and soon after we fired another gun and hoisted the signal for a pilot. Off Ft. Gaines the smokestack of the monitor *Tecumseh*, sunk by a torpedo while passing the forts was to be seen. Fort Morgan was almost a mass of ruins. From the sea it does not show how severely it had been handled. The shattered and perforated walls of the lighthouse drew our attention as we approached, the wall in one place being gone for nearly half its circuit. The whole point about the lighthouse was scattered with charred timbers and other wreckage. Our land forces were encamped on the Point. Their white tents and baggage train were a pleasant sight to us. A salute was being fired by Ft. Gaines. probably in honor of our victories at Atlanta. We stood in close under the stern of the *Hartford*, flagship of Admiral Farragut, and cheered her as we passed, then anchored a short distance from her at a little after 1 P. M. A draft of 30 men was distributed to ships lying here. A view of Fort Morgan from our anchorage shows a slope of earth furrowed and upheaved out of all semblance to regularity, while an occasional small patch of the original grassy surface accentuates the ruin. The buildings were almost entirely demolished.

Thursday, Sept. 22, 1864. We got under weigh at 6 A. M. for Pensacola. It commenced to rain just after we got our hammocks last night and we stood holding them in our hands an hour hoping the rain would cease and give us a dry deck to spread them on. We were then ordered to spread them upon the berth deck. The air below was hot and foul and I was glad to find a dry spot under the hurricane deck where I could bunk down and breathe pure air. We came to anchor at the Pensacola Navy Yard at noon. Ft. McRae and the navy yard are greatly injured, the splendid dry dock filled with rubbish, its gates demolished and its steam pumps removed or destroyed. In contrast stands Ft. Pickens, grim

and defiant, ready for instant action. At 3 P. M. we were
transferred to the frigate Potomac, receiving-ship of this
station. Here we still have to spread our mattresses on the
upper or spar deck with only a "housed" awning (the outer
edges lowered to resemble the roof of a house) for a shelter
from the rain.

Saturday, Sept. 24, 1864. My little Freddie is four years
old to-day and I long to see him. The dazzling-white beach
and strange trees have a pleasant but tantalizing appearance
to us who cannot get ashore. Regular navy discipline is
enforced here, for which we are thankful. Still I am anxious to get into my own ship where I can have the privileges
and cleanliness there found. Here we are only "recruits"
to be watched and disposed of in the easiest possible way.

Sunday, Oct. 2. Twenty years ago to-day I came into
Norfolk, Va. in the old Cyane from a cruise in the Pacific,
little thinking I should ever re-enter the service, especially
in support of the Government against some of my former
officers. I am drafted for the "double-ender" Port Royal,
Lt. Commander Gherardi, commanding. The double-enders
have both ends bow-like—each end supplied with a rudder
to enable them to navigate narrow rivers without turning.—
The Port Royal is stationed at Mobile Bay and we are to be
sent to her on a tug tomorrow. My ear has been troubling
me so much at times ever since I got hurt that I have had to
go to the doctors for relief from the pain. At each time a
blister behind the ear has rendered it hard to tell whether
the pain came from inside or outside the skull, for the blisters have had no "orders" to come off.

Monday, Oct. 3. We were sent on board the tug at 7 P.
M. and started at 11 P. M. We were wedged like beasts
on top of a deck load and got neither hammocks nor sleep.

Tuesday, Oct. 4. We arrived at Mobile Bay at 7 A. M.

I found my clothes-bag ripped open and my best suit stolen. My "ditty box," containing my sewing implements and the pictures of my family, had been broken into and the things not taken were strewed about the deck. Our things were in a pile where only the tug's crew could get at them, yet no investigation was attempted. Others were in the same predicament. I am glad to get on my own ship at last, where such things will cease.

Wednesday, Oct. 5, 1864. I find the *Port Royal* a small vessel of only 705 tons and very light draft; yet she has a heavy battery of eight guns—two IX-inch smooth-bore (100 pounders,) in broadside; one X-inch smooth-bore, (150-pounder,) on a pivot carriage aft; one VI-inch rifle, (100-pounder,) on a pivot carriage forward; two V-inch rifles, (60-pounders,) in broadside forward; and two 24-pounder brass howitzers. Last night was rainy and the berth deck hot and stifling. I consequently rose with a severe headache, but had to help at holystoning the decks for two hours before breakfast. We are to coal ship tomorrow and this would seem to be the refinement of unnecessary labor, but it is only by such means that we can keep the ship free of pests of all kinds.

Thursday, Oct. 6. "Scrub and wash clothes!" was the order passed after hammocks were stowed this morning. In washing clothes two or more messmates will chum in the use of a bucket and after the decks are wet down each one will spread his piece upon the deck, rub it thoroughly with a generous coating of soap and then scrub it with a brush on inside and outside. Rinsing is done either in the bucket or under the deck force pump. During the whole process the deck is awash with soapsuds and the men barefooted and with trowsers rolled high up kneel at their scrubbing. The beneficial effect of this mode is two-fold. Not only do the

clothes get a sopping and scrubbing that dislodges unwelcome
intruders, but the deck and bulwarks receive a good clean
washing afterward. After breakfast we commenced to coal
ship and finished at 6 : 30, then scrubbed the decks with sand
before lowering our clothes-lines. I stood my first anchor-
watch from 10 to 12 P. M.

Friday, Oct. 7, 1864. We spent the forenoon "cleaning
ship." The *Selma* came in from New Orleans. She was
taken at the battle of Mobile Bay. There is constant signaling between the Admiral and Army and we seem to have
a share in it.

Saturday, Oct. 8. A stiff "norther" commenced at midnight and at 3 A M. we had to let go another anchor and
pay out to 45 fathoms of chain. The barque *Alamo*, of
New York, went ashore and being light was left high up on
the southeastern beach inside the bay. The tug *Buckthorn*
buried her bows at every sea as she came in this morning
from Pensacola. She brought us some provisions. I drew
another pair of pants at a cost of $9.11 on a special requi-
sition to replace those stolen. The monitor *Manhattan* is
swept by every sea, but emerges "smiling in the Storm King's
face." Her crew have taken refuge in a scow towed astern
but are getting considerably shaken up by its tossing. The
gale will probably clear the land of any yellow fever.

Sunday, Oct. 9. The gale has abated but it is still cold.
We performed the usual Sunday's holystoning of the deck.
A gritty stone five inches thick, and having a flat under surface of about 10 x 15 inches, bound with a rope and ropes at
the narrow sides to drag it by, is hauled back and forth with a
see-saw motion over the wet and sanded deck till the whole
surface has been scoured. The custom of always using it
on Sunday has given it the name of holy-stone. All places
that cannot be reached with it are scoured with similar stones

about the size of the Book of Common Prayer, and from being used in a kneeling position they have been dubbed "prayer-books" by sailors.

Monday, Oct. 10, 1864. All hands scrubbed hammocks and the recruits scrubbed their blankets. The *Sebago* came down from Dog River Bar, nine miles from Mobile, with an officer and two men killed and three men wounded in a fight with a battery, she getting aground while on picket in the channel abreast of the battery during the night. The *Monongahela*, Capt. Wm. E. Leroy, one of my officers on the *Erie* and the *Cyane* of long ago went to sea at 11 A. M.— We are taking stores from the *Buckthorn*. The store steamer *Bermuda*, formerly a blockade runner, came into port this morning and the messes were allowed to send aboard to buy fresh stores.

Tuesday, Oct. 11. The *Metacomet* came down the bay from the front this forenoon. I heard at noon that the 2nd Maine Cavalry was at Fort Morgan and wrote to brother Louis who is Surgeon in it. The letter went on board the flagship to be forwarded.

Wednesday, Oct. 12. The *Pinola* came down the bay last night. We exercised at the big guns in the morning and our Division with Sharp's rifles in bayonet drill in the afternoon.

Thursday, Oct. 13. We got under weigh at 8 A. M. for the front, reached the fleet at noon but did not come to anchor till 2 : 30. We fitted boarding nettings and were called to fire quarters in the afternoon. At 5 : 30 we up anchor to go on picket, anchoring in the western channel below some obstructions placed by the rebels across the main channel. Others of the fleet took stations to prevent any vessel either leaving or entering Mobile. The *Octorora* started down the bay soon after we arrived, we being her relief. At midnight the alarm rattle on the berth deck was sprung for quarters and we exercised at the big guns a short time, with other maneuvers interjected, as might occur during a sudden night attack upon us.

Friday, Oct. 14, 1864. When hammocks were called this morning we found the ship at her old anchorage. The *Sebago* was aground again under the eastern shore. The *Metacomet* and the Mississippi double-turret monitor *Winnebago* – were at their old moorings but went with us to support the *Sebago* and tow her off if necessary. She got off by her own exertions and unmolested. The rebels are burning off a piece of woods in the range of a new battery (Spanish Fort) upon a hill on the eastern shore at the head of the Appalache channel. One of the rebel floating batteries close to Mobile is trying its range with shot and shell, but they do not reach half-way to us.

Sunday, Oct. 16. A flag of truce that had been flying a short time was hauled down with the firing of a gun from the rebel gunboat *Morgan*. It is misty and cool. Picket duty at night as usual.

Monday, Oct. 17. Another flag of truce from the rebels, and after it closed several shots from the *Morgan's* guns that did not come anywhere near us. It is cloudy and cold.

Tuesday, Oct. 18. Last night the petty officers came to me to be "steady cook" to their mess, I to be allowed 37.5 cents of ration money per day for the extra labor. This is duty excusing me from deck duty by day except for drills and when all hands are called for any special duty. I had taken my week's turn at cooking for my own mess and they had seen my work. I accepted. Last night a small boat with a single person in it was seen rowing for the ship, but on getting into the current it was swept down the bay. I was one of eight sent in a boat to pick him up. In the haste to get us off no signals had been agreed upon to guide us and

we failed to locate him and on our return to the ship learned
we had not gone within half-a-mile of him. We found hard
rowing in the teeth of the gale on our return.

Wednesday, Oct. 19, 1864. There was an alarm at midnight that a rebel gunboat was coming down. We got to
quarters so speedily, our battery "cast loose and provided"
that the captain praised us. One unlucky fellow of our gun's
crew, a ward room waiter, let his pistol go off. The captain
was forward inspecting the readiness of each individual and
came rushing aft to know if anyone was hurt. Finding no
one hurt and only the unlucky waiter scared he burst out :-
" Oh, you blunderbuss !"   " Oh, you lubber !"   " Who
ordered you to fire?" His pistol was taken from him and
his station changed. This morning the captain explained
to us the principle of a shell and the manner of handling one.
Our ship has not been repaired during its thirty months of
continuous active service. Our boilers leak so under steam
pressure that the pumps are started every half-hour when we
are under weigh. It is thought she will go to New Orleans
for general repairs very soon.

Friday, Oct. 21. Three refugees came off in a boat of
their own manufacture. They pushed boldly out into the
stream and the night being dark used the rebel campfires to
guide them and trusted to luck to reach some of our vessels.
Their boat was nearly full of water when they reached us.
They came near detection by a cavalry patrol stationed along
the beach to prevent refugees putting off to us. They give
doleful accounts of rebel life.

Monday, Oct. 24, 1864. The *Selma* went down the bay
a short distance for target practice with some new sights to
her guns. Upon hearing the firing the Mississippi monitor
Chickasaw and the little dispatch boat *Cowslip* were sent up
to us, the former to our assistance if needed, the latter to

return with a report of the cause of the firing. These Mississippi monitors differ somewhat from those of the Atlantic seaboard in that their decks are more convex to secure headroom below with a light draft to the vessel. They are so short and broad and the decks so convex that they are called "Mud-Turtles" by the sailors. They are being fitted with great, many pronged forks called "torpedo rakes" that may be lowered in front of them to catch any torpedos the rebels are said to be sending down the current of Appalache Channel, which has not been obstructed by piles as has been the western or main channel. I give here a home-made cut of

A MISSISSIPPI-RIVER MONITOR,

or "Mud Turtle,"

with her rake raised as when not needed. These monitors are our main dependence in serious work as they are impervious to anything the rebels have.

Wednesday, Nov. 2. Last Sunday I had a very severe pain in my head. It was rainy, the men took refuge on the berth deck and there was such a continual noise that it made me almost crazy. The doctor ordered me into my hammock and gave me a sleeping potion. I was unfit for duty all of the next day. Last night five men of the crew of a one-gun battery stole a boat and came off to us after we had returned to our station in the morning. They were within 200 yards of us at one time during the night but feared to approach or hail. In the morning they had drifted five miles away. We saw them a mere speck as we were coming to anchor and an armed boat was sent to investigate. They were the second set of five to come off from that gun's crew in the same boat. It had been set adrift after the first five came off. It had been picked up by its former owners and has again been used to reach our lines. We set it adrift now hoping the remaining five of the gun's crew may bring their officer the next time. The others were to have come off at this time but their officer remained awake sitting at the fire too near to where they lay asleep and these did not dare try to rouse them. The shore is lined with small batteries but they are very scantily manned, they tell us. They repeated the story of a torpedo boat nearly ready to come out to attack us. Forewarned we are forearmed, and as the moon will soon give us light they will find it hard to catch us napping and will not be likely to try except during dark, rainy nights. At such times we take extra precautions. The watch on deck is held with sidearms at the big guns, and armed boats with their crews sitting in their places are held alongside the ship ready to shove off in chase at the first warning of a cigar-shaped thing. When we reached our anchorage in the morning we found the *Metacomet* had sent a boat a long way down the bay inshore for another refugee boat. They were getting dangerously near a rebel battery and our ship was ordered to up anchor and go to their rescue. The refugees were contrabands, three men, a woman, and a child. We towed them to the anchorage and they went on board the *Metacomet* in her boat, that ship flying the senior officer's flag under Lt. Commander Jouett. When the tide turned we set that boat adrift to benefit the next party wishing to pay us a visit. This is the third day of rain and of armed lookouts on gratings slung over the sides of the ship just above the water's edge to give notice of the approach of the long expected torpedo boat. It was my turn from 12 to 2, but I had not been on lookout over fifteen minutes when the officer of the watch brought a man to take my place as punishment for missing his muster when the watch was called. Last Monday one of the steerage officers came to me offering me the rating of steerage steward, they not being satisfied as to the honesty of the present one. That would make me a petty officer and what is called an "idler" from having no deck duty or watch at night. It would give me $20 a month of wages and $7.50 of ration. My present receipts are $27.25 a month and in cooking for the men I do not feel as a servant. I told him I disliked to take the man's position from him if he could be induced to do better. When the man learned of their intention he was penitent and they retained him.

-*Thursday, Nov. 3, 1864.* A short time before 4 A. M. an alarm was given that the torpedo boat was coming down upon us. We slipped our cable and the watch cast loose our battery while the watch below were rallying to quarters.— We saw no more of it, whatever it was, although we were at our station for some time after daylight getting our anchor.

Friday, Nov. 4. This morning six stout contrabands, all brickmakers, came aboard from a sailboat which they stole two miles from shore and carried to the water. They had a musket and quite a quantity of tobacco with them. We are fitting the sailboat over for a dingey or chore-boat. In the afternoon the *Owasco* came up to relieve us and after supper we went down the bay to the fleet.

Saturday, Nov. 5. We hauled alongside a coal ship and took in coal. We did not finish and will have the cleaning ship to do over again after filling up on Monday.

Saturday, Nov. 12. Last night we came up to the front again. We had been lying at Ft. Morgan for a whole week and our mess has had oyster stew for supper every day, the boys calling it nice, but without milk I could not make it nice to my taste. There was none left for the cook's tidbit at any time, which may have had some influence upon his opinion. Mobile looks very much as it did when we went down the bay and probably will for some time to come. It seems to us as if the policy of our Government were to keep as large a force of rebels here as possible by a show of our navy without any great accompanying land force and thus prevent their reinforcing Hood. While stowing away the capstan bars last night I trod upon a nail that has made me so lame that I was sent below in the morning watch. The little *Cowslip* came up in the forenoon and the *Metacomet* soon after fired a truce gun and sent a boat to meet one from the *Morgan*.

Wednesday, Nov. 16, 1864. I am off the sick list to-day. Our ~~Ten~~ days of enforced quiet and poultices have made me anxious to get about again. Four contrabands came off in a small boat, having run away from a plantation thirty miles above Mobile on the Tombigbee River. They followed the banks of the Tombigbee and Mobile Rivers till nearing the city, then kept around it to Dog River and finding this boat three miles above its mouth packed it around the rebel pickets to a point on the bay where they found no pickets and launched their boat for us and freedom. They reported the roads out from Mobile lined with people last Monday leaving the city under the impression we were about to make a descent upon it. Four white men came off this morning to the *Metacomet* and report that Lincoln is re-elected. This is conceded by them to be a heavy blow to Confederate hopes, they having an idea that if MacClellan had been elected they could have secured peace upon their own terms. A new list of prices for clothing has been posted, making cloth pants (of satinet) $12.38 and other things in proportion, at which rates

a man's pay will hardly clothe him. In place of calling the
watch at midnight the rattle was again sprung for quarters.
This is done to accustom us to taking our stations promptly
and with coolness, for we never know whether the rattle is
for earnest business or only drill. The captain does not trust
the inspection of the men at the guns to the officer but goes
to each man and examines him critically, occasionally asking
a man a question as to his particular duty in certain contin-
gencies and explaining the man's duty if not understood.—
To-night he had gone forward inspecting the men and on his
return was inspecting the officers. We noticed that Ensign
H. of our gun was quite fidgety and saw he was without his
pistol. It was amusing to witness his uneasy movements in
his efforts to hide the emptiness of his holster. We pitied
the man knowing he would get a dressing down before us.
I could not resist the impulse to slyly offer him the pistol from
my belt which he accepted and placing it in his belt returned
to his position before the captain arrived. Being a nervous
man he could not carry out the deception with coolness and
received a thorough inspection from Captain Gherardi, who
felt sure something was wrong with him. Turning to us he
gave each a searching glance but no one showing concern he
passed on. This forenoon Mr. Snair, officer of the pivot
gun near us called me to him and told me never to do that
again, but let every one, officer as well as man, suffer for
his own carelessness. Had it been detected I would have
been severely punished, he said. Mr. H. is a volunteer officer, and is one of the kind that cannot get the "drill" into
his head, so that Mr. Snair has to drill our division with his
at small arms practice, the bayonet and cutlass drills. The
Cowslip came up from The Fort this noon with dispatches.

Sunday, Nov. 20, 1864. For the past three days there
have been frequent flags of truce. A well-dressed man at

first came off to the *Ossorora* to get a pass to see Admiral Farragut. A boat was sent down with him and before night he was up again and has been going and coming ever since. Ostensibly his errand has been to get permission to run a cargo of cotton to New York—a queer request as we are not yet in possession of Mobile. Some think that he and "The Brave Old Salt" have something else to talk about besides cotton, or the dispatch boat would not be placed at his service so readily. Last night was quite foggy with some rain. Two deserters from the rebel gunboat *Morgan* came off to us, just missing capture by hearing the voices of their picket boat's crew. This morning another boat was seen far down the bay with a single man in it and the little *Cowslip* went for him. He had given up trying to stem the current and had taken in his oars to float down to the fleet. Another lot of refugees brought off a Mobile paper with a statement in it that Lincoln's re-election was certain.

Wednesday, Nov. 23, 1864. We have been having a "norther," with freezing weather. Water striking the decks in washing them yesterday and Monday mornings froze at once and we had a jolly time sliding. To make things more uncomfortable to us than usual lookouts had to be doubled at night. The watch on deck were allowed to seek shelter behind their guns but the crews of the picket boats which were kept rowing around the ship at night suffered greatly, being exposed to the force of the gale and drenched to the skin by the waves that half filled the boats at every circuit. I was fortunate in having a grating lookout but suffered exceedingly from wet and cold though partially protected from the wind and rain by the overhanging swell of the ship's quarter; in fact there was little choice of position anywhere. And this is the Sunny South! The wind came up from the south this morning and brought warm weather. Last night we were reinforced by a gunboat, a mail boat, and a tug, so that we have three gunboats, two mail boats, two tugs, and a monitor. Refugees state that 1000 men could take the place any day, showing that our efforts to keep reinforcements from Hood had failed. Eastern papers state that the new battery on the eastern shore had driven our gunboats from that side. This is untrue. The eastern shore is picketed every night by a gunboat just as the western shore is so as to prevent egress or ingress at either channel by blockade-runners, the several picket vessels returning to the general anchorage at daylight where they would be in a position to act promptly in either direction. That battery commands only the upper half of Appalache Channel and a little, very shoal one close to that shore hardly fit to be called a channel and cannot throw a shot more than half way to the bar at the mouth of the channel, below which is our anchorage. This bar and that at Dog River are what prevent our going up to the city with anything but the lightest draft. When the city is taken it will have to be done by the army, and they know it. Our going to New Orleans is set at rest for the present by finding the source of the leak in the boilers, and moreover the *Cowslip* is alongside discharging coal into us as if we could not be spared just now to go down the bay for our coal.

Saturday, Nov. 26, 1864. Yesterday eight or ten sail were in sight from our masthead down the bay close in to the western shore. The *Selma* and *Cowslip* came up last night and this afternoon the Admiral's dispatch boat *Glasgow* and a monitor arrived, so that we have the *Octorora*, *Sebago*, *Kennebec*, *Port Royal*, *Selma*, two monitors, two armed dispatch boats and an armed tug. The rumor is that Sherman is marching upon Mobile, that Canby has landed on the western shore, that they have pontoons for crossing

Dog River. and that an attack on Mobile may be ordered at any moment. (All a feint to call the rebels back from opposing Sherman on his march to the sea which he commenced from Atlanta ten or fifteen days ago according to refugees.)

Monday, Nov. 28, 1864. The little *Cowslip* was attacked by a new rebel battery on the western shore but fairly drove them out with her 30-pdr, Parrott rifle and two 24-pdr. brass howitzers. She would not stand any such foolishness.

Wednesday, Nov. 30, 1864. An army transport came up yesterday and anchored a long distance from the fleet, giving color to the rumor that Sherman was within twenty-five miles of Mobile, but late last night we got under weigh heading down the bay which we would not have done were Sherman coming here. On anchoring we put out the fires, another sign that we would not be needed at the front very soon.-- We were somewhat astonished to find only the *Richmond* of 26 guns at anchor here. Farragut with the *Hartford* had sailed from Pensacola for New York on November 20th. The *Metacomet* is at New Orleans for repairs and the rest are supposed to be on the coast of Texas.

Sunday, Dec. 11. To-day a draft of 22 men was sent to the *Richmond*, the present flagship of the station, now under Commodore Thatcher. We start for New Orleans when the gale now raging abates. Water again froze on our decks and we had to resort to holystoning with dry sand in place of scrubbing with water.

Wednesday, Dec. 14. We arrived at New Orleans at 3 A. M. We left Ft. Morgan on Monday, reached the mouth of the Mississippi at daylight and passed Fts. St. Philip and Jackson about noon yesterday. Just before dark we began to see orange groves yellow with fruit. I had seen no such display since leaving Rio de Janeiro ~~forty~~ twenty years ago. An apple orchard loaded down with fruit is a beautiful, cheering

sight, but the color of the orange is so striking that the eye
is captivated at once. I have had to draw of the Paymaster
more flannels and shoes. Everything received at the time I
shipped, amounting to four months pay is gone entirely, also
several articles since drawn. That is to say, I have served
the Country 3 1-2 months in war time and will have to serve
as many more months to pay for clothing already drawn, by
which time the present stock will be in rags. It is a general
wish that contractors and congressmen might be compelled
to serve with us until the latter were willing to furnish the
seamen in the navy with the same clothing in quantity and
quality that they give to soldiers and marines. It is unjust.

Tuesday, Dec. 20, 1864. We have had our 48 hours of
liberty ashore, commencing Sunday. I spent each day on
shore returning to the ship at sundown to spend the night,
reporting with a request to be allowed to finish my liberty
next day. I visited the famous Custom House and the no
less famous market, strolled through some of the best streets,
and gathered some of the Spanish moss that gives such a
ghostly appearance to the double line of trees in the middle
of Canal Street. The oleanders growing in the open ground
in front of the houses had been badly frosted during the late
northers. Flowers and shrubs in Jackson Square Park or
Garden were in a sad state from the freezes. I signed my
accounts with $21.13 due the United States, my extra duty
pay of $15 for cooking going to pay my debt to Government.
A raw marine recruit with lighter duties and less exposure
doing the same extra duty would have had about $75 due to
him.

Thursday, Dec. 22. All but the petty officers of the ship
were transferred to the *Metacomet.* The carpenters and the
caulkers were still busy about her new deck of oak when we
came aboard. The change had been made to give her more

strength in a seaway; her extreme length and light draft has
made her weak-backed so that she buckled to the seas. As
stores and provisions were to come on board we were set at
work as soon as we could get into our working clothes. We
expect to sail on an outer blockading cruise as soon as the
ship can be gotten ready. Lt. Commander James E. Jouett
is a very energetic officer, and his 1st Lieutenant, Actg.
Vol. Lt. Henry J. Sleeper is a Down East whaler, so we are
sure of taking prizes if energy and hard work can accomplish
such result. Our other officers not including engineers are:

Asst. Surgeon E. D. Payne,   (From Pa.)

Actg. Asst. Paymaster H. M. Harriman.

Acig. Master Clifford C. Gill—wounded in boat attack on
    Battery Tracy on night of April 11-12, 1865; resigned
    a lieutenant June 19, 1882.

Actg. Master Henry C. Nields—Mentioned by Farragut for
    conspicuous bravery at battle of Mobile Bay; died a
    Lt. commander Dec. 13, 1880.

Actg. Ensigns James Brown, Rufus N. Miller.

Actg. Master's Mates J. K. Goodwin, Charles Harcourt.

Actg. Gunner James Laman, (appointed *Aug. 10, 1864.*)

We thus had but one *regular* officer on board, yet there
was no lack of discipline or effective work on the part of the
ship whenever called upon to act.

Sunday, Dec. 25, 1864. The carpenters got through late
last night and we sailed for Mobile Bay to-day with a monitor in tow.

Thursday, Dec. 29. We filled the ship brim-full of coal
on Tuesday. Yesterday was stormy and we put in the day
at cleaning ship. To-day we sailed at 6 A. M.

Friday, Dec. 30. We sighted a steamer burning bitumi-
nous coal, considered by us a sure sign of an English ship
and a blockade-runner, but darkness coming on we lost sight

of her. Our Paymaster was the first to see her and reported her from the masthead. When hailed, "Can you make her out?" he got the joke upon himself by shouting, "She's a prize! She's a Prize! She's burning black coal!" He meant to have said that she made a black smoke. By night it blew fiercely from the southard and during my lookout at the bow in the first watch the ship pitched in a'way to un-load my stomach of its accumulated bile; but in the morning watch I was enabled to retrieve my character as a seaman by being among the foremost to help secure an anchor that had broken adrift and was pounding the bow of the ship most dangerously. Every sea came on board and some of the heavier ones would sweep us off our feet and aft nearly to the break of the hurricane deck. Mr. Gill had to call for volunteers, so many of the forecastlemen of the watch were showing the white feather. Jack Lee, Capt.-o'-the-forecas-tle, and one of his able seamen, John Hudson, stuck to their duty as forecastlemen and took the most dangerous position at the rail, while Capt.-o'-the-Afterguard Collins, and his able seaman Dana, a man small of size but gritty, with the writer assisted Mr. Gill inboard. We got both the anchors on deck at last, relieving the bow of the ship of their weight, so that she rose from her plunges more readily. Our First Lieut., Mr. Sleeper, standing upon the hurricane deck could see the ship squirm like an eel.

Saturday, Dec. 31, 1864. The gale continues to be very severe. We sighted a schooner under close reefs and gave chase, losing sight of her during a heavy squall of rain but afterward caught sight of her under bare poles. When the launch was called away to board her Mr. Gill ordered me into the boat as one of his regular "fighting boat's-crew." In the boat were Lee as coxwain, Hudson, Dana and myself, with three others of our watch upon one side of the boat and six

picked men of the starboard watch sitting upon the thwarts
on the other side.   We were destined to pass through many
rough experiences together and learned to depend upon each
other under all circumstances.   There was not a shirk or a
coward among them.   We took possession of the schooner,
Mr. Gill finding her papers rather too old to be regular.—
She was the *Sea Witch.*

Saturday, Jan. 7, 1865.   We have had a stormy cruise
and have taken only two small prizes, the second one being
the *Lily,* a large scow decked over and schooner rigged.   In
the cruise we went down the coast till sighting the Mexican
shore, then came back to Galveston, or rather outside that
place, it still being in rebel hands.   Here we met the supply
boat *Morgan.*   I sent a letter home containing $6.   (It did
not arrive there.   (A strange fatality befell every money letter I sent while in the service.)   We got some fresh stores
from the *Morgan* and then sailed for Sabine Pass which we
reached to-day.

Wednesday, Jan. 11.   We are at sea again after coaling
ship under great difficulties, the sea being very rough and
we working all hands by day and by watches at night.   Our
ship was moored a short distance from and abreast the coal
schooner.   One watch would go on board her to fill the tubs
and hoist them out of her hold while the other remained on
board the ship to receive the full tubs, empty them into the
wheelbarrows supplied by the collier, and dump them down
the coal scuttles for the engineer's crew to stow away.   The
coal was hoisted and transferred by whips from the mastheads of the two ships.   The whips were joined at the tub
and after a tub was hoisted the whip from the other ship was
hauled upon to draw the tub on board, and the hoisting whip
eased off or lowered at the same time.   This would be all
smooth work in a smooth sea, but when the two ships rolled

away from each other the tub would take a flying leap into the air and then with the reverse roll of the ships would at times take possession of the deck, clearing it of men and wheelbarrows and hold possession till a chance offered for a rush to overpower it. This took time and we made slow progress. Coxwain Jack Lee and I were stationed at the schooner's hatchway to receive the empty tubs as they came back from the ship to be re-filled, and guide them down the hatchway to the tub-fillers below. We did some dodging as well as catching and more than once made a visit with the tub to the hold of the schooner to the surprise of the shovelers standing ready to fill up. In changing the watch one midnight at the height of the gale Lee and I stepped into the bow of the launch as it rose with the sea. We picked up in the stern sheets where we had been thrown by the surge upon the boat as it fell with the sea and the long painter or towline, fastened at the fore chains, suddenly tautened and jerked the boat forward spitefully from under us. At the next surge a contraband came aft in a graceful diving attitude and "landed" between the boat and ship. He would have been crushed or drowned had we not instantly seized him and hauled him into the boat. It was done so quickly that the poor fellow had no idea how he came in the stern sheets under a pile of shipmates whom we had received very much as we had received together the empty tubs for the past four hours. At the next surge we had plenty of help, for it takes a true man-o'-war's-man but a moment to recover his wits on board ship or boat. He gets accustomed to such incidents and his whole training tends to enable him to meet them with coolness and success. Last night Collins and I had a wheel watch from 12 to 2, ready to steer should the ship drag her anchors or snap the cables and break adrift. About one o'clock one of the quarter boats became swamped

and I was sent down with a bucket to bail her out. Being
already full she sank with me to my waist and the officer
began to think with me that it was going to be a tough job,
no less than bailing out the Gulf of Mexico, so he ordered
me out. I came out thoroughly wet and stood 2 1-2 hours
more of watch in my wet clothes. I got so chilled that I
lay awake till all hands were called in the morning. In the
morning after breakfast two men were sent down to try the
feat and one of them, not taking my precaution of a rope
about the body was washed away from the boat but the other
swam to him and both were hauled on board wetter than I
had been. Mr. Sleeper had been watching the work with a
smile in the corner of his eyes and then suggested that perhaps the water would run out of itself if the boat were hooked
to its takles and the bow hoisted first. It was done and the
anchor being aweigh we put to sea. We learn that the *Sea
Witch* had 32-lb. shot for ballast and a lot of powder, while
the *Lily* had quinine, percussion caps, and rifle powder on
board, making them sure prizes. We took the scow in tow
for Southwest Pass to cast her off there for some tug to tow
to New Orleans for condemnation and sale. The wind and
sea went down soon after starting and we had a pleasant
passage. We are bound to Pensacola for repairs and to fill
up to our complement of men.

Friday, Feb. 3, 1865. We have remained at Pensacola
Navy Yard since the middle of January having our forward
deck re-caulked and the copper re-placed and fastened by a
diver. We received a new commander, Capt Crosby. We
coaled up by wheeling it from a pile in the Yard to the coal
scuttles on deck, and to-day we put to sea on another cruise
for blockade-runners. While at Pensacola I sent home a
letter with $10 in it. (The usual fatality attending it.)

Tuesday, Feb. 7. We made the land last night 30 miles

last of Sabine Pass and anchored two miles from the beach. This morning the supply steamer *Bermuda* came in sight and running down to us put aboard fresh meat and vegetables for the men and other stores for the officers. We both then raced to Sabine Pass, we beating them thirty minutes in the thirty miles. She brought us news of the taking of Wilmington.

Wednesday, Feb. 8, 1865. We went to sea last night, but to-day is so rough that we are making for the land. It is understood that we have orders not to push the ship into heavy weather unnecessarily, for we may soon be wanted to cover the landing of troops when the ship will need its full strength to withstand the shock of heavy firing. Moreover we are getting of the opinion that blockade-running is about given up as we have not seen a suspicious vessel since leaving Pensacola. We anchored with the fleet off Galveston in the afternoon and learned they had made a raid inside the forts one night and had cut out two blockade-runners loaded with cotton and just ready to run out. A third was run ashore to the westward of the bay and one of our gunboats was shelling her.

Friday, Feb 10, 1865. We got under weigh at noon in company with the *Bienville* which claims to be the fastest on the station. In the race that ensued we gained at the rate of a mile each hour. We overhauled one of the schooners taken at Galveston and on her way to New Orleans for her condemnation and sale. The weather is fine and warm and the sea smooth, just right for our ship to show her best foot at steaming. In heavy weather the *Bienville* would perhaps leave us astern.

Saturday, Feb. 11. My frequent wettings with salt water and exposure are resulting in boils and salt-water sores. I had to go to the doctor yesterday with a large boil upon my

knee-pan that was giving me much trouble to get about at
my duty. I was put on the sick list and had a poultice put
upon it. To-day it was opened and again poulticed, being
greatly inflamed.

Sunday, Feb. 12, 1865. We are at anchor at New Orleans again. The weather is warm and pleasant. It is the
general opinion that we go to Mobile from here very soon.

Monday, Feb. 13. We are taking in coal and ammunition, as also our broadside guns which had been left here on
going upon the cruise for blockade-runners.

Friday, Feb. 17. We are still at New Orleans but expect
to sail to-night with a monitor in tow. Orders are that no
one be allowed to go ashore. A draft took place at New
Orleans on the 15th and sums as high as $2500 were paid
to substitutes. The boil on my knee came to a head and
burst last night, and I put in some sound sleeping after it.

Sunday, Feb. 19. We arrived at Mobile Bay with a monitor in tow and afterward went to the front.

Sunday, Feb. 26. We have been here a week and nothing
of importance has occurred as the weather has been stormy,
with heavy rains. There are here only the *Metacomet* and
Octorora, both double-enders, the propeller gunboat *Sciota*,
(these three being schooner rigged,) the monitor *Winnebago*,
and the armed tug *Pink*. Last night one of our boats went
up Appalache Channel and in front of the rebel batteries to
sound for the depth of water. They found only seven feet
of water on the bar, which prevents our trying to pass, as
we draw over nine feet. A black smoke is rising down the
bay showing that a monitor is coming up. She evidently is
coming to relieve the *Winnebago* for her to go down to coal
as that monitor is apparently stirring up her banked fires to
start her engines. We are all keeping a sufficient head of
steam to enable us to move at an instant's warning, for it is

learned that the rebels have another torpedo boat ready to come out against us. The first one was intended to run a short distance under water. It is said to have been taken to Charleston and was very effective in sinking herself and *her own crews.* A strict lookout is kept by us to prevent a torpedo boat reaching us. Thirty-seven armed men are on guard in boats and in all parts of the ship, blue-lights ready to ignite and the rest of the watch with side arms on stand at their guns. Under a flag of truce the rebels yesterday sent a lot of packages to their friends, our prisoners at Ship Island. Our boat was sent to meet them and I had a close view of the rebel flag. It is represented below.

THE REBEL FLAG.

The boats met and after a distant salute by the officers they came together, side by side. The boxes and parcels were silently passed into our boat, they shoved off and we returned to our ship, the white flag was hauled down, and we were enemies again.

Sunday, Mar. 5. There have been frequent truce flags flying the past week and last Friday an Army boat came up

with a lot of prisoners for exchange, returning below last
night.   Another monitor came up this morning and the
Octorora went below.   The remaining monitor is stripping
herself of her torpedo rake to go below, so it is not probable
that we intend to attack just yet.   The rebels ought to feel
like the boy told to stop after school to take a whipping, but
perhaps think they can "lick the master" and feel indifferent
about the time of commencement.   Captain Crosby orders
services read every Sabbath, which gives that long respite
from work.   Several of our men crawled ashore on the hawser at New Orleans the night before we were to sail, with the
intention of having one more good time and returning before
daylight.   They overstayed and were brought on board by
the police in response to offered rewards.   They have been
kept in double-irons on bread and water till now.   Yesterday they were court-martialed for desertion.   The Court
did not comply with certain rules and the revising authority
dissolved it and remanded the men to their duty, Captain
Crosby making great show of anger at the Court's failure to
comply, warning the men that for any succeeding offense he
would see to it that the Court proceed regularly.   They had
already "paid the fiddler" pretty roundly for their dance
and were thoroughly frightened.   Our 1st lieutenant is an
energetic man and though he works us hard is inclined to
favor those that he sees are always ready to do their full
duty, and is sure to impose extra duty for any shirking.   In
furling sails the afterguard have the mainsail to furl.   He
had seen me furling it alone several successive times and at
last called me down when I had it half furled, saying that
he would see if he could not make others do a *little* of the
work.   He mustered the afterguard of both watches and each
man, commencing with the captains of each watch, had to
furl the sail in turn and loosen it for the next man to furl,

until every man had performed the duty to his satisfaction. He told them at first why he disciplined them and then sent me forward. The boys took it pleasantly, knowing they deserved it. A new station bill was made out, and to-day we were called to furl sail under it. I had received orders to take my station and do that duty only, and when I took my place and answered my muster as to "stand by the lee vang to slack it if necessary," there were smiles among the officers—the men forward had had their laugh over the joke on the afterguard as they studied the station bill. Seamen will understand its nature but landsmen may have to be told that the slacking of that rope would be very rarely, if ever, needed. My stations now are mostly light and easy, requiring a person of intelligence and integrity. My hardest task is being one of those selected to stand upon gratings close to the water's edge on dark, rainy nights armed with Spencer magazine rifle, revolver and cutlass, with orders to "first use your Spencer against any cigar-shaped thing coming toward the ship, then use your revolver and last your cutlass, but *stand your ground*." At target practice it developed that I was one of their best off-hand shots, hence this station and that at quarters to stand by the relieving-tackles ready to steer in case the wheel became useless, and act as a sharp-shooter in close action.

Thursday, Mar. 9, 1861. Commodore Thatcher came up to-day in a small dispatch boat and in it reconnoitered the rebel batteries, drawing their fire as he made the circuit of shore line. Only one shell gave evidence of decent marksmanship, it passing about twenty feet above the hurricane deck of the little boat as she sped swiftly past, exploding as it struck the water. He then returned to Fort Morgan.

Saturday, Mar. 11. A fleet of gunboats, monitors, and tin-clads came up, so that there were here seven gunboats,

five monitors, and four tin-clads. These tin-clads are Mississippi River boats of very light draft, clad with boiler-iron
to protect the crew and troops upon them from infantry fire
and armed with two 30-pdr rifles in the bow and several brass
howitzers in broadside. They form quite effective boats for
operations in shallow waters. (I have recently seen a statement coming from the editor of the *Engineer's Gazette* that
these "tin-clads had four screw propellers, the first adoption
of multiple screws for propulsion." I have no recollection
of noticing any difference between their mode of propulsion
and that of the *Cincinnati*, a sketch of which I give farther
on. Both may have used several screws of small diameter
to propel them, a device necessitated by their light draft,
while the old stern-wheel paddle-boxes were allowed to remain for storage purposes and to draw the fire of the rebels'
artillery. In motion their wake would be the same.) They
were named as well as numbered, but were designated by
the number painted on each. The monitors were the *Milwaukee*, *Kickapoo*, *Chickasaw*, and the *Winnebago*. Besides
these we had the ram *Osage*, a Mississippi-River iron-clad
of the Fremont pattern, more heavily plated than a tin-clad,
yet drawing only 2 1-2 feet of water. The *Chickasaw* and
Milwaukee were sent to feel the batteries lining the western
shore while the others steamed slowly along the east shore.
At 2 P. M. the *Osage* fired two guns, the shot striking the
water a short distance ahead, when the Commodore steamed
over to them. The eastern batteries did not return a single
shot, but in the meantime a white steamer was plying from
the town to their heaviest, or Water Battery, at the foot of
the hill overlooking Appalache Channel, apparently carrying
troops. (See the map, page 39.) Upon the western shore
Missouri Battery, just below the obstructions, opened fire
on our monitors but was soon silenced with shells that struck

with quite good accuracy in their midst. Battery Buchanan, of seven heavy rifles, opposite the upper end of the line of piles driven diagonally across the channel was able to send a shell at times to near the lower end of the obstructions, but most of them fell short of that point. A battery built upon piles in front of the city commanding both the western or main channel and the near approach to the city by Blakely River from the east was hardly able to send a shot as far as Battery Buchanan. The *Morgan* remained silent. So far we had it our own way, and at 5 P. M. the monitors were recalled. We cleared for action when the fleet appeared in the forenoon but were not kept at quarters long and had a fine view of the afternoon's proceedings. The tin-clads left us at night. Their part of the work and also ours appeared to be to stand ready to go to the assistance of any monitor disabled while in action.

Sunday, Mar. 12, 1865. This morning we found that two of the monitors had disappeared. One of those remaining has been reconnoitering the eastern shore. Otherwise all is quiet and Sabbath-like.

Monday, Mar. 13. A rebel flag of truce came down this forenoon and the mail boat soon after went down the bay with dispatches. All the extra gunboats and all but one of the monitors have left us. Saturday's demonstration made the rebels show their hand, so that we now know very nearly what we will have to encounter in our advance if attempted at once. Any delay by us enables them to increase and to perfect their present eastern shore defenses.

Thursday, Mar. 16. The dispatch boat came up early in the morning with an answer to the rebels' flag of truce of Monday and we sent in it in by a flag of truce soon after.

Sunday, Mar. 19. We came down the bay last Friday night to coal up ready for the attack which is to be made in a few days. The advance of the Army landed on the eastern shore near Alabama City on Thursday and with the 2nd Maine Cavalry from Pensacola had a slight engagement with the enemy. There are here some half dozen monitors and the Fremont pattern of iron-clads, the *Osage* and *Cincinnati*. The *Osage* was present at the demonstration of Saturday, the 11th instant, but the *Cincinnati* did not arrive here till last Friday night, having been on duty on the Mississippi River until now. She is one of the fleet of armor-clad gunboats used in taking places on the Mississippi and its tributaries. She is well adapted to that purpose, being of light draft and mounting 14 guns, some of them, if not all being 30-pounder rifles that would be quite effective at short range against the 32-pounder smooth-bores of the rebel forts. I took a sketch of her which I reproduce by a cut of my own manufacture.

FREMONT'S IRON-CLAD RIVER-GUNBOAT CINCINNATI.

Monday, Mar. 20, 1865. This morning there were lying at anchor with us off Fort Morgan ready to steam up to the front the gunboats *Genesee* and *Albatross*, the *Cincinnati*, tin-clad *No. 42*, and three monitors. The others had been already sent to support the advance of the army that had landed on Thursday. All got under weigh at 10 A. M. and

followed Commodore Thatcher in his dispatch boat *Glasgow*.
After passing a monitor on duty off Alabama City on the
eastern point of the bay we commenced to shell the woods.
We found that many of the fuses to a lot of 200 percussion
shells had been tampered with, only five out of sixty-two
bursting, rendering them useless except as solid shot. As
solid shot, however, they mowed swathes in the trees that
must have made staying in that vicinity rather unpleasant.
The other vessels had better luck, nearly all bursting in the
woods in front of our advancing troops. We saw one shell
pass through the roof of a large, square house and set fire to
something in the rear of it. One shell of ours made a large
doorway through a neat little cottage on the bank. This
brought a severe reprimand from Captain Crosby, who does
"not believe in shelling private houses." When we neared
the upper fleet the *Itasca*, *Octorora*, *Sciota*, a monitor, the
tug *Pink*, and even the diminutive tug *Ida* took a hand at it,
dodging around among the larger vessels to carry orders and
barking like a little pug imagining he is taking a very prom-
inent part in a melee among the big dogs. Our carpenter
had recently built a small platform at our stern for one of
our boat's howitzers, and our Gunner, Mr. Lemon, was at
work mounting the gun as the *Ida* passed. Her gun's crew
could hardly wait to get past our stern before firing. The
unexpected explosion behind them with the passage of the
shell close to their heads made Mr. Lemon and his gun's crew
dodge, amusing those on the tug. Shaking his fist at the
perpetrators of the joke Mr. Lemon went on with his work.
He could afford to laugh with others at the occurrence, for
his warrant came to him through coolness and efficiency at
the passage of the forts. At my particular station I had
nothing to do and could watch the proceedings. A little
skiff pushed off from the shore apparently intending to visit

some of our vessels, but the men acted as if badly frightened
upon a near approach to any of our fleet. At times they
seemed very green at the oars, lifting the blades high above
their heads and making other curious movements. Again,
they would rush into the very line of fire of some vessel as
if insane. As that ship at once moved ahead enough to get
beyond the line of the boat in every instance, and as each
curious movement of the boatmen seemed to precede some
change in action of certain of our ships, I concluded that the
boat's crew knew what they were about, and that the captains of our ships and the army knew what they meant, also
that the little *Ila* was on hand if the change was not made.
The monitors and Fremont iron-clads were close in shore
and needed no boat to transmit army signals to them. The
lighter gunboats took stations farther out, while we had to
lay off still farther and fire at elevation to pepper the woods.
Not a single shot was returned and at 6 P. M. we hauled off
and anchored with the upper fleet. After dark we got under
weigh and steamed down to some place unknown to me, but
supposed to be at Fish River where our troops had gone into
camp. Very rainy all night and the watches got soaking
wet in short order. The army boys must have unpleasant
beds on such a night.

Tuesday, Mar. 21, 1865. We got up our anchor before
daylight and steamed down to the lower fleet at Ft. Morgan.
We find that the jar from firing has made the ship leak so
that we have to keep a steam pump going all the time. We
worked with the hand pump three-fourths of the time before
starting the steam pump. At 10 A. M. we started up the
bay again, reaching the upper fleet at noon. At 3 P. M. a
dispatch boat brought news that the main army was landing
at Fish River and we were ordered down with the *Genesee*,
the monitors, and *No. 42* to cover their landing. At about

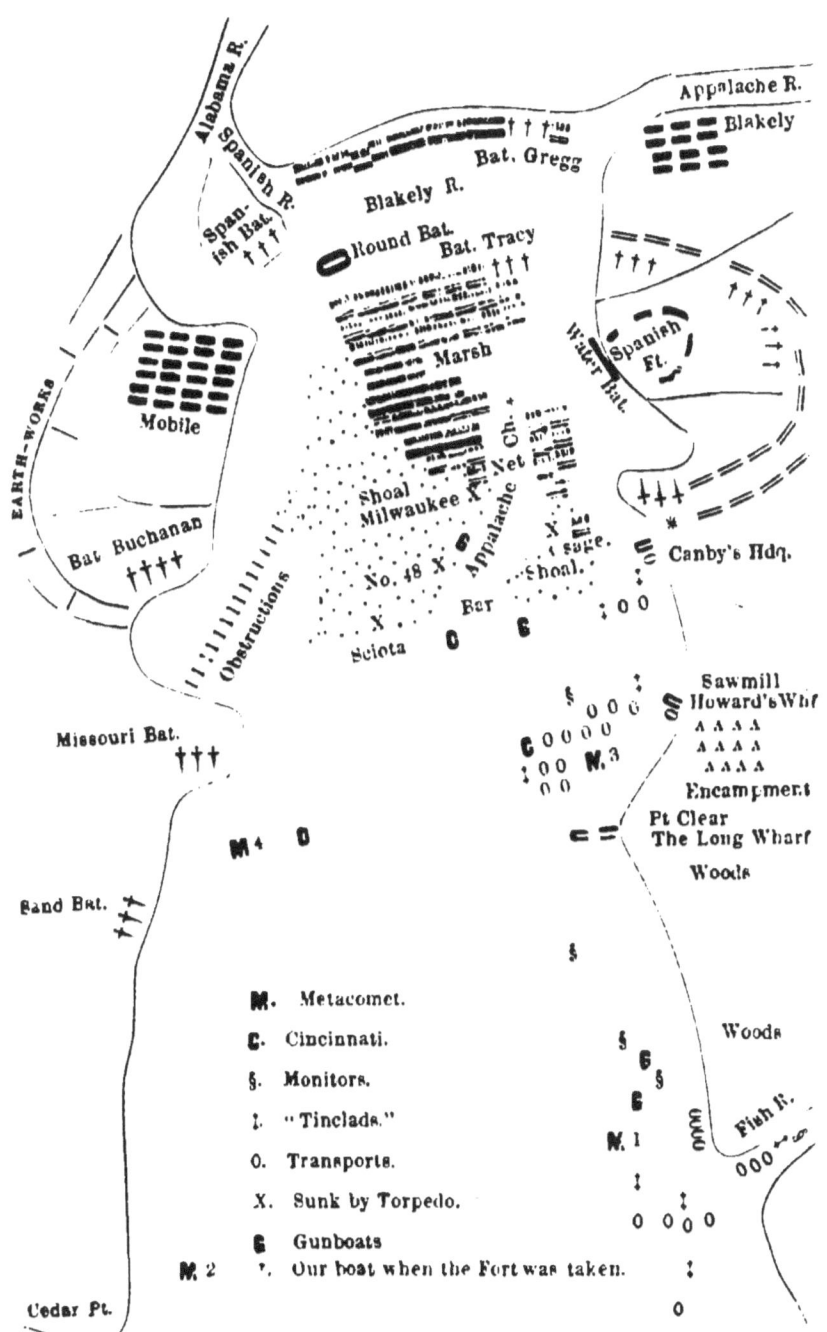

Alabama R.

Appalache R.

Spanish R.

Blakely

Bat. Gregg

Span-ish Bat.

Blakely R.

Round Bat.

Bat. Tracy

Spanish Ft.

EARTH-WORKS

Mobile

Marsh

Water Bat.

Bat. Buchanan

Shoal

Milwaukee X

Net Ch.

Appalache

Canby's Hdq.

No. 48 X

Shoal.

Sage.

Obstructions

Bar

Sciota

Sawmill

Howard's Whf

Missouri Bat.

Encampment

Pt Clear

The Long Wharf

Woods

Band Bat.

M. Metacomet.

C. Cincinnati.

§. Monitors.

1. "Tinclads."

0. Transports.

X. Sunk by Torpedo.

6 Gunboats

'. Our boat when the Fort was taken.

Woods

Fish R.

Cedar Pt.

4 P. M. we commenced to shell the woods ahead of the army
and fired forty shells before 6 P. M.   We got our supper
after 7 o'clock and lay here (at M¹ on map) all night.   The
troops landed without opposition and are quietly occupying
the woods, their camp-fires burning brightly and the extent
of smoke above the trees showing that the force is large.

Thursday, Mar. 23, 1865.   In the two hours that I was
on lookout last night five transports arrived with troops and
shot into the little bay at the mouth of the river.   They had
been landing at the same rate all day yesterday.   The 2nd
Maine Cavalry had a sharp fight with the rebels on Tuesday.
morning showing that our shells alone have kept them from
giving our troops a warm reception at their landing.   The
army transports loaded with troops continue to shoot into
the river from down the bay quite regularly each half-hour.
a new one arriving almost as soon as landing space is clear.
A tin-clad and a monitor are lying in the river just above
that landing for protection, while the rest of the fleet cover
the landing from the bay shore, where stores seem to be the
lading.   ·

Saturday, Mar. 25.   Last night we took a picket station
at Cedar Point, on the western shore (at M² on the map) in
sight of Ft. Morgan light.   We could not see that any of our
troops were here, though rumor says that Gen. Steele was
to land at this point.   We returned to the eastern shore in
the morning at earliest dawn and anchored some distance
below the mouth of Fish River.   After breakfast our boat
took a party of our officers ashore hunting.   Being my turn
to keep boat I did not get nearer than a quarter-mile to the
dry land.   Those who went ashore had to wade that distance
and some of the men who waded barefoot got badly cut by
the oyster shells on the bottom.   Our officers got five dirty,
lean, small land-pikes which they called wild hogs.   They

had certainly been wild enough, but their ears showed that some other man had already put his tally upon them. We got to the ship a little before supper time hungry as hunters, ate our dinners which had been kept warm for us in obedience to a rule in the navy, and then finished off with the pot of tea at our sides already poured for our individual use but by another rule must not be touched by us till the whistle of the boatswain had uttered its third or "pipe down" note for supper. Refugees on board say that the army will meet no resistance until our ships can go no farther, but afterward the resistance will be stubborn.

Sunday, Mar. 26, 1865. After a deal of signaling with the Army we got under weigh and played about among the fleet, giving instructions verbally to follow us in line of battle to cover the army's advance to Howard's wharf, which we are told is the highest that ships of our draft can skirt the shore. We came to anchor (at M^3 on map) a little below that wharf after running our nose into the mud a little way above it. The army followed without the least opposition and went into camp abreast of us. While coming up we fired but three shells. The targets were hit so effectively in each instance that none others were needed. The captain of our forward pivot gun (a VI-inch rifle throwing a shell of 100 pounds) was named Granger, said to be a nephew of Gen. Granger. Capt. Crosby, now Rear Admiral Pierce Crosby, retired, asked Granger if he thought he could take a slice out of the middle of a long wharf running out to a boat-house in deep water a mile ahead. Granger had fired that gun every time since the ship went into commission, and the result of his first shot was that about twenty feet of the planking and timbers went flying through the air from the middle of the "bridge" (see map) connecting the boat-house with the land. "Good!" shouted the captain. "Now, Granger, put one

into the boat-house!" Granger did so to the consternation
of a section of artillery secreted there. They fled for the
land with their guns in tow, but coming to the gap found it
too wide to jump with their guns. They left them and took
to the water in great haste to reach the shore by wading.—
On coming within sighting distance of piles of sawdust at a
mill just above Howard's wharf Granger was told to put a
shell into the sawdust pile close to the shore. Granger at
once kicked up such a dust about them that another lot of
artillery men dusted out of their hiding place. They must
have thought with the Irishman "Arrah, Sam, somebody
must have towld yez now!" They possibly would have been
quite correct, for the owner of the large, square house that
we had put a shell through had been hounded by them for
showing a white flag and was standing at the captain's side
to pilot the ship as near the shore as our draft would permit.
In the afternoon there appeared to be a consultation of the
leading army and navy officers on board our ship. At the
same time a train of pontoon boats came up in tow of a river
boat.

Monday, Mar. 27, 1865. The launch was sent with a
seine to fish for torpedos alongside of and near to Howard's
Wharf. We caught no torpedos but did catch a mess of fish
for the ship's company. The Commodore came up at noon.
We learn from one of the signal corps at the wharf that the
army had some skirmishing with the rebels on the back road
which runs three miles from the beach and had a few men
wounded, but had met with no opposition to speak of. On
yesterday the rebels landed 4000 troops at the hill battery,
which they call Spanish Fort, and at 1 P. M. to-day commenced to shell our advance. It is raining, making work
in the water doubly unpleasant. Another train of pontoon-
arrived this morning, also a large river transport loaded with

troops. We have here the four monitors *Chicasaw*, *Kickapoo*, *Milwaukee*, and *Winnebago*, the Fremont iron-clads *Osage* and *Cincinnati*, the tin-clads *42* and *48 (Rudolph,)* the propeller gunboat *Sciota*, and the double-enders *Metacomet* and *Octorora*. The two tin-clads and others of the fleet seem to be forming a chain of boats near the army at landing points on the eastern shore from Gen. Canby's headquarters to Ft. Morgan. After dinner Mr. Sleeper, took the launch, first cutter, and whaleboat up the eastern shore line. He took the whaleboat to sound that little passage to see if our monitors could go by it to help the army. We were to drag for any torpedos the rebels might have placed there. We found no torpedos and no passage except for the lighter tin-clads and transports. We went up to the point of land where the left of our army line was in position and Mr. Sleeper in the whaleboat went around the point in the dusk of evening to see if the rebels could reach our army with anything heavier than we could meet them with. That boat's crew saw the infantry fight, but we saw only the steady, clock-like action of a battery close to the bank abreast of us which kept up a continuous roar with their pieces. Our cavalry got among torpedos yesterday, but those who placed them in the ground were caught and compelled to take them up again. We were well soaked with the rain. We have an advantage over the army boys as we could don dry clothes when we reached the ship at 7 P. M. They dry themselves by their campfires.

Tuesday, Mar. 28, 1865. I have been on duty twenty-six hours in the past thirty-two; in a boat most of the time. A new boat's crew of twelve picked men was selected for the launch last night in anticipation of a stretch of serious work. The discarded ones of the old crew feel sore about it. We started at daylight this morning to cut small trees and stake out a passage for the monitors to go up Appalache Channel

to the help of the army which is almost constantly engaged.
We had but four hours of sleep last night after a hard day's
work dragging for torpedos.   We were started at five o'clock
without a morsel to eat since seven o'clock last night, and
continued to work until 10:30 A. M., when our stakes were
set.   Officers sometimes forget that men are apt to work as
they are fed.   We had worked cheerfully cutting the stakes
expecting to be allowed to go on board the ship and get our
breakfast as we passed the ship at breakfast time, but when
we found that we were not to get anything to eat until the
stakes were set our strokes became feeble and slow.   Mr. Gill
(hard G) who is the officer of our boat noticed this at once
and wanted to know if we had anything to eat before we
started.   Finding that we had not he said "It shall not
happen again while we are working at this business if I can
help it.   Remember that I am in the same fix and the sooner
the work we are ordered to do is done the sooner we get our
grub."   This put a different face upon the matter, for Mr.
Gill was a popular officer, and the boys put more force upon
their oars, finding they were punishing him and themselves
instead of the one to whom they wished to show disapproval
of his treatment of them.   We reached the ship in season to
eat our breakfast and dinner together after the others were
through eating, and just in season to start again at 1 P. M.
to drag the channel for torpedos.   I had come aboard with
a severe headache which a cup of coffee before we started in
the morning would probably have prevented.   Nearly cold
boiled rice and salt beef with the pot of cold coffee from our
breakfast ration made rather an unsatisfactory meal after a
fast of nearly eighteen hours, all but four of which had been
spent at labor.   The rebel gunboats had commenced to shell
our troops about ten o'clock and our monitors were ordered
to go up Appalache Channel to meet them.   The rebels did

not wait to be met but put back to Mobile before our monitors reached the bar. About 3 P. M. the rebels opened fire
from their Water Battery on our boat which was just below
the Marsh Channel. They planted one shell where we had
been but a few moments before and its explosion just under
the surface drenched us with water and half filled our boat.
" Pull steady, boys ! Don't miss a stroke !" said Mr. Gill.
" Every officer in the fleet has his glass upon us. We will
take care of the torpedos and the Commodore will take care
of us," and proceeded to bail out the boat with one hand
while holding the end of the drag-rope with the other. In a
short time he added—" There goes the signal, boys, for the
Milwaukee to cover us." We feathered our oars with the
utmost nicety, every oar at a horizontal as it went forward
for the next stroke. Two of the monitors soon steamed up
past us to near the head of the channel, drove the steamers
away and silenced the water battery by a 15-inch shell that
burst within it. While returning to anchor just below our
boat, thinking it must be clear of torpedos, the *Milwaukee*
struck a torpedo abreast of her after magazine as she swung
to her anchor, and commenced to sink very rapidly in nine
feet of water. In less time than we could turn our boats and
reach her side from a distance of not over 250 yards her stern
was two feet under water and on the bottom, while the bow
was as far out of water and stuck in the mud at the side of
the channel. They had given her full speed at once and let
the chain run out to push her into the shoal at the side of the
channel at "Milwaukee, X" on the map. The Engineer on
duty obeyed the signal of "four bells" before the accompanying order of "Every man on deck !" The man stationed
in the after magazine was pulled out of it from under water
by the powder passers and helped on deck. The forward
compartment was clear so that the men lost nothing, but the

officers saved nothing. The discipline was excellent, there being not the least sign of panic on her deck. There was a little dog on board that seemed greatly confused by the unusual state of the ship and I asked an officer if we might take him on board the *Metacomet* until they were established in better quarters, promising good care of him on the part of our shipmates. When bidden to go to me the little fellow curled himself down in my lap, glad to find a refuge. He would occasionally place his paws upon the gunwale of our boat to watch the work on board, then look up into my face with an expression of inquiry plainly asking "What is the matter with my old home?" Getting a pleasant word from me and a patting from my mates he would curl down again in apparent content, but we noticed that he watched every movement of the officer giving him into our care, as ready to return to her deck as were the few men who stepped into our boat at the invitation of Mr. Gill when we first reached her side and before we knew she was already on the bottom.— We remained alongside while their officers were signaling to the Commodore for instructions, and then resumed our work at dragging. After everything had been made snug the men were put on board the *Winnebago* by other boats that were sent from the fleet for the purpose and the officers were given quarters above water. When we got back to the ship at 7 P. M. I was too sick and tired to eat my supper. I felt about used up. A half hour of sleep lying upon the bare deck was very refreshing and I ate my supper to be ready to start again at 8 o'clock for an all night's work divided into dragging and picket duty.

Wednesday, Mar. 29, 1865. At 8 o'clock this morning I had been on active duty thirty-eight hours out of the past forty-eight, rowing a boat nearly all the time. Troops are still coming up by transports and the front of the army is

engaged almost constantly with the enemy at Spanish Fort.
To-day we were pained to witness another disaster. While
going to the front to take part in protecting the army from
the shells of the rebel fleet the iron-clad ram *Osage* struck a
torpedo at the eastern side of the channel at "Osage X" on
the map, and sank at once. She had two men killed and
forty-five wounded. She is a complete wreck. We begin
to think these advances to shell our troops are a device of the
rebels to draw our ships into the influence of their torpedos
to destroy them. They run away after getting our vessels
to enter the channel, where we feel sure they send down a
fresh supply of torpedos every night. Mr. Gill proposes on
another night to go up higher on picket than his orders say,
to see if we can catch them at it. These torpedos are simply
powder barrels half full of powder and encircled by several
percussion fuses in such positions that a blow against the
barrel anywhere will explode one or more. The barrel is
kept below the surface by a chain and hemispherical weight
whose flat side resting lightly upon the bottom allows the
current to work the sandy mud from under it and float the
torpedo, always submerged, gradually down stream until it
reaches still water at the channel's edge ready to do its foul
work of destruction. This accounts for their presence just
after our drag-ropes had passed over a locality. The bight
of our ropes dragging along the bottom is sure to catch the
torpedo by the chain between the weight and barrel and hold
it securely while we row across the channel to shoal water.
Here a man from each of the two boats dragging together
drops carefully overboard to hold the barrel firmly while a
third man bores a hole in its side with a copper-coated augur.
Water is then allowed to enter and the thing suffers death
by drowning. The use of a steel augur before passing Fort
Morgan caused us the loss of two boats and their crews, the

rebels coating the inside of their barrels with material for exploding by friction.

Thursday, Mar. 30, 1865. We were called away at 3 : 30 P. M. yesterday, just half an hour before supper, to drag for torpedos all night. It rained and blew hard from the north, wetting and chilling us through. We were getting no torpedos and at ten o'clock Mr. Gill returned to the ship to get a lighter boat, hoping we might be allowed to go aboard to get our suppers or at least for something to eat. We got orders instead to "Shove off and return to work!" When we went alongside the *Kickapoo*, our rendezvous for changing duties with the picket boats Mr. Gill told the officers of that monitor of our supperless condition. Her officers were not backward in expressing opinions on the matter and we got a cup of hot coffee and a biscuit apiece by order of the "ranking officer" present. (It is barely possible that this came to the notice of Commodore Thatcher through a requisition for the amount of the *Kickapoo* Paymaster's stores of coffee, sugar, and bread "expended" for us. Officers find ways of bringing grievances to the attention of headquarters without reporting acts of their superiors. At any rate we did not have to test the *Kickapoo's* hospitality again.) Mr. Gill told us to snatch a couple of biscuit from our messes before entering the boat another time and that he would get the coffee and sugar from the army store-boats on the way up. We started from the *Kickapoo's* side for our picket station warmed and cheered in spite of the norther and its cold rain, for not only our stomachs but our hearts had been warmed. We went up Blakely River till we saw the rebel boats and watched them some time, then floated down stream again. We hear that the army has cut off all communication by land with Mobile. If so we expect our monitors will soon go up above the channel and the torpedos, thus by one bold stroke

cutting off their communication by water and compelling an
early surrender of the fort and batteries on the eastern side.
The longer we stay below the Marsh Channel the more of
our ships will suffer from torpedos. We got back to the
ship at 6 : 30 this morning after fifteen hours boat duty in the
teeth of a norther. The *Octorora* was gotten over the bar
to-day by removing her battery and heavy articles; but in
getting her forward pivot 100-pdr. rifle back again the mast
of the *Pink* was broken, which causes a delay in any forward
movement on the *Octorora's* part.

Friday, Mar. 31, 1865. The *Octorora* is shelling the
rebel gunboats at long range, they having commenced again
to shell our troops. It is said there are about 12000 troops
at Spanish Fort. Last night our picket boats got hold of
what appeared to be a hawser lying on the bottom across the
channel near the head of the Marsh, but which they were not
able to raise. It is thought that it may be their intention to
tauten it when we attempt to advance above that point and
perhaps to float a nest of torpedos against it for our benefit.
Its finding suggests a similar contrivance to stop their torpedos at the foot of the Marsh Channel and save ourselves
much work at dragging and perhaps some ships. To-day
we have been preparing a net of ratlin stuff (tarred rope a
little larger than clothesline) to set a little below the marsh
to ward off torpedos from the anchorage of the monitors
after they go up to that point. I signed accounts with the
Government having $11.29 due *me*, after six months of war
service, but as I will have to draw a new supply of clothing
early in April I will then be in debt again.

Saturday, Apr. 1. We were called away last night *after*
supper in company with the 2nd cutter for a special duty.
Yesterday the soldiers, more adventurous, or perhaps under
less severe discipline than we are, pulled in and cut out an

old steamboat hulk kept for a hospital by the rebels and in
face of the rebel batteries towed her down to the mouth of
Blakely River.   As she was useless to us and in a position
to be used to menace our picket boats the *Winnebago's* boat
boarded and set her on fire to-night.   The soldier boys' dash
was rather ill-timed, as the episode prevented our making
an intended raid to-night to cut out a barge loaded with
ammunition.   It illustrated the necessity of strict obedience
to orders in war and the un-wisdom of unauthorized separate
action.   We anchored just below the burning hulk with the
rest of the picket boats of the fleet for the remainder of the
night.   The 2nd cutter's crew were greatly disappointed as
this was a special detail and their first inning in the game.
On reaching the anchorage of the fleet this morning we found
that our ship had gone over to the western shore to coal up
at a schooner there.   Were it not for our breakfast waiting
our arrival we would have been in no great hurry to reach
her deck, for no one is excused at coaling ship and we were
therefore sure to lose our morning's nap on the bare berth
deck before nine o'clock quarters.   We get our hammocks
only by special order and for the forenoon only.   We often
drop asleep sitting in the boat holding our oars at a level in
floating silently down stream, though with open ears to act
at Mr. Gill's order in guarded tones.   Most of my notes are
written while we are floating idly down.   Our army is giving
the rebels in the fort no rest, keeping up an incessant fire by
day and night.   They say the torpedo game is played upon
them also, the torpedo shells being found all along the front
of their line in great number.   After all her labor in getting
over the bar the poor *Octorora* is still in trouble.   She is fast
aground and all her heavy battery has to come off her again.
A southerly gale will float her, but it seems to us as if these
fierce northers would never cease.   They have driven so much

of the water down over the bar that the few inches to spare
under her bottom is reduced to a minus quantity. Refugees
from rebeldom charge us with having brought our northern
weather with us to oppose them.

Sunday, Apr. 2, 1865. Last night we dragged all night
without getting anything, though our other boats got two
before we arrived, which was at dark. Our boat was sent
in the afternoon to carry cots for the wounded men of the
Rudolph (tin-clad No. 48,) which was struck by a torpedo
while lying at anchor in the midst of our fleet that had gotten
over the bar. The water extends half way above her lower
deck.

Monday, Apr. 3. We were again dragging the whole of
the night and were allowed our hammocks all this forenoon.
Some deserters from the *Morgan* say the rebels are hurrying
away all their cotton and stores from Mobile and think they
intend to evacuate soon. Our monitors still lie at anchor
a little above the bar with their rakes down to catch any of
the torpedos that may come down upon them. In the afternoon we had to go after the store-scow of the *Milwaukee*
which had broken adrift. We had a long, exhausting pull
against the wind and current, and were given our hammocks
all night.

Tuesday, Apr. 4. We were in the boat most of the day.
On our return we found that a call for twenty volunteers to
man a mortar scow to shell Spanish Fort had been made and
filled. Granger and his whole gun's crew were the ones to
be accepted. They will be stationed at the point we visited
near to Gen. Canby's headquarters one evening under Mr.
Sleeper.

Wednesday, Apr. 5. Last night we picked up a torpedo
only 300 yards ahead of the *Octorora* which has no rake for
protection. The *Octorora* lies not far from *No 48* on the

map, and this torpedo had passed clear of the line of boats
that were dragging the channel from the marsh to the bar.
Soon after we reached the ship this morning the mortar-scow
men went in her to their new quarters. This relieves us
of boat duty for a time unless we are sent in another boat.
Because of our boat being away we lose our morning's nap,
told that we will get our hammocks tonight. Thinking this
a good time to have something done to relieve a nearly constant pain in my left ear which was getting about as bad as
the right I went to the doctor. He put a blister behind that
ear and let me run. Yesterday we commenced an immense
net to be 1000 feet long, but to-day we see nothing of it.
Instead, we have a lot of empty beef barrels on deck which
we are slinging for buoys to the net when it is placed across
the channel at the foot of the marsh. We of the launch are
a sleepy set, especially as the others push in ahead of us on
purpose to relieve us of as much of the work as possible, on
account of our all-night's work. Our ship now lies at "M³"
on the map. The *Cincinnati* is anchored a little farther out,
near the outer edge of the transports and is fitting a torpedo
rake to be ready to go up with the others after the net has
been stretched across the channel.

Thursday, Apr. 6, 1863. Last night we laid our buoys
across Appalache Channel at the lower edge of the marsh, a
little over 600 feet wide at that point. I have another blister behind my left ear to-day. All hands are preparing a
net and anchors to lay to-night. Mr. Sleeper went with us
to oversee the work and at near midnight chided Mr. Gill
for his loud tones in giving orders, saying that the rebels
would hear him. Mr. G. answered that he had to speak loud
to keep his boat's crew awake; for they had been on duty
since Tuesday morning without sleep. This was true so far
as Mr. Sleeper's orders had been obeyed, but during those

seventy hours every available opportunity for stealing a nap had been utilized to its fullest extent. We knew that all the boat duty put upon us was needed, and did it cheerfully; but we felt that we were entitled to some sleep during the day after an all night boat duty and stole it at every chance. There has seemed to be cool feeling between the two officers since we got our midnight supper on board the *Kickapoo* and appearances indicate that we are being quietly blacklisted with our officer. We showed that we could do good work if we were sleepy, though the pulling and hauling came rather tough on my raw blisters.

Friday, Apr. 7, 1865. It is cloudy with a raw north wind again. We got through with our last night's work at 3 o'clock this morning and were allowed to lie down on the berth deck until breakfast at eight o'clock. To-day we are making drag-nets to catch torpedos with. This will make harder work for the boats' crews, and less effective—if they use them, which is doubtful.

Saturday, Apr. 8. Some of the crew are at work making drag-nets. A party is ashore cutting and trimming trees about twenty feet high to stake out a safe channel up the marsh. To-night we staked out a passage up the marsh and then went on picket. While on picket last night Mr. Gill let four of the twelve oars rest apeak by turns so that we slept sitting on our thwarts nearly one-third of the time after midnight. Those that were dragging took over thirty torpedos from the net we set Thursday night. There were twenty boats engaged in the marsh channel during the night. The *Octorora* went to just below the net and fired a saluted salute into the Water Battery to-day in honor of the taking of Selma, and anchored there to stay. I am having another large boil coming, this time on my instep. It commences to swell badly and is quite painful. A bunch on the back of my hand from the last one has not gone down yet. The boys are nearly all in a similar state of eruption, caused by the marsh water we have to work in, we think. We are all sticking to our seats—though Hudson has to sit sidewise— for our work is getting interesting, feeling sure that something will break loose when the monitors come up to the net, and we want to be in at the death.

SUNDAY, APRIL 9, 1865. At 3 A. M. our boat was at the little cross opposite the Water Battery on the map on page 39. We had been watching steamers plying between Mobile and Spanish Fort, but could not make out which way they were carrying their loads. The army had been making repeated assaults during the night, evinced by the lines of infantry fire creeping up the hill. Suddenly the firing ceased and shortly afterward three bonfires were seen to blaze out within the fort, their positions forming a triangle, at which Mr. Gill looked at his watch and said "Three o'clock; the fort is ours, boys!" The Water Battery was shortly after lighted up and rockets were sent toward the middle of the channel to Mobile. At this, three quick flashes as of powder thrown upon a fire at Gen. Canby's headquaters answered the joyful signal. (A member of the 124th Ill. Inf. Reg. claimed that *they* took the fort on the evening of the 8th by following along the beach at low tide "which was *six feet* at that point," [!] entering the fort from the side next to the town of Blakely, and following the works from the north to the east without seeing anyone till they met some of another regiment coming in like manner from the south by the east side, and that Gen. Canby did not know the fort was taken till wakened to hear their report of its capture by them.) This is the substance of his yarn in the *National Tribune* some years after, and doubtless was as it appeared to him, but he will have to tell it to the marines as the sailors of that

fleet can hardly believe there could be so great an excess of
tide at the head of Appalache Channel over that at the foot.
Such a tide with us would have saved labor and ships, and
enabled the army to have walked into Mobile at once under
our escort.   The soldiers on the south side certainly thought
they were opposed by something more substantial than spirit
firing up to three o'clock this morning, and we saw the last
steamer pass by loaded to the guards just as the rockets shot
out after the retreating foe.   That part of the army fighting
on the south side was not slow to find out that *the fort was
evacuated;* nor was Gen. Canby unless our eyes deceived us
regarding the powder flashes.   He probably got less sleep
during the seige up to that time than we of the *Metacomet's*
launch.   Their report coming while enjoying his well-earned
slumber very likely confirmed his supposition or belief that
the north side was evacuated first, hence those on the north
side could walk in unmolested, while active work was going
on upon the other side of the hill.   What he saw and what
we saw taken with what the army boys on the south side did
completes a record of the night's events.   We returned to
the ship early with the news, and after quarters and inspection
were over had our hammocks for all day and all night.

Monday, Apr. 10, 1865. We were started out before
breakfast and took up a line of seine set some time ago by
the other picket boats above the monitors' anchorage.   It
took us until ten o'clock, when they all steamed up to just
below the marsh net and anchored near the *Octorora.*   On
returning to the ship from taking up the net I went to the
doctor with my foot and instep greatly swelled and blue in
color.   He ordered me to lie still and poultice with a cake
of hardbread soaked in some medicated solution he gave me.
News came yesterday of the fall of Richmond.   The New
Orleans *Times* quotes from New York papers that " The

War is Over." We hope so, but do not see the work here quite done yet.

Tuesday, Apr. 11, 1865. The launch was away all last night, going up Blakely River nearly to Round Battery in dragging for torpedos. They got no torpedos but captured a rebel picket boat. I lost that much, but the boys want me back as the fellow sent in my place " was a sneak or a coward," and as the swelling has gone down some, I shall take my place to-night. Yesterday afternoon the *Morgan* and another rebel boat came out and took part with Batteries Gregg and Tracy in exchanging shots with our fleet and the captured Water Battery, but were so warmly received that they shortly after returned to Mobile. We now have only the two marsh batteries, Gregg and Tracy to oppose our monitors going directly up to Mobile with the army by a passage cleared of torpedos.

Wednesday, Apr. 12. All our boats were on picket last night. Going up to Batteries Gregg and Tracy we found them being evacuated and rushed in to capture their crews. The *Metacomet's* boats were among those to land at Tracy. Who took Battery Gregg I would not say, though we sailors always *supposed* some of the boats of our fleet had that honor. We *know* that we run *somebody* out of Battery Tracy and do not believe it was any of our army. They got out in a hurry, leaving matches to a lot of shells which exploded a moment too soon to seriously injure anyone. In the rush Mr. Gill's revolver went off, the ball going through his own foot. Our officers were very blind when we came on board the ship this morning, and we have articles of spoils from that battery ranging from a dead hog to a barber's shaving chair and footstool with all its kit. I got some rebel muster rolls, descriptive lists, a musket and bayonet, a case of fine water colors and a letter written upon a coarse, ruled paper, to her husband by a plucky wife in Houston Co., Ga., where they "had to drink pond water; had the chills," and other troubles and privations, but would not sell the land to live on. My spoils were soon stowed away, but when the doctor came to look at my foot it had become so swollen again that I had to confess my night's spree. He ordered his steward to lash me in my hammock if I offered to stir without his permission. After breakfast we got under weigh in company with the *Cincinnati*, *Sebago*, *Sciota*, *Itasca*, the tin-clads, the Commodore's dispatch boat, Gen. Canby's boat, and a lot of transports. We all steamed over to the western shore and went to quarters. We had left the *Octorora* and the monitors at the foot of the marsh channel to guard that passage, and a part of the army were at Blakely and at the captured batteries. When the doctor came below prepared for work I begged to go to my station, telling him I had only to see to covering the after hatches and then stand by the relieving tackles, also that I couldn't possibly stay down there if it was to be an action. He at last gave me leave to go, but charged me not to move around much. I found a mess of it about the gratings, my darkie assistant not knowing the proper place for each quarter had gotten them mixed, and men were going from the guns to straighten them out, while Mr. Sleeper stood at the edge of the hurricane deck waiting its being done to enable him to report the ship all ready for action. As I hobbled along buckling my cutlass and pistol belt I dealt out the pieces in a hurry to the men, then the tarpaulins, and touched my cap first to Mr. Sleeper, then to my division officer, Mr. Gill, to whom I should have reported. There were broad grins on more faces than theirs as Mr. G. touched his cap to confirm my report and Mr. Sleeper turned to Capt. Crosby to report the ship ready for action. Mr. Gill was also stumping about on one foot and a cane. The stop to the signal reporting this was broken and we were ordered to fire. Granger sent a shell into the garden of a man named Ferguson where Sand Battery had been, but was not now, as it was already on the road to Mobile. A white cloth was at once waved. (Mr. F. afterward showed us a piece of that shell, saying that "he didn't like that kind of garden seed and thought he better show a white rag to let us know he didn't want any more.") One of our boats brought him off to the Commodore, then the army transports landed some troops while we steamed up opposite Missouri Battery. A boat sent ashore here brought word back that Mobile was evacuated. We were then ordered to leave our side-arms at our quarters and leave our quarters. Thus ends the block-ade and seige of Mobile. The negro that John Lee and I saved from death while coaling off Galveston died last night of consumption. The doctor had tended him faithfully, but the sudden shock of immersion in the chilly water when he was overheated by shoveling coal in the schooner's hold and the fright were too much for him. A coffin was made for him this morning and he will be buried ashore in the livery of his country. Going on deck after dinner I found that we were anchored about a mile below Missouri Battery, (at M⁴) and the troops were landing and marching to that point. At 2 P. M. we up anchor again and went back to our old posi-tion on the east side of the bay.

Sunday, Apr. 16, 1865. We have lost a vessel a day by torpedos for the last three days. Friday the dispatch boat *Althea* went under water, yesterday the tug *Ida* was sunk, and to-day the gunboat *Sciota* has her spar deck just above water. She was crossing from the west to the east side of the bay a little after 4 P. M., and while skirting the shoal at the point marked "Sciota X" on the map struck the tor-pedo just beneath where the petty officers' mess were eating

supper. Five of them were killed. (When Old Vets. spin
their yarns from memory they are apt to get facts mixed, if
not enlarged. In telling of the sinking of the *Sciota* I have
always thought I was correct in saying that *all* of the petty
officers were killed except the ones on watch. I was some
surprised when putting my diary into type to find the record
gave the number as *five* only. It would seem that my own
yarns—from memory—will sometimes have to be taken *cum
grano salis*. It explains the honest discrepancies in stories
told by those who kept no diary at the time of occurence of
the incidents. I think my written copy will stand the test.)

Sunday, Apr. 23, 1865. There has been little stirring to
note during the past week. On Monday we were trimmed
with flags in honor of the surrender of Gen. Lee. We went
to Pensacola that day for coal and stores. On Tuesday we
coaled ship and took in provisions. Wednesday we returned
to Mobile Bay and anchored at our old position at M⁴, below
Missouri Battery. Thursday the boats were all out dragging
for torpedos, but found none. Friday we hoisted the launch
upon deck for repairs, nearly all her crew being already on
the doctor's hands for the same purpose. On Saturday I
"discharged the doctor," that is to say, I asked to be let off
the sick-list which then contained ten per cent of the ship's
crew. In the afternoon I planed the launch's oars into good
shape and got my foot quite sore and lame. At night I had
an armed lookout or sentry duty for the first time in about a
month, having had boat duty by night in the meantime.—
We received the news of the assassination of the President
on Friday and we have worn our colors at half-mast, a sad
contrast to our appearance on the passage to Pensacola last
Monday. I understand that the rebels have sent in a flag of
truce, asking what terms will be granted them in case they
surrender, and the answer was, the same terms granted Lee

by Grant. The whole talk here now is of "When shall we get home?" In my letter of this date to my wife I write "Tell Freddy pa has gotten the ' rebels most all fighted.'"

Friday, Apr. 28, 1865. Word came that a rebel steamer had run past New Orleans to put to sea. We got under weigh and went down the bay expecting to go in chase. At Fort Morgan we found the *Brooklyn* had gone and we came to anchor. While we lay here the supply steamer *Bermuda* came in on her way from Galveston. All the men whose terms of service had expired were sent on board for passage north. This was disheartening to those of us left behind, as we took this as evidence that the time for this ship to be sent north was still distant. We have been giving the ship a great overhauling, both inside and outside, scraping and painting everywhere. We returned to Mobile to-day, and anchored at our former position M⁴ on the map.

Saturday, Apr. 29, 1865. To-day I was in the boat that is dragging the western channel for torpedos. It was a welcome duty as it gave me a chance to see how we removed the line of piles obstructing the western channel, and how our sunken ships were raised. A tug was anchored a little distance above the piles, from which a boat carried charges of explosives and dropped them beside the piles, a wire connecting them with a battery on the tug. When ready to fire the boat returned to the tug, the water about the piles boiled furiously and the piles shot upward, fell over on their sides and floated down stream. We also saw the army boat *St. Marys* being raised by the "camels" used here to float the large cotton ships over the bar. These camels are large, square, wooden tanks with one side hollowed in to fit against and partly under the side of a ship. They are brought to the whole length of each side of the ship, then flooded until barely afloat, fastened securely to each other and the ship,

and then pumped out by powerful steam pumps, taking the
ship with them as they rise. The *St. Marys* is an iron boat
that I am told was formerly on the New York and New Orleans Steamboat Line. In addition to this ship the Army
has lost by torpedos the dispatch boat *Gen. Banks*, and the
stern-wheel river boat *Robert Hamilton*. These make a loss
of three vessels for the Army, and six for the Navy by torpedos since March 28th.

Saturday, May 6, 1865. Yesterday we had $5 of "grog-
money" served out to us, $3 of which went for my share of
food supplies purchased of the supply boats to help out our
regular navy ration, which seems to go not so far as usual.
To-day our watch received $5 as liberty money and were set
ashore for forty-eight hours of liberty. I wanted to see the
earthworks and the vegetation, but soon found I would not
be allowed outside the city limits. The city itself was bare
of everything. A one-legged rebel ex-soldier stumped about
among the boys, bragging and offensively saying that they
" 'low'd they 'd been whipt, but they wern't conquer'd *yet.*"
The boys were sorely tempted to whip him until he, at least,
was conquered into silence. I had to tell him that we did
not want to conquer him ; we only set out to keep him in the
Union and make him behave,—and that was just what we had
done. It shut him up for the moment, apparently unable to
gather his wits for a retort, and the boys finished him by a
shout of derision. He let them alone after that. On the
wharf were a lot of guns from the Selma arsenal, with piles
of loaded shells and other war material. Boys were getting
a stock of powder,—perhaps to celebrate the coming Fourth
of July with—the sentry taking little notice whether they
purloined from time or purcussion shells. They seemed to
know which were safe to handle, for they took from time-fuse
shells only. The monitors were lying in Alabama River,

opposite the city. The *Sciota* had been raised and was at
the city bank of the river and being repaired. The new
planking shows that about fifteen feet square of her side had
been crushed in. There was little else to interest me in the
city. I also knew that unless I returned to the ship by the
same boat we came on 1 would have to wait till to-morrow.
I returned to the ship disgusted, and reported for duty.

Tuesday, May 9, 1865. To-day we received 105 men
who had been sent home from the Pacific with still several
months to serve. Several not needed to fill our quota will
be sent to other vessels.

Thursday, May 25. We were suddenly shaken up by an
explosion of great force at Mobile. The warehouse holding
the stores of war material taken from the rebels was blown
up, doing a great amount of damage to the city and shipping.
Though seven miles distant our ship was shaken as if struck
heavily. It was evidently the work of some rebel.

Tuesday, June 13. Word was passed to-day for those
whose time of service had expired to go aft. They were
told they could have their discharge here or wait a few days
and be sent home by the first boat going north, also that a
transport would be going every few days. I put in an application for my discharge on the ground that as the rebellion
is crushed my services are no longer needed, and that being
a farmer and not a sailor by profession my service in the
navy has been, and must necessarily continue to be at great
pecuniary sacrifice to me, and hardship to my family. I am
not at all confident of a favorable result, though the doctor
in handing in my application was heard to say that I was
really unfit for service through increasing trouble with my
ears. I cannot get an answer before July 4, and should I get
my discharge I will have due me little more than enough to
bear my expenses home. Should I draw nothing more I will

have \$24.50 of wages due me and \$4.50 of grog money, or about \$29. All I shall have gained will be the satisfaction of having served my country in her time of need.

Thursday, June 23, 1865. Mr. Sleeper seut for me and asked me several questions which I give as I understood at the time of utterance. It will be borne in mind that I had on for pants the parts of two pairs pieced together and with a hole already breaking through at one knee. It will show the state of my hearing. He asked me :—"Can you keep a hole sewed up?" "Yes, sir," I said, looking at my holey knee and inadvertently placing my hand over the spot, being at the time stooping to hear him better as he sat back in his chair. The Paymaster and another officer present laughed, the former saying, "He doesn't understand you." "Can you keep a ship's hose sewed up?" came next. "I cannot say, Sir. I am neither a shoemaker nor sailmaker." They all laughed and I looked extremely foolish. "What did you think I said?" I told him, and they had another long laugh. "What kind of a Captain-o'-the-Hold would you make?—I am talking of a ship's hold—h-o-l-d—and neither holes nor hose." "I couldn't promise to be very expert, Sir, as I have never served in that capacity." "Can you s-t-o-w things so that you can find them again?" "Yes, sir."— "Can you find a thing in the dark that *you* stowed away?" "I think I could, Sir." "Could you keep everybody out of the hold?" "Yes, Sir, if I had sole charge." "That is sufficient." When I knew what he was talking about I could manage very well, but the expectation of a reprimand for a hole in my trousers led my understanding astray.

Friday, June 24. This morning the Boatswain told me he had orders to show me the stowage of the hold and put me in charge. I spent the remainder of the day in cleaning out rubbish, scrubbing, and whitewashing. I was messed and mustered with the petty officers. I have felt gratified to know that not a man on board but expresses himself as glad that I have the promotion. My pay is $25 a month, and I have no duty except to take care of the hold. I have no watch at night, being what is called an "idler." My station at quarters is in the shell-room to hook on shell as needed, and in case of fire to stand by the stop-cock for flooding the forward magazine when ordered. Evidently I need not expect my discharge till the ship goes home.

U. S. S. Metacomet, Philadelphia, Pa., Aug. 16, 1865.—After a long waiting the order came for us to sail for this port, and we are here. The hold is empty, clean, and as sweet as a thick coat of whitewash can make it. Inspection is over and we are now receiving a fortnight's furlough, with the privilege of selecting the Boston, New York, or Philadelphia Station as the place for reporting at the end of that time—"those of you who return—*those of you who* RETURN!" as Capt. Crosby expressed it with an emphatic repetition. This was understood to mean that Uncle Sam will not cry or hunt for you should you not return. Few understood it in its meanness, tempting these men to commit the crime of desertion that the country which they had defended at the risk of their lives might take advantage of their action to avoid payment for services already rendered. and to prevent all claims for unpaid installments of bounty, or pensions for injuries received while in the service.

Dracut, Mass., Aug 17. Home at last, all the way from Philadelphia by rail. At Pawtucket Bridge I called at Carter's Store and asked if there was any one going my way that I could get a ride home with. Mr. Carter said, "Your wife is in town," and looking across the street added, "There's your ride at Butler's now." I went over and found my wife telling Mr. Butler that she expected me home any day. On turning to go out she exclaimed, "Oh! Joe!" and was in my arms instantly. How we enjoyed that ride home! At home Sidney climbed upon one knee, Bell upon the other, and little Freddie was almost heartbroken when I told him to "Wait a minute;" but when I put my head down between the others and told him to put his arms around my neck his countenance underwent a great change as he found he was the closest to me. Such a hug he gave me! A happy day to all of us.

————o————

CHAPTER II.

——

IN THE NAVY AFTER THE WAR WAS OVER.

——o——

U. S. Receiving Ship Ohio, Charlestown Navy Yard, Thursday Aug. 31, 1865. I arrived on board the *Ohio* from my furlough this afternoon and had some difficulty in being accepted as the individual described, and the clerk seemed determined to read "C. H." as coal-heaver in place of Capt.-o'-the-Hold. Mr. Gill, my old officer in the launch passed by just then, and his hearty shake of the hand satisfied the clerk. Out of about twenty who were to report at this station only five do so, all petty officers :–John Powers, Boatswain's Mate; John O' Brien, Paymaster's Steward; George H. Gabriel, Surgeon's Steward and Nurse; John Hudson, Cooper and launch-mate; and myself. There are

three or four vessels here fitting out for foreign stations, and
we who have two years to serve cannot expect to remain here
very long. On the way from home I called on Gov. Andrew
at the State House. After asking me a few questions he
endorsed my wife's application for my discharge and I put
it in the mail before reporting on board. I doubt if my first
application was forwarded to Washington from Mobile.

Wednesday, Sept. 27, 1865. 1 was not surprised to get
a letter from my wife saying that the answer to her application was :-"As many men have been discharged as the wants
of the Service will permit."

Wednesday, Nov. 1. I am drafted to start to-morrow
afternoon for the *Princeton*, the Receiving Ship at Philadelphia. There are two-hundred of all grades in the draft.

---

*On board U. S. S. Ticonderoga, Philadelphia, Pa.,—
Saturday, Nov. 11.* We were sent on board this ship in
the afternoon and were stationed at once. I was named as
Main-mast-man, port watch, having with one other man the
charge of the rigging about the mainmast, to see to leading
out all ropes whenever orders are given to haul upon them,
to coil them up afterward, and to keep everything about the
mast neat and always clear for running. It is a desirable
station, but requires a man able to hear well. The gang of
shore carpenters were smoothing down the quarter deck with
adzes and I borrowed a plane of them to smooth the space
about the mast that would belong to my mate and myself to
keep clean. Our Executive Officer, Lt. Commander Allyn,
(now deceased) watched me to see what I was going to do
with it. He let me work and seemed pleased that I did it.

Wednesday, Nov. 15. We straightened things out generally on Monday and bent sails yesterday. The decks were

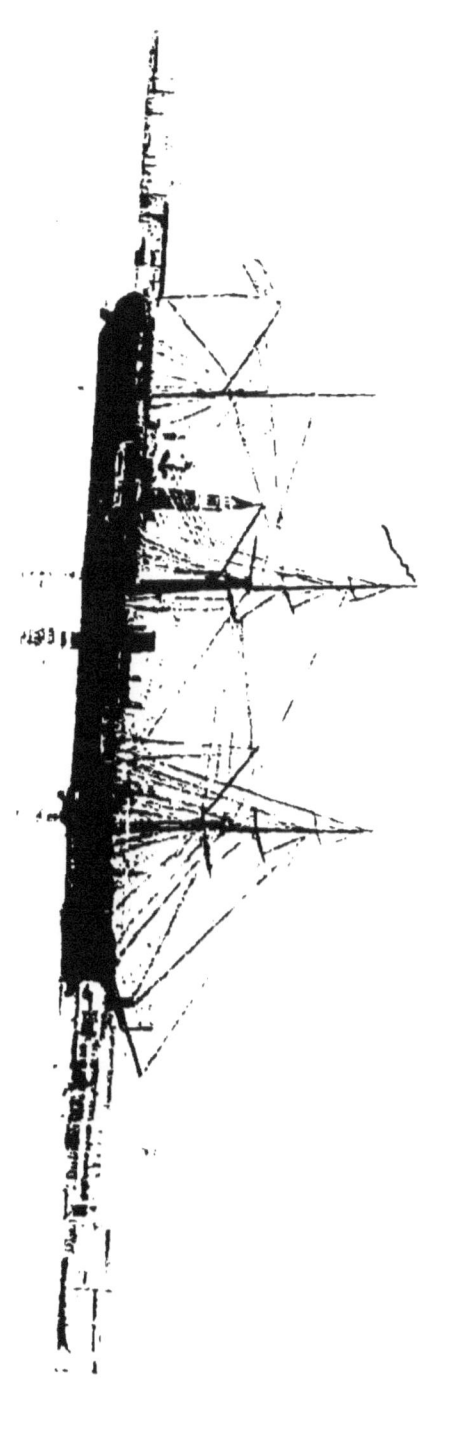

holystoned this morning for the fourth consecutive day in order to get them smooth. In the afternoon the officers gave a grand ball on board. It is rumored that we sail for the Meditterranean in a few days. The *Ticonderoga* is a bark-rigged propeller, carrying two XI-inch (200-pdr) shell guns on pivots, two IX-inch (100-pdr) shell guns in broadside, two 60-pdr rifles forward in broadside, with two 24-pdr and two 12-pdr brass boat-guns mounted on carronade slides in the waist, which we use for saluting. During the war she carried a VI-inch (100-pdr) rifle on the top-gallant-forecastle, her broadside battery was ten IX-inch shell guns, and the two XI-inch pivot shell guns that could be fired from either side. Being long and narrow, with a draft of but 16 feet, her war battery was rather more than Government cared to risk on her upon a cruise across the Atlantic. She had rolled so heavily while off Charleston, S. C. that ten feet had been taken from her lower-masts, hoping that with the reduction also in the weight of her battery she might become more seaworthy, and withal more comfortable in a seaway.

Monday, Nov. 20, 1865. We unmoored and steamed down to Fort Mifflin and took in ammunition, then continued down to the Breakwater and anchored. I drew $20 of my pay and sent it home in a letter. (It never arrived.) I also made over half-pay to my wife, to commence on Jan. 1, 1866, for one year. On the way down I went to the Surgeons for help from increasing deafness. Dr Gunnell, the Chief Surgeon gave both ears the first examination they had received since the injury occurred over fourteen months ago. After syringing them out carefully and thoroughly he examined them through an instrument sending in a beam of light by one tube while he looked through another. He found the scar upon the drum of the right ear and told me that the use of that one was destroyed, but he hoped to save the other, which probably had its auditory nerve affected through sympathy. The drum of the right ear appeared to have been ruptured.

Saturday, Nov. 25, 1865. We got up our anchor and went to sea at 6 A. M. The weather is very fine and we hope for a pleasant passage. We have a very pleasant set of officers, and the men seem disposed to keep them so by cheerful and prompt obedience.

Sunday, Nov. 26. The fine breeze of yesterday has increased to a fresh gale and the ship rolls heavily, keeping the deck full of water and dispelling our pleasant anticipations.

Monday, Nov. 27. Still blowing heavily, with the sea breaking over us continually. The ship rolls her hammock nettings under at every heavy surge.

Tuesday, Nov. 28. Last night was very stormy indeed. The hatches were battened down and every sea plunged over the bow and formed a cascade falling from the top-gallant-forecastle upon the spar deck, keeping it half knee deep in water.

Wednesday, Nov. 29. Before the sea could subside from the last gale another set in from a different direction, and we are having a distressingly unsteady sea. Rolling tackles and extra lashings are everywhere. Last night the other watch in shifting the main topsail let one of the reef-tackles get foul in bending the new topsail. When we came on watch we were ordered to set the sail with a close reef. The men could make no impression at hauling out that reef tackle. I was looking aloft trying to make out where it was foul and did not hear Ensign Wadleigh call me as mainmastman till he called me by my name. When I told him I thought it had a turn around certain other ropes he ordered me to lay aloft and clear it, which I did very quickly. To-day Mr. Allyn told me he would have to change my station from the mainmast and put me in the fore top where I could follow the motions of others when I did not understand an order, adding that the change was not made for any fault of mine, but solely on account of my defective hearing.

Thursday, Nov. 30, 1865. Still blowing as fiercely as ever, and we are rolling and tumbling about worse than we have been at any time before. At 5 A. M. the truss bands to the lower yards commenced to work loose and were taking chips out of the lowermasts at every roll. The foresail was set and the teeth on the inner face of that band of iron took chips three-quarters inch thick and five inches long out of the mast. It was my watch below, but lying close to the hatchway and awake I heard Mr. Allyn order the boatswain's mate to call "All hands save ship!" I threw on my pants and was on deck almost before the call was uttered. As I reached the deck Mr. Allyn caught me by the shoulder and shouted in my ear, " Port watch furl the foresail!" The order answered for others as well as myself, for the ladders were full of men as eager to respond as I, and we lay aloft as fast as we could, the gale pinning us to the shrouds one moment, and the roll of the ship toward us forcing us to hang by the rigging till the upward roll gave us momentum and tautened the shrouds so that we could mount again. We had hardly reached our places on the yard before a cry was raised that the mast was going, and we were ordered to lay down from aloft. Those of us already on the yard found this not so easy to do. Being first on the yard I had laid out to the yard arm and, not hearing the order, passed the leach of the sail in to the next man for furling. Those not already on the yard obeyed the order to lay down with greater alacrity than they had mounted the rigging ; (such are to be found in nearly every crowd) but the passing of the leach to the next man was continued to the bunt of the sail, and we got it furled before attempting to leave the yard. Finding the mast still stood, though the yard surged fearfully, the men who went down were ordered aloft again, and once on the yard worked with a will and we saved both the sail and mast. At the yard arms it seemed as if the waves would reach us at nearly every heavy roll. There were some quite narrow escapes from being jammed between the yard and shrouds in attempting to leave the yard after the sail was furled. I lost my foothold at my attempt, but a sailor is always safe if he has a hand hold, and as the ship rolled the other way my feet caught the rigging and I was all right. Finding the carpenter's gang at the cat-har-pins trying to catch the nuts of the binding bolts to the truss were short a hand to handle a monkey wrench I remained aloft to help. We were two hours aloft before it was secured. I got one of the chips which had to be picked out at the risk of fingers before turning the nut, and this work had to be done while the yard was at rest pressed against the lower rigging at either side. Although with bare head and feet I did not suffer, for the weather had become quite warm. The men of our watch were mustered after the sail was secured to see if there had been any skulkers in the watch. As I failed to answer to my name Mr. Allyn ordered a search for me, saying that I was the first one on deck and aloft. No one had seen me come down from aloft and they began to think I had gone overboard. At the call of my name by the boatswain's mate the Carpenter answered for me that I was aloft helping him, and all became serene. They had experienced some of the delights of having a deaf man on board to be bothered with. We were at work all day getting rolling tackles, extra lashings, preventer stays and backstays everywhere, especially wherever anything depended upon the strength of iron about the rigging. The gale abated somewhat in the afternoon.

A few hours more of such weather would very likely have proved fateful to some of our big guns. We would sooner lose our masts than these pets, for we want to show them to our cousins across the water. It is said they have nothing to equal them over there.

Friday, Dec. 1, 1865. Another gale is buffeting us about at its own pleasure. Department orders were not to use the propeller over forty-eight hours after leaving port, except in case of emergency. Capt. Steadman decides that emergency compels us to start steam to prevent the ship becoming a wreck. Everything alow and aloft is made as secure as is possible by the expenditure of rope for lashings and we take things easy, let the seas pounce in upon us, shake ourselves and try to laugh with our mates at our duckings, but finish with a sullen grin and a wish that the designer of this ship '' had died before he was born,'' or that the ship had rolled the sticks out of her off Charleston, and her bottom also.

Saturday, Dec. 2. The weather was fine in the morning, but the afternoon finds us plunging into the seas and taking in water over the hammock nettings after the usual style. The men aver we are aboard the *Flying Dutchman*. We have had no sail set for the past two days. The carpenters find they can do nothing to secure our lower yards until we arrive in port and have a steady ship so that the trusses will not grind the mast as fast as they compress them. Boat-swain Briscoe and his mates are trying with rope lashings and tackles to secure the yards so that we may be able to set the sails again ''whenever we are favored with a calm,'' as he expresses himself.

Sunday, Dec. 3. Our lower yards are secured so we can set the topsails and we are trying them. To-day is pleasant, though somewhat cloudy.

Monday, Dec. 4. The wind rises with the sun, and the

sea is at its old game of vaulting in upon us from either bow
or gangway. Our decks are never dry.

Tuesday, Dec. 5, 1865. Last night while under reefed
topsails an eye of the parral to the fore topsail yard broke,
letting the yard sway away from the mast and from side to
side, the broken ends of the jaws of the yard striking the
mast at each roll of the ship accompanied by an uplift of the
bow as if determined to shorten our masts to accord with the
breadth of beam. Another substitution of rope in place of
iron was in order. The gale abated in the afternoon.

Wednesday, Dec. 6. I am forty years old to-day. I am
counted an old man among sailors, but they admit that I am
as spry as the youngest and can stand as much hardship as
the most rugged of them. The weather is quite moderate
and the ship moves along under sail very demurely.

Thursday, Dec. 7. A stiff fair breeze is blowing and
we are making good progress toward our port, heading for
Fayal, in the Azores.

Friday, Dec. 8. Being at masthead lookout this morning
I had a fine view of the Island as we approached it under
steam and sail, favored with a fair and gentle breeze. On
rounding a promontory upon the southerly side of the island
we opened the bay and town of Fayal. Opposite to it and
protecting the bay is Paica Pica, a lofty cone, rising with
quite regular sides to above the clouds. The ship fired the
usual salute while I was aloft.

Sunday, Dec. 10. We are coaling ship in the rain. We
took in sixty tons before noon. The coal is dusty and all
wore sufficiently blackened faces and hands to take parts in
a negro minstrel show. Even after that sailor's luxury, a
fresh-water-wash, streaks of black showed under the eyes
and on the edges of the eyelids, giving us a comical appearance at evening muster. We were black-streaked but were

none of us black-listed. That would not have amounted to anything as all were in the same predicament. In fact one not having that countersign would have been called upon to explain his whereabouts during coaling.

Monday, Dec. 11, 1865. We commenced coaling again as soon as the lighter came off, which was not till 10 o'clock. We took in fifteen tons and then cleaned ship. It is still rainy. My deafness is very troublesome in such weather. To-day Midshipman DeLong (of Arctic fame and death) was mustering the men at coaling by the watch numbers, at the same time continuing the work. As I did not answer to my number Peter Wood, the Capt.-o'-the-top pointed to me where I was at work, and "All right, he's deaf," was Mr. DeLong's response. The doctors still drop a mixture into my ear three times daily. Lately they make no examination in the morning, simply order the mixture continued.

Wednesday, Dec. 13. We have made what repairs we could here and to-day set sail for Lisbon at 6 P. M., going out by the eastern passage between Paica Pica and the Island of St. George. It made a very pleasant view.

Thursday, Dec. 14. The breeze increases to a gale and we are under close reefed topsails and storm staysail.

Saturday, Dec. 16. The wind and sea have been very high the past two days. Our two lifebuoys were wrenched from their lashings and lost last night.

Sunday, Dec. 17. *"All Hands Bury the Dead!"* was the call of the boatswain and his mates this noon. Our Surgeon's Steward, named Mellen, an Assistant Surgeon during the war, was found dead in his hammock this morning and we are called to perform the last rites over his body as we commit it to the deep. The sea ran very high, and as the grating was tipped at the stroke of "eight bells" for the body to be launched from the gangway a huge wave met and like a ravenous shark swallowed it before our eyes. The poor man is said to have been disappointed in his betrothed, who married another man while he was at the front, and he tried to drown his disappointment in drink. It is said that our surgeons took pity on him and got him this subordinate position, hoping by the means to wean him from his habit and his sorrow. It proved a vain attempt, as an inspection of the Dispensary stores showed that he had drank the wine and alcohol, and had even used large quantities of morphine. Some of our men had served in the same ship under his care, and their invariable custom of addressing him by his former title of "Doctor" or "Mr." was followed by all of the men. They had known him as always cheerful and taking good care of them and they endeavored to show their continued respect and their sympathy without intruding upon his evident sadness.

Wednesday, Dec. 20, 1865. This is our third day of fine weather and fair wind. The ship has been under full canvass most of the time and the deck continually wet.

Thursday, Dec. 21, 1865. It has been squally and rainy all day, we shipping seas continually. We are trying the ship at beating against a heavy head wind and do not find her a fancy sailboat. Narrowing of the beam for swiftness under steam destroys a ship's power under sail in a great measure. Either the one or the other must naturally be auxiliary until an effective mean has been discovered. A cruiser in war must have sail power to enable her to keep at sea for an indefinite period and not be compelled to enter a friendly port for coal, yet still have sufficient steam power to overhaul or evade an enemy. For the defense of our coast steam may predominate even to the exclusion of sail wholly, but even then a breadth of beam is necessary to enable the ship to carry her battery in safety. In this respect most of our ships designed for use on our coast during the rebellion were extremely faulty. On board this ship we have hardly dared cast loose our guns at sea in the best of weather from fear that the pivot guns, at least, would get beyond control and plunge overboard. They were powerful to look at, but would have literally "left us in the lurch" of the ship, and in the first lurch at that, we sailors believed.

Friday, Dec. 22, 1865. The wind is high and the sea is rough. I had the lookout forward in the last dog watch, and while the rest were aloft furling the foresail I had the chance to report the first light on the European coast. We were about a hundred miles away from our proper striking point. All sails were furled and steam started on a south course.

Saturday, Dec. 23. At 2 P. M. we arrived off the bar at the mouth of the Tagus, thirty miles below Lisbon, and hove to for a pilot.

Sunday, Dec. 24. No pilot came off yesterday and Capt. Steadman concluded to stand in without one. Just in season to claim his fees a man claiming to be *un pilota* came off to us and we moored ship at Lisbon at 1 P. M. We found no Admiral Farragut, nor any American man-o'-war in port.

Monday, Dec. 25. We saluted the Portugese flag with twenty-one guns, also gave one of thirteen to an official.

Saturday, Dec. 30. We have been busy repairing ship since our arrival and today have been painting. It is one of their holidays and we have helped them celebrate by our hoisting the American ensign at the fore and mizzen masts with the Portugese flag at the main, and by firing salutes at noon and sunset. I went to the doctor again yesterday on account of my left ear, telling him it not only pained me and throbbed more than usual but was quite sore externally. He told me that the auditory nerve was diseased and that there was no help for me; that he was very sorry for me and would do what he could to alleviate the pain, which was all he could possibly do, and that I could not expect to hear any better. We have had $2 in American gold served out to us from our grog money account. Our mess put in $1.25 of this for a New Year's dinner. Of course I followed suit though knowing I could get much more gratification out of the ten pounds of figs I bought for 25 cents of our money, a handful of which I allow myself after each meal for other reasons beside the pleasure of eating them.

Monday, Jan. 1, 1866. We have been saluting the old year out for the past two days and have commenced saluting the new year in, saluting twice daily. I hope we will get through soon as I am one of those detailed as saluting guns' crew. We find it a continual bother.

Tuesday, Jan. 2. The Armorer has spotted me as a good hand to blow and strike for him. I have been at that work two days now—when not saluting. We are repairing the iron-work broken during the gale. If the ship keeps up her vicious habit of breaking things I may have added that trade to my list of accomplishments before I reach home.

Sunday, Jan. 7. We up anchor to go to sea to-day, but the engine broke down as soon as we started it and we had to anchor again.

Tuesday, Jan. 9. We made another attempt to get to sea and succeeded, though the engine broke down at a most critical point, only a quarter-mile from the reef just outside the mouth of the river, with the swell setting us on. We got sail upon her in season to avoid it and stood out to sea. I have been in charge of the hold four days while the captain of the hold is sick.

Thursday, Jan. 11. We passed Gibraltar with studding sails set and a very light breeze. I signed accounts with $60.20 due me up to Dec. 31, just 17 cents more than when

I came on board this ship, though I have drawn $20 of my pay at Fort Mifflin to send home.

Friday, Jan. 12, 1866. It begins to breeze up with the wind ahead, so that we are beating to windward along the southern coast of Spain within sight and *feeling* of Grenada's snowy peaks. Our engine broke down just abreast of the entrance to Gibraltar, but our captain did not stop for any repairs.

Sunday, Jan. 14. We are beating under double-reefed topsails, foresail, main-trysail and fore-top-mast-staysail, sighting the same peaks ahead as we near the Spanish coast, evidently gaining nothing on our course. It is cold and I am half seasick from being in the hold most of the time. I have been in the hold for the past nine days doing the work of the capt.-o'-the-hold, who is on the sick list with a badly swelled arm from a boil. At 8 P. M. the gale had broken, the wind going down rapidly though still dead ahead. The ship has been making water faster than the hand pumps can dispose of it readily, and as the engine is now in order the steam was started to pump and to push the ship ahead on her course with all sail furled.

Monday, Jan. 15. A light, warm breeze sprang up from the west at 9 A. M. and all hands were called to make sail. All the square-sails and port studding-sails were set. Soon after noon the wind had hauled to the northward enough to let the fore-and-aft sails draw, and they were set, but at 8 P. M. it was calm again, with all sail furled and steam was pushing us ahead at a grand rate. This morning we were 540 miles from Nice and Ville Franche, the latter being our port.

Tuesday, Jan. 16. A cold breeze from the north is so nearly ahead that our fore-and-aft sails would not fill on our course. We had general exercise at quarters, as has been the practice since leaving Lisbon. We had not been exercised on the trip across from fear of losing our guns, but being all old hands they find we know what to do every time. At 10 A. M., while at quarters, we passed the Island of Majorca, 340 miles from our port. We passed Minorca at sundown, only a few miles distant to the east of us. In the old days Port Mahon, in the southeast corner of this Island, used to be a favorite resort and a naval station for American men-o'-war.

Wednesday, Jan. 17, 1866. A gale commenced with a squall at 9 A. M. All hands had just been called to clean ship, we expecting to reach port early tomorrow morning. The decks had just been wet and sanded to be holystoned, when a barrel of coal-tar broke adrift from its lashings and after staving its own head in against one of the guns took upon itself the task of "cleaning ship" in its own peculiar style. It was intended to be used for painting the anchors, cables, and other iron-work; but it seemed disposed to run amuck and paint every thing except the anchors and cable. The white bulwarks and all the running rigging coiled about the foremast and fore rigging received a generous application. The problem with each man was how to arrest the barrel without himself getting tarred and barreled. Some of it splashed over the coping of the fore hatch, which is some three feet high, and for a time it was feared it might reach the galley fires. Hose were laid to put out the fires in case it reached dangerously near to them. Some came into the hold, but I soon stopped that by putting on the hatches till the berth deck cooks got the fore hatch covered with its gratings and tarpaulins. The barrel was easily captured after the tar had run out; then all the squilgees in the ship were used to prevent the stuff reaching the quarter deck and to force it into the scuppers and overboard. In the hold we were not idle. Barrels and boxes broke adrift repeatedly in spite of our constant watchfulness. Planks stowed in a rack overhead shot out spitefully and dangerously near our heads as we were shoving their neighbors into place. The captain-o'-the-hold was so much better that he could help me considerably. When Dr. Hyde took him to task for his exertion during the melee, he said :—"I thought it was an emergency requiring the use of my steam, sir."

Thursday, Jan. 18, 1866. I was told this morning to take the place of the ship's cook, who got a finger jammed during the ship's riotous behavior yesterday. I find this no sinecure, the work continuing from 3 A. M. to 8 P. M. I greatly dislike the having to get into the hot coppers, (large, square tanks of boiler-iron,) to clean them out after cooking the men's dinner in them, so that I may boil their tea-water in the same tank. One copper is for fresh water exclusively; the other is filled with sea water to boil salt meats and any thing where the water is not to combine with the food to be cooked. This morning the gale abated about as suddenly as it came on. We have been in sight of the Alps all day, and at sundown made fast to a mooring buoy close under the beetling ridges of the Sardinio-French town of Ville Franche.

Friday, Jan. 19. A view of the place by daylight leads one to infer that the town is taking on new life. In all parts of it are new or unfinished houses, and even the ivy-grown walls of some of the ancient ones appear to have been rejuvinated as if just wakened from a Rip Van Winkle sleep of ages. Great public improvements are in course of construction. Along the sides of the ridges on either hand are walls and terraces, the steep sides of the ridges quarried out for carriage ways of easy grades, with cone-shaped heaps of the rubbish tipped down the mountain side in many places. It looks as if Napoleon is trying to found or colonize a city in the new territory ceded him by Victor Emanuel for services in the Lombardy campaign against Austria.

Friday, Jan. 26, 1866. A new French iron-clad, named *La Teressa*, pierced for six broadside guns and having a semi-circular breastwork forward, decked over apparently to form a top-gallaut-forecastle, came into port at sunset.

NAPOLEON'S IDEAL IRON-CLAD.

She looks like a capsized vessel that has had a fence built a few feet from each side of her keel to keep her crew from being washed off her bottom, and two jury masts, a smoke-stack and other appointments erected to see if she would do better that side up. One of her masts is a derrick, though it might answer as a main boom were it not for the small, iron smoke funnel or ventilator just abaft that mast. It is provoking some amusing criticism among our ship's crew. Only two other vessels are in port, both small, and had run in from the gale evidently. They appeared to be waiting for wind enough to get out again. I see no signs of commerce being carried on here, and those going ashore for officers' mess supplies find a great lack of everything they want. I hear that the *Colorado*, flagship of the squadron, sailed from here for Lisbon two days before we arrived, and that we are to follow to-morrow.

Saturday, Jan. 27, 1866. We put to sea at 10 A. M. I was sent to my watch at 8 P. M., I having accidentally capsized a jug of wardroom officers' milk placed in my way by the wardroom cooks while I was getting the mess-cooks' kettles of skouse ready to put on the fire in the morning. I am not sorry to be relieved from the detail, as it was doing the work of a $45 man at about one-third his pay, with no extra compensation.

Sunday, Jan. 28. A fine day with a cool breeze from the southwest. We had quarters, inspection, Divine Service, and reading of the Articles of War at muster; after which we were told that we had behaved so well we would be given liberty as soon as we got to any place where we could stop long enough. This was consoling after listening to Articles terminating in "shall suffer death, or such other punishment as a courtmartial shall adjudge."

Monday, Jan. 29. At midnight we were abreast of Minorca, and daylight found us in sight of Majorca on our port beam. At general quarters exercise this forenoon I got a bayonet thrust in my finger while "repelling boarders." In the afternoon we were exercised in the first principles of fencing. We set all sail at 5 P. M. and shut off steam. It had become calm again at midnight and all hands furled the sails as an exercise when changing the watch. Steam was then started.

Tuesday, Jan. 30. A fine, warm day, the sea scarcely ruffled. They are taking advantage of this fine weather to

perfect us in all kinds of drill before meeting the Admiral.
We had general quarters and fighting-fire drills in the forenoon. In the afternoon we were drilled at facings and at
marking time. I was sent from drill because I could not
hear. The Spanish coast is just discernable to our right.
We met and exchanged colors with a steamer at 4 P. M.

Wednesday, Jan. 31, 1866. Cloudy and inclined to be
rainy. All hands were called to clean ship after breakfast.
which means that we will probably go into Gibraltar. We
sent down topgallant yards and mended the furl of our sails :
that is, we smoothed out all wrinkles and bunches in the furl
to look as neat as possible on going into port. At 4 P. M.
the African coast was visible to the south, stretching east
and west a long distance, while sails were in sight all around
us, coming from or going to "The Rock." The wind had
been freshening during the day, giving us the prospect of a
"nasty night," but it went down with the sun, and at 10 P.
M. it was calm and we were steaming silently along, keeping
a good lookout for becalmed vessels that lay in our course.
The striking of our bell for that hour wakened the watch of
of a small brig just ahead and close to our course, causing
a furious ringing of her bell and rush on deck of those below,
evidently thinking they were about to be run down by us.
Her position had been reported by our lookout some time
before and we were amused to witness their flurry. Their
lookout probably kept awake during the rest of his watch.
We anchored at Gibraltar at 11 P. M.

Thursday, Feb. 1. We saluted "The Rock" at 9 A. M.
and received a salute in return. The *Kearsarge* and *Frolic*,
of our fleet, are in port, the first we have met since leaving
home. We up anchor at 10 o'clock to take a berth nearer
town for convenience in coaling ship. The *Kearsarge* went
to sea in the afternoon.

Friday, Feb. 2, 1866. We got an early breakfast to be ready to coal ship. The *Frolic* went to the eastward at 9 o'clock this morning. She was a captured blockade-runner and an eyesore to the people here. The fog on the African shore leaves only the top of Mount Atlas clear and bare. Here and along the Spanish coast it is streaming up the hills and ravines like steam from many cauldrons. While coaling I saw a fine specimen of coal containing the rings of two trees that had lain side by side, the larger one fifteen inches in diameter. I laid it to one side for leisure to examine it. It caught the eye of the ship's writer, a Harvard graduate, as he passed by, and he was as interested in tracing out the rings and grain of the ancient wood as I was. How much pleasure can be derived from even the slightest knowledge of a science. It often renders interesting many of the simplest incidents that otherwise would be a mere blank. Scarcely another enlisted man in the ship would have noticed these lines in the black mass that told us so much of its past history. "O, it happened so," said one of the boys when the ship's writer was telling them how these rings showed that the coal came from the wood of a tree. His retort that "So did the world happen so!" was accompanied by a look as if he felt that he had been throwing pearls before swine. Mr. Wright was an amused witness to the affair and let it go on as we were not kept from work but were waiting for another lighter to come off. He confirmed our words that this coal once grew as wood in an English swamp. That settled it. The wind had freshened so that we had to give the ship more chain and the sea was so rough when the second lighter came alongside loaded to the gunwales that we had to let her drop astern. She had shipped so much water that she sank just astern of us, her Spanish owner kneeling in the bow praying to the saints till the boat sank under him instead of throwing overboard coal from the bow. This southeast gale is the only wind that can trouble vessels in the bay of Gibraltar. An English steam frigate came in from sea this afternoon and anchored close under the mole. The gales here rise in squalls, are short and sharp, and subside as quickly. It is calm again this evening.

Saturday, Feb. 3, 1866. We got another early breakfast and succeeded in taking in our complement of 200 tons of coal during the day. A little before supper time we had emptied one lighter and another came up to take its place and I took its line to pass to the ship. The empty lighter had been pushed away from the ship until there was about ten feet of water between them. Expecting to find the ship close to me I looked up to pass the line to those on board, but not finding the ship where I expected it and looking up too suddenly, an action sometimes producing dizziness and a roaring in my ears, I lost my balance and having nothing to cling to would have fallen flat upon my stomach had I not jumped to strike the water feet first. When I came to I had been under water some time, for after a few kicks that sent me to the surface I found that messmate Williams and some others had stripped to dive for me, seeing that I remained motionless. A wave helped me to reach the gunwale and I got aboard the empty lighter without much help. The full lighter was some distance astern and they were using their sweeps to get alongside again. Mr. Clark had the deck and ordered me to come aboard and change my clothes. As I reached the deck he laughingly asked me what I jumped for. I said " I thought I needed washing, sir," and after he had his laugh out gave him the true reason. I was sent below with orders to get on dry clothes and finish washing my face as it was too streaked to pass muster. I had been shoveling dusty coal for three hours before taking to the water, and it seems that I had not remained in my bath tub, big as it was, long enough for complete ablution. We went to the coaling again directly after we had supper and finished soon after dark. Everything was left standing until morning.

Sunday, Feb. 4, 1866. We cleared up and washed down the deck before breakfast. After quarters, general inspection, and Divine Service we were set to cleaning ship. We hove short on our cable after supper and at evening quarters secured our guns for sea.

Monday, Feb. 5. All hands were called to up anchor at 11 o'clock last night, and at midnight we were plowing away for Lisbon with our steam rotary plow. This morning our watch washed clothes and while washing decks at 7 o'clock commenced making sail. The Rock still looms up in the distance and several sail are in sight coming out or going in to "The Straits." Coming on deck this noon we found the ship close-hauled on the starboard tack, making an almost direct course for Philadelphia instead of Lisbon. At musket and cutlass drills this afternoon and evening I was sent away by our Division officer, Ensign Wadleigh, on account of my difficulty in hearing orders and my apparent ability to use those weapons effectively. All sails were furled at 4 P. M. and steam started, heading N. W. by N.

Tuesday, Feb. 6. All hands were cleaning ship in the forenoon. The sea was rough this morning, but at noon we were passing the light at the mouth of the Tagus, 24 miles from Lisbon, and in smooth water. We unbent all the light sails and sent down their gear to make the ship look neat and trim aloft on going into port. At 3:30 P. M. we let go our first anchor, and at 6 o'clock were thoroughly moored in the broad expansion of the river opposite Lisbon, and a short distance astern of Admiral Goldsborough's flagship, the *Colorado.* Goldsborough had succeeded Farragut. In port were the *Canandagua*, recently from Boston, and the *Kearsarge*, both bark rigged, respectively one and two sizes smaller than the *Ticonderoga*, the principal difference in size arising from their respective lengths.

Wednesday, Feb. 7, 1866. We scrubbed hammocks this morning. All the boats' masts are being scraped and their sails bent for use. The launch was hoisted out of its chocks ready for lowering and I was set to cleaning her out, which means that I am to be one of her crew. A crew of petty officers is selected for drill in disembarking howitzers from the two largest boats, and probably there is to be a general fleet exercise at landing men and marines, the men acting as soldiers. Saluting is going on all around upon the arrival of a Prussian war brig.

Thursday, Feb. 8. Holystoning decks. A mail came on board, but nothing for me. I was sent into the spirit-room to whitewash and re-stow it. I appear to be made the ship's "general-utility-man." It somtimes works in my favor, this time relieving me of the work in receiving provisions and stores going on at the time.

Friday, Feb. 9. At quarters to-day we thought we were sure to have our expected drill at landing troops, taking our hint from the actions of our officers. It passed off with our getting everything in readiness for that or any other drill the Admiral might order. The axles of our broadside gun-carriages were greased ready for quick work whenever the Admiral came aboard to inspect us. By signal from the flagship we loosed sails with the fleet, and at 1 P. M. furled them upon the same notifiaation. We beat the fleet at both. A sailor's pride is in the character of his ship for smartness. He will undergo any amount of drill with pleasure in order to " beat the fleet" at any general fleet exercise ; and to beat the flagship is his especial endeavor and delight. The men learn to judge when an order is about to be given and they will steal aloft in sufficient numbers to "get everything ready for running," and the flagship is almost sure to have the bunt of her sails half-formed when the signal is broken for the fleet to furl sail. This was our first meeting with the fleet, and the quartermaster on watch kept a bright lookout for and reported these signs of activity at once. Hence, when a series of rolled signal flags was being run up on board the flagship a little before our noon hour was up our master-at-arms passed the word "Everybody on deck!" and we knew just what it meant. The berth-deck was cleared quickly of every man fit for duty except himself. "All hands!" could not be called by the piping of the Boatswain and his mates without detection by the Admiral, nor could any man show himself above the hammock-nettings, or forecastlemen touch a rope on the top-gallant-forecastle, but those who were to furl the jibs were lounging close by, ready to "lay out" at the word of command and every rope was led out ready to be manned the instant the order was given. Our success gave us note with the ships of every nation witnessing the trial. Our officers, from the captain down, are as elated and proud of our success as we are. The clouds and barometer show that a storm is at hand, and we shackled chain to our best sheet anchor. The lateen sails of the fishermen and small coasters as they float in a nearly horizontal position on either side of their masts form quite a pretty view as they scurry into port from the threatened storm. The sails, poised some distance above the boat call to mind a novel of ~~Marryatt's~~ Cooper's, "*THE WING AND WING.*"

In this position the sails have a lifting action upon the boat
and they are quite weatherly in running before a gale on that
account.   They look like so many great gulls sailing with
poised wings close to the surface of the water ready to seize
an object floating there.   At a first glance in the distant
twilight one may be hardly able to tell whether it is a bird or
boat.   My home-made cut will give some idea of the resem-
blance.   We took in fresh water to-day and some was stolen
in transfer from the boats to the water-tanks in the hold by
men for a fresh-water wash.   It was amusing to see them
use it in succession with added supplies of soap until it had
become anything but "fresh."   I preferred to draw a buck-
etful from alongside after the tide had been running out for
some three hours and was quite fresh.   We had watched the
line of river water meet and gain mastery over the salt tide-
water, plainly shown by an agitated line creeping down to
us, the ship swinging to its influence as it passed us on its
way to the sea.   A current of five miles an hour was found
when the log was thrown, and the water with such a current
would be reasonably fresh, yet the water they used was far
better to them for being purloined from the ship's stores.
After supper we sent down top-gallant yards with the fleet
and beat them again.   This fixes our status as the smartest
ship on the station.

Saturday, Feb. 10, 1866.   I slept soundly all night for
the first time in a long while, my ears having been troubling
me exceedingly of late.   I was sent in the spirit-room again
to-day.   Mr. Allyn finds that the smell of the liquor doesn't
affect me.   We received our inspection visit from the Admiral, and he witnessed our drills at quarters, fighting fire, at
making and taking in sail, shifting topsails, and even had
us fish the foremast, (strap joists of wood around it with
ropes, like splinters around a broken arm.)   He expressed

himself as highly pleased with our appearance and behavior.
Everything was done promptly, speedily, without a hitch or
flurry of any kind, and without noisy commands.

Sunday, Feb. 11. 1866.   It is a very rainy and a very
windy day.   Most of the men-o'-war sent down top-gallant
masts or housed topmasts, but we hold on to ours.   We did
nothing but house awnings.   This is done by fastening the
outer edges to the sides of the ship low down, so as to shed
rain.   The water runs off and falls upon the deck and goes
overboard through the scuppers.   Not all of it, for it is the
sailors' time for getting his fresh water scrubbing all over in
water caught from the awnings.   Don Quixote would have
found plenty of occupation in an endeavor to stop windmills
here to-day.   The hills all around us are crowned with them
whirling furiously in the gale, many of them apparently at
work grinding.   The motto here seems to be "Grind your
grain while the wind blows."   We find no quiet Sabbaths
like those of New England anywhere we go.

Monday, Feb. 12, 1866.   The gale had abated somewhat
this morning, though it still rains at intervals.   We had no
exercise at quarters as the housed awning would have inter-
fered with the working of the guns.   I was sent to the hold
to help break out planks and oars for the carpenters in the
forenoon.   There was no ship's work in the afternoon, and
the men were allowed on the berth deck on account of the
rain.   I made a cap for sea service in place of one given a
messmate who had lost his last one overboard while aloft.

Tuesday, Feb. 13.   We had to break out the hold again
to-day for some rice and other things complained of as unfit
for food.   Coffee, bread, rice, and other things, enough to
support a small family three months were condemned by a
"Court" and thrown overboard.   We had been fitted out at
Philadelphia with the remains of stores brought home by

vessels after the war closed and some of it was very poor.
The regulations require that every stick of wood shall be ex-
amined before being put on board a ship for fear of wood
destroying insects getting aboard to multiply, but food destroying insects did not appear to have been guarded against
so thoroughly when fitting us out.   Very likely the authori-
ties acted on the principle of the darkie who covered his hat
very carefully from the rain and worked in the rain with his
wooly pate unprotected.   When asked if he was not afraid
of getting sick by working with his head uncovered, his answer "Hat's mine, head's Massa's" was about as sensible
as allowing weevils and maggots to go on board a ship and
stock its hold and bread-room with their progeny in order to
save that amount of stores to the Government, thinking it
was only sailors who were expected to eat them.   Word is
passed to have all letters for home in the mail-bag to-night.
The *Canandagua* goes to England and the Baltic, while we
go to Gibraltar and expect to visit twenty-two different ports
of the Meditterranean before returning to Lisbon.

Wednesday, Feb. 14, 1866.   We unshackled the chains
from the mooring swivel before breakfast and brought one
chain to the capstan ready to run up one anchor when the
signal is given by the Admiral.   In the presence of the Admiral we have to wait for permission even to lower clothes
lines, no matter how sudden may be a shower in its coming;
There were frequent spits of rain all day and no signal to up
anchor coming we removed the chain from the capstan and
let it run down into the chain locker at sunset.

Thursday, Feb. 15.   We got under weigh at 11 A. M. in
company with the flagship, the *Canandagua*, and *Kearsarge*,
leaving the storeship *Ino* a fixture here.   There are papers
aboard giving an account of the picking up of our lifebuoys
and the supposed loss of the ship.   The buoys were torn

from their lashings by a heavy sea December 16th, on the passage from Fayal to Lisbon. It must have been a time of anxiety to our friends until the news of our safe arrival reached them. After getting an offing the *Canandagua* left us and steered to the northward, bound for English waters, and will probably visit Baltic ports this summer, while we stood to the south with the flagship and the *Kearsarge*, with a prospect of visiting twenty-two Meditterranean ports after filling with coal at Gibraltar. The gallant little *Kearsarge* is keeping closer in shore and farther astern, bound for Cadiz we suppose.

Friday, Feb. 16, 1866. All sails were furled at 8 A. M. We were expecting to be piped to breakfast, but the signal from the Admiral read " Furl all sail!" instead. It didn't make any difference in the result, however, for we beat the flagship handsomely. The *Colorado* was two cable lengths ahead and we could see no signs of preparation made by her men, and sails being set the test was a fair one, for neither crew could do anything toward furling by stealth as when the sails hung in festoons. The *Colorado's* crew will get all the exercise they care for, probably, before we meet again. The forecastle was short of men from sickness and I was one of our topmen sent to help furl the foresail. Not hearing the order "Down booms!" I got caught between the studdingsail boom and fore-yard and squeezed like a lemon in a lemon squeezer. The boom not coming down well the man at the inner end rode it down with his weight. I could not even squeak and would have been seriously injured had not the man outside me called instantly to those on deck to hoist up that boom again.

Saturday, Feb. 17. All hands cleaning ship in the forenoon. I got a harder squeeze than I supposed yesterday, as I feel quite sore about my ribs and am spitting blood at intervals. The doctor thought some small blood vessel in the right lung was ruptured and wound a bandage around my chest tightly several times, telling me not to exert myself for a few days. The Admiral hove to at noon and sent us into port. We anchored at Gibraltar at 5 P. M. and hoisted the seniority flag, the storeship *National Guard* being there.

Sunday, Feb. 18, 1866. The sentences of a courtmartial on four of our men were read at muster this morning. One was fined two months pay and deprived of liberty ashore on the station for jumping overboard and trying to swim away while drunk. Another got drunk while on duty ashore and resisted a marine on board who attempted to take him in custody and tore the coat of John Margerum, another marine in the scuffle to overpower him. He was fined two months pay, $2 for the coat, and deprived of liberty at the next port where liberty is given. The third man smuggled liquor on board and sold to the first and fourth. He received the same sentence as the first man ; while the fourth man, for simply getting drunk upon the smuggled liquor without being very disorderly was given ten days confinement in double irons. After supper we rigged stagings for coaling ship to-morrow.

Monday, Feb. 19. We took in 90 tons of coal. I still continuing to spit blood occasionally the doctor tightened the bandage and let me run, though the bandage hurts my sore ribs at every pull upon a rope. We got under weigh at 7 P. M. for Malaga.

Tuesday, Feb. 20. We anchored in the outer harbor of Malaga at 8 A. M. and then loosed sails to dry. I was in the sail-room to-day overhauling sails to transfer some spare sails to another room. The rest of the men were scraping and slushing (greasing) masts, or other work of the kind. Being sent on these details by order of Mr. Allyn the men can only growl when it relieves me from a share of some unpleasant work, though they are free to acknowledge that it does not always work in my favor, and that I never shirk or hang back from any duty when on deck. Charlie Norwood and Tom Webster, two native Americans from Maine, reminded them at dinner time that it didn't give me a fat job though it was a "slushy" one when I had to do the ship's cook's work, and Capt.-o'-the-top Pete Wood silenced the growlers when he told them that not one of them would be trusted to do the things I had to do even if they could do them, and they would be in the sick bay now if they had my squeeze on the fore yard. "That's so!" said one, and they turned to growling at each other for suggesting such a thing. They are not disposed to be unfair about anything, but have to be shown wherein they are at fault when the thing does not work in their favor. They will be inclined to favor me quite a while now, at least until this mess growl is forgotten.

Monday, Feb. 21, 1866. We gave our hammocks their fortnightly scrubbing. We receive our clean hammocks the night before and return the scrubbed ones at inspection of them at quarters after they are dry. The bedding is aired monthly by fastening in the lower rigging by the middle with the mattrass and blankets opened out to the sun and wind. We saluted some Spanish officers that visited the ship. Our XI-inch guns excite great interest. They examine outside, they look into the big muzzles of these guns and then at each other as if they were ahead of their time ; and they are. The *Frolic* lies inside the breakwater and her boats' crews are on board occasionally. This forenoon 24 names were called for going ashore on liberty, and my name was among them. We were supplied with half-a-month's pay each in Spanish gold and told to get ready to go ashore after dinner for a 24 hours' leave. While at the mess cloth spread near the top-gallant forecastle Norwood jokingly said, " Stuart, now don't run away till we have a chance ashore." My answer was "What I may do will not hurt your chance," but it seems that some of the officers were in hearing, for when we were mustered in the gangway to be set ashore Mr. Allyn looked at me and asked if that was the best suit I had. (It was better than the rest by a mustering jacket; all new but the frock.) He said I didn't look well enough to go and I couldn't go ashore looking so. I told him I would be glad to wait until I had finished a new mustering frock and take my turn another time. I was told I couldn't wait and could not have it another time; so I responded, "Aye, aye, sir," and walked forward in an extremely erect manner. They tell me they expected Mr. Allyn to call me back and punish me by the way he looked after me, but that he turned to Mr. Wadleigh and said, "He's a spunky fellow, anyway." He intended to nip my supposed deserting scheme in the bud. Boatswain Briscoe met me on my way forward to know what was the trouble and offered to lend me a frock of his sailor mustering suit when a seaman, and when I told him of Norwood's remark he offered to go my security. I told him that "I would rather stay aboard until my officers learned to respect and trust me than to have any one go my security, and that I would stay on board till Mr. Allyn was satisfied that I had no intention of deserting and put my name on a liberty list of his own accord—I certainly should not ask for liberty until then." I would have liked to see the country, noted as it is for its raisin grape, but the city, according to reports of the *Frolic's* men, is mean looking and has nothing worth seeing except the cathedral. It is probably a fair sample of small Spanish and Portugese towns; a collection of one or two room cabins of adobe or sun-dried blocks of clay about four times the dimensions each way of our brick, and white or yellow-washed on the outside, with the bare and filthy earth for a floor, infested by mangy curs, fleas, and other vermin, and plastered with mud on the inner walls. The roofs are covered with the only cleanly material about them—fire-burned, gutter-shaped tiles, arranged to form lines of gutters from the ridge to the eaves, each alternate line inverted after this manner :— ∿∿∿ to lead the water into the line of gutters on each side. The country is quite hilly, the hills steep and full of ravines, and only an occasional tree to be seen. While I was sewing upon my new frock to-day one of the sleeves and my scissors disappeared. No trace of them could be found among the men who were sewing near me. Someone wanted a patch, badly.

Thursday, Feb. 22, 1866. It being Washington's birth-day we hoisted ensigns at our mastheads at daylight and at noon fired a salute in honor of the day. It was so rainy we did not wash decks in the morning. The liberty men are coming off singly and in pairs, and most of them are drunk and dirty, if no worse. The material for our fresh soup was so scanty that the ship's cook with other petty officers went to the mast with a complaint and obtained some rice to put with it. Instead of 250 pounds of fresh beef there were 175 only, and of vegetables the supply was even more scanty as also unusual in kind for a soup. One-half-bushel green peas in the (not edible) pods, six carrots, one good-sized squash, one peck of onions, and one bushel of potatoes cleaned out the market according to the Paymaster's Steward who bought the material. It was intended for 220 men. The smacks, small sailing vessels, and even steamers have been running into port for shelter all the forenoon. A lady, wife of the *Colorado's* Chief Engineer, came off in the last boat at 2 P. M. as we were getting under weigh, and as the sea was very rough she was hoisted with the boat and helped on board after it was run up. In the evening we were off *Capo De*

Gata, or Cat Cape, with a gale blowing in our teeth and the snowy peaks of the Sierra Nevada sending down chilly gusts that made us quite uncomfortable.

Friday, Feb. 23, 1866. Morning found us still plunging into a heavy head sea and abreast the same cape. In the afternoon the lady passenger was nearly washed out of her berth by the sea bursting in her cabin deadlight. Hatches are battened down, for great seas are tumbling in upon us over our bows and gangways, flooding the decks two feet in depth at times; in fact plunging over the combings of the fire-room hatch which is three feet high. At 2 P. M. things began to break in earnest and we were forced to steer into quieter seas under the shelter of the cape. The gale began to subside at sunset and at midnight we resumed our course.

Saturday, Feb. 24. This morning found us with the sea smooth again. I ate my ration of bread skouse with good relish this morning, for I had fasted since Thursday noon on account of seasickness produced by the storm. We did not anchor at Carthagena until 7 P. M.

Sunday, Feb. 25. From our anchorage the city looks to be quite well built, with a wall running along the shore the greater part of its length. There is a little knoll near the city that has a cave under it, and as the gales sweep in from the sea the water rushes into its mouth with much splashing and roaring. We find here a Spanish 90-gun ship, a frigate, and a 16-gun brig; also our own little *Frolic*. She sailed from Malaga the day before the storm and reached this port before it had fairly set in. There is a Belfast, Me. ship in port short of men, and her captain was aboard begging for ten men to take the ship home. He did not succeed in his endeavor. Men would have been willing to go if they could have protection of an officer with them, but they were shy of a ship whose captain for any reason could not keep his crew.

Monday, Feb. 26, 1866. To-day we have been kept very busy breaking out and re-stowing the hold to get four small water casks for a catamaran or floating staging for working around the sides of the ship. It seems as if nothing ever came handy in this ship's hold. Eight men were sent into the hold to help the captain-of-the-hold. About half of the eight would help its captain look on most of the time, while the rest did the work. The Boatswain came down to see to the re-stowage, and as I was forcing a barrel into place by my feet against the barrel and my shoulders braced against whatever I could find, he exclaimed, " I never saw such a man ! You work with your hands, feet, head, and shoulders all four at once." John Hudson told him " Nobody ever had to go into the *Metacomet's* hold to help break out after Stuart had charge." Our captain-of-the-hold is as good as they will average, but the average man-o'war's-man is rarely capable of much effective head-work. It began to blow at sunset and I jokingly remarked to a shipmate that this ship could not remain in port in such weather and that we would have to get to sea before eight bells. At six bells (7 o'clock) the call to up anchor came, and at eight bells our watch took the deck with the ship diving into a heavy swell, making her way out to sea. The deck was soon half-knee-deep with water. Our port was to leeward and we were congratulating each other on very soon gaining an offing and would then put the helm up and slip along with dryer decks under sail. But this was a delicate operation in a heavy sea for our top-heavy ship. It nearly proved disastrous. Suddenly, with no warning she rolled her port hammock nettings under and the water rushed on board the whole length of the ship, and flooded the berth deck, fireroom, and even the steerage and wardroom with water. We almost hoped to see the masts go over the side, and we would have even spared one of our

pets, the pivot guns, were it not that the men were in the lee
scuppers where its eight tons of iron would have crushed
them in its course through the bulwarks. Everything made
so secure that it could not get away cracked and whistled
with the strain, and everything not securely lashed brought
up in the port scuppers mixed with legs, pump-brakes, arms,
feet, halliard-racks, heads, and spittoons, all in a confused
medley, with the water pouring upon and bearing them down.
The ship lay in this position a moment as though surprised
with us at this sudden and most furious assault from her
old enemy; but she gathered herself for the recoil—and recoil she did—sending everything over to the other scuppers
with an addition to the number of men by those who had
forced their way up the hatches under the impression that
the ship was on her beam ends and filling. They were in
season to catch a pouring bath from over the starboard rail.
Their hammocks had swung so as to strike the deck beams
above them with force. We gathered ourselves the best we
could and held on to the nearest stationary object—except
the pivot gun,—looked for what might come next, and waited
for orders. By this time the ship had gotten before the wind
enough to be out of the trough, and soon getting steady she
gaily raced the waves on her course. One of the watch below was seen wearing a spittoon on his head as he was on
the point of stepping upon the ladder to return to his hammock. He hadn't stopped to dress when he came on deck
and he looked so comical in spittoon and short-tailed frock
stepping over the combing of the hatch three feet above us
that he was greeted with a roar of laughter. "Loose the
fore-top-sail!" came the order, and we found the ship was
going nearly east. We passed two lights, (at Cape Palos,)
and the coast then trending to the northward our course was
changed accordingly. While on lookout between 10 and 12

I reported a dim light (at Cape Nao or Ship Cape) far to the north. Our topsail was then taken in and speed slackened. *Tuesday, Feb. 27, 1866.* In the morning we found the gale had abated and that we were lying to off the harbor of Alicante. We entered and came to anchor at 8 : 30, during a heavy fall of rain. At noon it was blowing quite freshly again. To-day completes half my term of service. Our boat, the 2nd cutter, took some of our officers ashore, but though we could rub our hands against the jetty wall we were not allowed to enter the city or even step ashore. We had the same satisfaction as the miser's son who was allowed to rub his bread against the cupboard door where the cheese was kept. If the portions of Spanish soil I have seen are fair specimens I wonder not at the backward state of its agriculture. Ragged, desolate edges of rocky, steep hillsides, destitute of a single tree or sign of vegetation, markets devoid of everything but a few vegetables, dried figs, roasted squash seeds, sour oranges, and FISH attest to this state. These crags are crowned by ruinous castles or fortifications. An extremely unfinished looking breakwater partially shelters small vessels from the storms that rise here with scarcely a warning. The rock for building this appears to have been quarried from an adjacent hill in the rear of the town, and they had removed the hill close up to the foot of a castle that crowned the hilltop, leaving almost vertical faces to those of its sides toward the city and harbor. Another hill a short mile farther away seems to have been more recently used, though appearances would scarcely justify one in claiming it to have been done at as late a date as the Pliocene Age. I reported my second installment of bounty as now payable and found it could not be paid except by an order from the captain of the ship. It is getting so rough at sunset that we are expecting to hear the call to up anchor at any moment to

worry out the gale at sea, though the more probable theory
is that the time allotted us to make the grand tour of the
Meditterranean is so short that the captain uses nights to go
from one unimportant port to another and stops only a day
where our presence is not needed by our consul.

Wednesday, Feb. 28, 1866. We went to the jetty again
to-day, but were no nearer stepping ashore than yesterday.
The character of the men entering our naval service is such
that officers dare not trust them until they have proved their
reliability. The few native Americans of trustworthiness
that do enter have to undergo the same test as others. We
cannot blame our officers for being unable to know at first
sight who can be trusted; for some of the best seamen are
unable to trust themselves where liquor is obtainable. In
no Service, either naval or merchant, does a seaman receive
so good treatment as in the U. S. Navy, yet there are some
nationalities that seem unable to keep faith if occasion offers
to break it. A desire for frequent change seems to possess
them and they do not even themselves know when the fit to
desert will take them. I finished my new mustering frock
this afternoon and it hangs to suit the most fastidious man-
o'-war's-man. We went to sea at 6 P. M. for Valencia, 160
miles distant.

Thursday, Mar. 1. We came to anchor in the harbor of
Valencia shortly after nine o'clock this morning. I went to
the captain asking for my bounty to send home to make a
payment on my farm, handing in the Selectmen's certificate
as evidence of my owning one. The Paymaster says that
his books have it that the full bounty of $300 has actually
been paid. I said "The second installment was not due till
two days ago, sir." "Bluff!" might have been read in my
look. The Captain said "Of course it could not have been
paid before it was due, but we cannot pay it till the error is

corrected, and the Paymaster will write to Washington for
the correction." He then read the Selectmen's certificate
aloud to the knot of officers who had gathered near enough
to hear what was going on. His reading it gave them to
understand that he thought this man will not run away, as
his selectmen say that "he owns a farm at home, and he is
strictly temperate and thoroughly reliable in every respect."
We have here a Spanish town on level ground. Single trees
and orchards studd the plain which extends back of the city
several miles in the form of a triangle. The hills rise suddenly from the edges of the plain, walling it in. It is well
watered by a stream coming through a gap in the mountains
at the apex of the triangle. The name, Valencia del Cid,
would imply that it was founded by Ruy Diaz "The Cid,"
Count of Bivar, a champion of Christianity and of the old
Spanish royalty in the 11th century; yet they are but now
building a breakwater to protect the shipping seeking shelter
or a mart.

Friday, Mar. 2, 1866. We up anchor at 6 P. M. for
Barcelona. At midnight we were passing a light to the east,
supposed to be Columbretes Rocks, the mainland showing
dimly on the western horizon in the light of the full moon.
The "switchtails" were running across the sky at sunset and
I prophesied wind and perhaps rain for to-morrow. Mr.
Wright asked me why I thought so. On my pointing out to
him the lines running across the sky like meridian lines on a
globe and many of them branching out like a switching tail
of a horse, he remarked, "Time will tell whether you are a
true prophet." I asked him to take note of it to-morrow.

Saturday, Mar. 3. We came to anchor in the outer harbor of Barcelona at 12 : 30 this noon, rolling our studding-
sail-booms out from the yards, the wind being quite fresh
with considerable sea running. Here is another attempt at

a breakwater, or rather two of them. Work upon one has apparently ceased long ago, though it is looking unfinished. They are still at work on the other. The line of snow on the mountain tops reaches to a lower level than heretofore, for we are some five degrees to the north of Cape de Gata, being now in the latitude of New Haven. At 2 P. M. we had to pay out cable to 80 fathoms, the wind still increasing and the ship rolling as if at sea. At sunset it began to calm down and at midnight we lay almost motionless upon smooth water.

Sunday, Mar. 4, 1866. All hands in our best blue suits for mustering, yet were called to up anchor to go into the inner harbor to moorings. We got moored and the decks cleaned again at 1 P. M. We were full of visitors all the afternoon. We had saluted the Spanish flag at 8 A. M. and had received that from the fort in return.

Monday, Mar. 5. We are painting the outside of the ship for the fourth time since leaving Philadelphia. A list of thirty men was read to go ashore on liberty for 24 hours.

Tuesday, Mar. 6. The liberty men come off slowly and behind time. We have been alongside the landing several times to-day, but it being my day to keep boat I did not get a chance to go ashore till after dinner, although one of the boys had promised to relieve me long enough to get some writing paper in return for a like favor received. They all intend to keep their word when they start out, but they find so many attractions, especially when there are liberty men ashore that they wait just a moment longer, or forget their promise entirely until the appearance of the officer of the boat causes them to hurry down to take their places. At this time Mr. Clark got down before part of the boys did, and I got permission to run up to a stall at the head of the landing to get some writing paper, which the men said they saw there. The woman in charge seeing me coming upon a run brought out a dirty tumbler and seemed greatly surprised that I didn't want to "take something." She had paper of a quality of good "news" paper, cut and folded like letter paper, and two sheets of spongy ruled paper. She told me there was a paper store just inside the city gate; but I had permission to go only that far and I returned to the boat to get permission to go there. I was told the boat was behind time already and must shove off at once. I stepped into the boat cheerfully and took my oar at once. After getting on board the ship one of my boatmates called me a fool for not going inside the gate and getting my paper, saying that Mr. Clark wouldn't have said anything if I had done so. We got into quite a discussion concerning its advisability, and sides were being taken among the messmates when a ward-room waiter came along inquiring for Stuart, the foretopman, and handed me a quire of fine quality letter paper and a bunch of envelopes, such as are used for foreign mail, saying they were from Mr. Clark. "Now, who's the fool?" was the remark of one of the men, and the jokes were on the other party. I had been well rewarded for my obeying the *letter* of my permission, and they had received indisputable evidence that officers appreciate prompt and cheerful acqui-escence in a refusal of favors asked. Some of the liberty men broke a wagon they had hired yesterday, and with oth-ers who had been locked up for "getting up a shindy" broke the station house door and escaped. Most of those coming off are in pretty good order for sailors, though they are quite "happy." One was too grand to come off in a ship's boat and chartered one with a crew of two rowers for the occasion and sat with tipsy dignity perched upon the sternpost of the boat. Some apprentices and marines were among those on liberty. One of the apprentices came off in a beastly state

of intoxication, made so by one of the men, unwillingly on
his part. Mr. Allyn investigated the matter, and I judge
from his countenance that the man will not get liberty again
very soon.

Wednesday, Mar. 7, 1866. The last of the liberty men
came off this morning, twenty-four hours over time. One
of them is a petty-officer. Another lot started soon after.
They had been held back until all the first lot had returned,
a rule that works admirably when boats' crews are allowed
to run up for a short time while the officer of the boat is on
his own errand, as some of these men will be on the list of
those held back, and they will find and coax the delinquents
down to the boat, and even use some force to keep them in
the vicinity, if needed, until their officer appears. A gale
is blowing with a chilly rain.

Thursday, Mar. 8. The gale has become quite heavy,
and as it blows directly into the harbor even vessels inside
the breakwater are as active in their rolling and pitching as
any old salt could desire. We found it rough at the landing,
the swell rolling in so forcibly that the Spanish boatmen had
hauled their boats out of the water. The fishing smacks are
scudding in under wing-and-wing for shelter. Occasionally
a spit of rain gives variety to the weather without improving
the temperature. After putting the liberty men ashore I was
sent into the hold to take charge while its captain was on
liberty. Quite a pleasant detail in this weather.

Friday, Mar. 9. Those on deck are coaling ship to-day.
Having little to do in the hold I repaired my portfolio, which
was in a very loose condition.

Saturday, Mar. 10. We are receiving water and at the
same time holystoning decks. This gives me the hatches to
the hold to scrub while attending to my fresh water tanks.
We got ready for sea in the afternoon and up anchor at the

setting of the sun. The liberty men had come off very drunk. One man brought down to the boat a quantity of liquor to treat the boat's crew and all but "Little Smith," an apprentice of our mess, guzzled it down in a hurry to get it out of sight before the officer appeared; as a result one of them is slightly drunk on duty for a second time to-day. At 8 P. M. I went to my deck duty, as by morning the proper person will have become sufficiently sobered to be able to do his own work. It takes at least twelve hours for an average liberty man to recover from a spree ashore.

Sunday, Mar. 11, 1866. We had a stiff breeze and a somewhat rough sea with heavy clouds and lightning to the north and east of us last night. It rained heavily with us at about 8 A. M., after which the sun came out warm and very pleasant, though at times hidden by masses of cumuli. The sea smoothed down with the breeze and we had quarters, inspection, and muster. In the afternoon we had Divine Service, led by a real "reverend" in his canonicals. This clergyman, his son and son's wife are passengers in the cabin. It is a small thing to mention, but my brightwork was highly praised by Captain Steadman at inspection this morning as being nicely kept. I had from the first been in the habit of using the smooth, round back of my shears as a burnisher and at this time had gotten every portion polished so that I had comparatively little trouble in keeping it bright. (This praise from the Captain started the scissors of the others of our gun's crew into energetic action, enthusing the crew of the after pivot gun, so that in a short time they watched the quick glance of visiting naval officers as they passed their guns and were proud of their work.) Our gun being just at the starboard gangway, and Captain Steadman knowing the pride a Yankee sailor takes in the trim appearance of his ship if he is not *forced* into the work of making her so, took

his opportunity, probably, to bring out the spirit of emula-
tion by a little praise.   Had all hands been compelled to do
this same work from their first entering the ship they would
very likely have been in the almost mutinous condition of
the crew of the frigate *Congress*, at Rio, in 1843.   Sailors
have some of the characteristics of mules.   A great deal of
work can be gotten out of them if they are made to think
they are having their own way.   It was only necessary for
Mr. De Long, of our gun, or Mr. Hitchcock, of his gun, at
their preliminary inspection of their respective guns before
quarters, to say to a man "Your brightwork rags must be
damp, your brightwork is tarnishing," to start the man with
a clean, dry cloth, even if it has to be the black silk neck-
erchief from his neck.   I finished reading the Massachusetts
Agricultural Report for 1859, taken from the ship's library.
Queer reading to put in a ship's library, but it proved very
interesting reading to me and gave me a subject for thought
on my lookout at night.   "Muck, and its use on the farm"
was treated in its pages so enthusiastically that I could not
but plan for extensive exchanges between my gravelly soil
and the rich peat of my meadow, to the advantage of both.

Monday, Mar. 12.   At 7 A. M. we were off the Island
of Sardinia and ran between it and a small island south of it.
At ten o'clock a target of five empty beef barrels with a sail
about ten feet square was dropped over the side and after a
mile of distance had been gained the ship was hove to and
the long roll called us to quarters for target practice.   At
his third shot Jordan of our IX-inch broadside gun struck
the barrels and demolished the target.   Of the fourteen shots
fired all would have hulled a ship of our size.   Jordan has
a Congress medal for distinguished services during the war.

Tuesday, Mar. 13.   Land was made upon our starboard
bow this morning at 7 o'clock.   During the forenoon we

drilled at shifting topsails three times. At the second time
one captain of each top was sent to the berth deck out of the
drill as if sick, and at the last time we were required to do
it without any petty-officer aloft in either top. It proved
satisfactory in each case, as was evident by the pleased looks
of our officers. We feel confident of retaining our laurels.

Wednesday, Mar. 14, 1866. We came to anchor in the
harbor of Messina at 10 : 30 A. M. It is a rainy day with
thunder and lightning in the afternoon.

Friday, Mar. 16. Yesterday we took in coal and also
sand. To-day we were visited by some high officials just at
noon, keeping us from our dinner. We do not enjoy eating
cold boiled rice and salt beef for any one, however noted he
may be. We got under weigh at 2 P. M. and steered to the
southward. The Italian shore is studded with villages, set
upon the hillsides generally, and occasionally are groves of
olive and fig trees about some old mansion, but not a forest
tree was to be seen crowning the many hilltops. As a natural consequence the soil is washed into deep gulches with
inclined planes at the outlets, and these are again cut and
re-cut until the whole face of the shore line as seen from the
Straits of Messina appears to be a confused medley of heaps
of dirt, gravel, rocks, and bare ledges.

Saturday, Mar. 17. We have rounded the "Toe of the
Boot" and are steering east, bound for the Island of Candia,
the ancient Crete. This afternoon I made me a cap for
going on liberty and special mustering wear. We have a
pair of canaries on board. With a quill whistle and tin cup
of water I inaugurated quite a bird concert with them. It
was supposed they had lost their song as they only uttered
an occasional chirp. After hearing my prolonged trilling a
few times from a hidden position they almost split their little throats in trying to outsing me. They thought they had

succeeded when I stopped, and they then tried to outsing each other.   No one showed more interest in the experiment than "Old Ti." the Captain's large Newfoundland dog, a genius in his way.   His full name is Ticonderoga, but he will answer to "Ticon." and prefers "Ti."   He has been trained to carry his dinner in a small basket from the cabin pantry to the "manger," (an enclosed iron-lined space in the extreme bows of the ship around the hawse-holes through which the chain cables or hawsers pass,) and after his meal is finished to return his basket to the cabin waiter.   He and the ship's cat are good friends, though his majesty "Tom" originally mistrusted his advances, it is said.   A share of Ti's dinner placed near him was too tempting an offer for Tom to refuse, and they now often eat out of the same dish. Ti is sometimes put through his gymnastics by the Captain's Clerk and seems to enjoy it as well as the rest until the stick is held so high that he comes down upon the deck with such force as to draw from him a yelp of pain.   While the decks were being washed one morning Ti wanted to go upon the topgallant forecastle, where he saw they had finished; but the step-ladders were unshipped.   He tried to go up by a rope ladder used by us at such times, but could not, and he barked for help.   We helped him up, and now he comes to me when he wants the same help, I being the first to understand his call.   He usually secures a safe retreat upon the Boatswain's locker on the topgallant forecastle at the call to " Wash down the decks !"   If caught below he often tries to climb without assistance and the men believe he will succeed in time.

Sunday, Mar. 18, 1866.   Land made on our port bow. We had the usual inspection at quarters, general inspection, and Divine Service in the forenoon, but no muster.   I got the Bible Dictionary from the library and read up Jerusalem as we hope to be allowed to go there from Joppa during our tour of the Meditterranean. The wind is nearly aft and we have studdingsails set.

Monday, Mar. 19, 1866. We were making and taking in sail nearly all the first watch last night. This morning we found land in sight on our starboard bow when our watch came on deck at 4 o'clock, and at 10 A. M. we anchored in the harbor of Candia, on the northern coast of that Island. Snow covers the tops of the mountains nearly half-way to the sea level. The oranges and figs here are the best I have tasted, but they ask us high prices for them. The costumes and government are Turkish. Visitors came on board us in large numbers during the afternoon. This we favor as it gives the people an idea of our power as a nation when they see such large guns on so small a vessel, and they will be apt to treat our countrymen and consuls with greater respect than has recently been their wont.

Tuesday, Mar. 20. I have to-day finished a complete suit of clothes that will pass muster for going ashore on liberty, and though my first trial since boyhood it is said to come up to the Yankee man-o'-war's-man's idea of a natty fit. We shortened cable at 5 P. M. and sent up topgallant yards ready for sea. At 7 o'clock the Captain came off in the 1st cutter, the gig returning with three men drunk. At 8 o'clock we were standing out of the harbor bound for Smyrna.

Wednesday, Mar. 21. At 8 A. M. we came to off Milo and took a pilot for Smyrna. At 4 P. M. we passed a large city to the west of us, supposed to be Syra, the ancient Hermopolis. At sunset a heavy gale set in, preceded by the switchtail forerunners all over the heavens.

Thursday, Mar. 22. "*Hard a-port!—Breakers under the lee bow!*" shouted the lookout forward just after midnight, and the ship came into the wind obedient to the helm, clearing the rocks by about twice her length only. A scene of apparent confusion began, the sails flapping and cracking like huge coachwhips, the watch below rushing on deck to aid without being called, and the men hurrying from one rope to another in obedience to orders to haul down and clew up the head sails, then to brail up the trysails. It is on such occasions that discipline and constant drill prove their worth. A maintopsail sheet had parted in the early part of the night, and although its sail being furled may have caused the ship to sag to leeward through a preponderance of head sail this made the ship swing more rapidly when the squaresails took aback, checking the speed at the same time. A timely lift from the propeller sent us ahead when needed and we were out of danger. One old salt got off the old saying, "A miss is as good as a mile." Mr. Hitchcock retorted, "That's all right, but in this case I prefer the mile to the Miss." By daylight we could have avoided it easily, but in a gale at night it is not so easy to distinguish between the normal cap of the waves and the spray of a breaker unless one expects or is warned of the probable presence of breakers. We are learning what a Levanter is. Topgallant yards were sent down in the first watch last night. This morning we found the ship was entering the Gulf of Smyrna when we came on deck and the gale was still blowing. At 2 P. M. we had dropped both anchors in the harbor of Smyrna. I was told by Mr. Allyn to hold myself in readiness for boat duty as a supernumerary in the 1st cutter. I have to appear at the gangway whenever that boat is called away, dressed in clean mustering clothes and the "Ticonderoga" ribbon on my cap ready to step into the boat if needed to fill the place of any absent member of her crew, with liability to be called upon for the same duty in any boat. This excuses me from any dirty work on board the ship and may be either an easy or hard work for me according to whether not any, or more than one boat is short-handed.

Friday, Mar. 23, 1866. We are having a warm and pleasant day after the storm. The launches were lowered and their sailing qualities tested. To-day the Yeoman left a lantern burning in the storeroom while he went on deck and when he returned found a partition on fire. It was quickly extinguished by help of some of the mess cooks without any general alarm, but of course had to be reported and investigated. He fears a courtmartial for criminal carelessness.

Saturday, Mar. 24. The *T. Ward*, of Berwick, Maine, sailed to-day for New York with our letters. For our drill this forenoon we had "Away all boats, armed and equipped." The boats' howitzers were lowered into the launches, marines filled the sternsheets of the boats, and we were exercised at sailing by signal from the ship. I was a launchman for the day. On our return I was ordered to change to a working suit and go into the fore passage and yeoman's storeroom to help him repair damages. He showed me where things were stowed, expecting nothing short of being disrated and that I had already been selected to take his place. He feels badly over the mishap, and we are all sorry for him.

Sunday, Mar. 25. Three coal lighters came alongside as we went to quarters and were sent away till to-morrow. It is said that we are within an hour's ride of the ruins of the Church of Ephesus, "where Paul once preached." *Perhaps* Paul may have preached at the site where the church now in ruins was afterward built, but it does not seem probable to me that the Christians had become powerful enough to erect so extensive a structure in his day as these ruins are said to indicate. Upon a hill-top just back of the city are the ruins of an immense castle, and beyond these, on the other slope, are the church ruins. On the near slope, within the precincts

of the city are several Moslem cemeteries, with their groves
of dark evergreen mourning cypress trees.   Within the city
are several mosques with tall, slim towers, called minarets,
having one or more stories of balconies surrounding them,
from which the muezzin call the faithful to prayer ; also one
cathedral shaped building and its tower, but nearly, if not
quite, all other buildings are flat roofed.   It is tantalizing
to be so near to such objects of interest and to be unable to
examine them.   The boats' crews report the streets infested
by beggars ; men and one woman seen were entirely naked,
squatting by the sides of buildings, their bodies covered with
disgusting sores.

Monday, Mar. 26, 1866.   We saw cars running along
the beach to the north of the city.   Engineers and firemen
obtain great wages on this railroad, which depends entirely
upon Englishmen and Americans for train hands.   For that
reason no liberty will be given here, though the men are too
disgusted with what has been seen to care to go on liberty.
Filth fills the streets and foul smells the air, the boats' crews
tell us.   Most of them refuse to drink the liquor there.   A
water boat came off to us this morning but was sent away.
That condensed from our steam is preferred as safer to use.
We received a visit from some distinguished naval officers,
judging by the amount of tinsel on their uniforms, and we
exercised with our after pivot gun for their edification.   A
salute as they left the side determined the rank of the senior
one to be that of a Captain by the number of guns given to
him.   A Turkish sailing frigate returned our salute.   This
afternoon the Turks are loading us with 75 tons of coal, we
looking on.   We are also taking in wood,—large, crooked,
and ant eaten.   I picked out a stick with a pretty lively nest
of ants in it and took it to the mast.   It was ordered to be
thrown overboard and a close watch kept for any more such,

an officer standing by to reject the load if any more were found.   Such visitors would soon have riddled our wooden walls.

Tuesday, Mar. 27, 1866.   We received more coal in the forenoon.   Though the wind became fresh with rain we let go from the mooring buoy and rode with a short range of chain by a single anchor until the coal was in and then up anchor and cleaned ship as we steamed out of port.   While on topsail yard lookout I had a fine view of a whole side of a range of hills with groves of orange trees covered almost completely with fruit which with the shining leaves painted the whole range in mottled green and gold, the gold predominating.   Nothing yet seen could compare with it.   A New England apple orchard in full bloom is a beautiful sight, but there are spaces between the trees and the coloring is not so vividly striking, nor so strongly in contrast with the barren desolation of the adjacent country.

Wednesday, Mar. 28.   We repeated yesterday's cleaning ship this forenoon and at 1 P. M. anchored at Pireus, the seaport of Athens.   We saluted the Greek flag, and also the French Admiral, receiving salutes in return.   We find here English, French, and Russian line-of-battle-ships, (74 to 100 guns,) with Austrian, French, Greek, Italian, and Turkish frigates, (30 to 50 guns,) and sloops-of-war, (ships of 20 guns.)   The most noticeable things in the harbor are the small sail boats plying about the ship while waiting for the passengers they had brought to visit us.—
There is a lateen sail forward like those at Lisbon on page 87.   The foot of the yard is brought to the stem-post as there, but the sail is split just forward of the mast to form a jib and mainsail on the same yard.   At

A HANDY RIG.

the stern a mast and boom are stepped for a triangular sail

the whole forming a very handy style of yacht rig that one person can handle readily. Upon their bows are the names of noted ancient Greeks in Greek letters, as–ΛΙΚΟΥΡΓΟΣ, ΠΡΩΜΗΘΕΥΣ, (Licurgus, Prometheus.)

Thursday, Mar. 29, 1866. I went to the landing in the 1st cutter to land some of our officers, but could not step ashore. The men-o'-war of other nations exercise at sending down topgallant yards and masts at night, and sending them up again in the morning. Luckily we have long topmasts, (topmast and topgallant masts in one stick) and are thus free from the nonsensical part of the exercise. Only boats and topgallant yards go up and down with the ensign of our ship. Our boats are hoisted to the davits, the topgallant yards tripped for lowering, and the ensign and day pennant hauled down in unison with all the other men-o'-war in port at sunset when a signal is given by the ship selected to lead. At 8 A. M. boats are lowered, to'gallant yards go up with the ensign, the stop of the day pennant is broken, and the small night pennant hauled down simultaneously with the others. Being so much smaller and our exercise simpler than theirs there is no rivalry between us and them. We finish our work quickly and then give our sympathy for the success of the English ship. We cannot compete with them in size of ship but when they visit us they stare at our guns in wonder. The English 100-gun ship is the *Gibraltar.* Several of her crew have been aboard us visiting, and had a "jolly time" treating our men with liquor they brought with them. The Austrian and Italian ships all have their yards a-cockbill, so I suppose it is Judas-Day with them. The starboard yardarms of the fore and mizzenmasts, and port yardarms of the main are raised to an angle of 45 ° and the ensign at half-mast as an expression of sympathy with the dismay and grief of the disciples at the betrayal of Christ by Judas. This port is intensely English. One might imagine it an English colony were it not for the Grecian flag flying from the frigate and the names given the boats. The building stone used in the town of Pireus shows that this is a limestone country. Very little marble seems to be used at the present time. There is a public square with trees and shrubbery, showing that they would grow if planted; but on every hand are naked hills with white rocks cropping out.

Friday, Mar. 30. Being at work aloft I had a fine view of the country from our masthead. Eight miles back of the town are the ruins of the Acropolis, which I give below. I see no prospect of getting a nearer view.

RUINS OF THE ACROPOLIS, ATHENS.

Pireus is in a little, land-locked cove southwest of the ancient city of Athens, of which it was the seaport, as it is now of the present capital of Greece, which is west of the ancient city and at the edge of an extensive plain dotted with groves of trees. Athens has a population of 28,000.

To-day is Good Friday and all the men-o'-war of Catholic nations still have their yards a-cockbill and the French Admiral fires one of his heaviest guns every hour. We sent up to'gallant yards and loosed sails to dry with the *Gibraltar*, neither of us taking any notice of the day.

Saturday, Mar. 31, 1866. The French Admiral visited us just before noon and we gave him a salute on leaving the ship. At 12 noon all the Catholic ships squared yards and the *Italia* fired a salute of 21 guns. After dinner we took several officers on board the Russian frigate ПCPCCЕЋTZ, translated by our men as *Nepercritz*, though the first letter of the name upon her stern is the Greek "P" and the third the Greek "R." Perhaps my translation may be as free as that, but I thought it might answer for *Peter the Great*. It was built at New York by the same firm that built the *U. S. S. Brooklyn*, of the West Gulf Squadron. The Russian ship carries fifty 42's, throwing round shot of seven inches in diameter. The *Italia* is an armored frigate of thirty guns on her main deck. The 4 1-2 to 5 inch armor plates extend three feet above the water line her whole length, but above that height only from the foremast to the mizzenmast, leaving five guns of a side without other protection than the wooden bulwarks. They both have vertical prows without projecting cutwater.

Monday, April 2. We received $4 of our grog-ration money and each put in $1 of it for luxuries for the mess, as potatoes and onions. There was a great hue and cry this afternoon that the Captain's dinner had been stolen, and all the galley and officers' cooks and stewards were put on the black-list on that account. It developed, however, that the Captain's Steward had carried the dinner aft without any one noticing it and had then gone ashore for something lacking for that special occasion. Being delayed, the dinner was missing. Upon his return things were righted, with much jollification at the galley and probable relief at the cabin as the Captain had a gentleman and lady to dine with him.

Tuesday, April 3, 1866. We left the port of Athens at 8 A. M. At 4 P. M. the snowy hills of Candia were seen, and when I came from lookout at midnight we had passed a large town on the southern coast, (perhaps old Caenopolis,) and the land was trending to the northward, illustrating the small extent of this noted country.

Wednesday, April 4. This morning we found the sun on our right hand and we were making good time for Trieste, Austria. We are scraping the coat of paint from our gun carriages and giving them a coat of fancy blacking that will make them look like a dandy's boot just from the hands of his bootblack; a monkey would grin at his face in the guns now. A little land bird is flying about the deck this noon, giving pleasure to every one by his presence, all anxious to make friends with him. Several low islands are upon our starboard bow covered with shrubs of some sort. We are hardly up to Zante yet, still the shrubs may be grape vines of the variety bearing the seedless grapes called Zante currants. The days begin to grow warm, the nights are still quite chilly.

Friday, April 6. I signed accounts with $71.81 due me on the Paymaster's books. They tell me the bounty is a separate account, so that my signing this pay account can not affect my claim for the installment of bounty due Feb. 27, last. We drilled with muskets in the forenoon. At 5 P. M. we were passing islands on both sides and I am told we will continue to do so until we reach our port. The old Boatswain had us all up in the top to teach us how to set the to'gallant studdingsails but did not get them set to satisfy him before they were ordered taken in. If another ship had

been in sight they would have gone out quickly enough, but
the two captains of the top rather resented the sending of
the boatswain aloft to teach even the apprentices so simple
a thing as setting a sail.   It was done as a reproof to them
for an accidental delay in setting the sail.

Saturday, April 7, 1866.   While we were cleaning ship
for entering port this forenoon I was ordered to the ship's
cook's duty again ; he had cut his thumb open and was put
on the sick list.   Only a few days ago I had an application
from the Paymaster's Steward to help him while his "Jack-
o'-the-Dust" was sick, but begged off on the ground that any
one could do that work, and my topmates were feeling that
they were doing more than their share of work through my
details to do work excusing me from deck duty.   With the
help of Woods, my top-captain I got off then, but at this
time the ship's cook carried the matter to the mast and we
had to give in.   Woods then wanted to have me stand watch
at night when on special duty, repeating the complaints of
the topmates that I didn't do deck duty more than half the
time.   He was told he could have me when not otherwise
employed or that I would be made a supernumerary and be
excused from deck duty altogether.   The growlers cooled
down at that.

Sunday, April 8.   We arrived at Trieste at 7 : 30 A. M.
and made fast to a mooring buoy.   At quarters we were all
surprised to see the Yeoman take a place as one of the crew
of the howizter in our division, evidently as a punishment
for his carelessness of a while ago causing a fire.   We are
all glad he is to be let off with a simple blacklist of extra
duty, for the men all like him.   We had many visitors of a
good class on board during the afternoon.

Monday, April 9.   I am at work on deck again.   Grog
ration money was served out to us in the morning, giving us

spending money and for mess purchases. All hands are at
work scraping spars and masts. Although the oldest man
in the top and almost the oldest man in the ship Woods sent
me to commence scraping at the truck while the boys were
set to scraping the booms upon the yards. The Boatswain
gave Woods a raking down for doing so, though I had said
nothing about it to any one. In fact I had offered to do it
to shame the growlers if possible. It worked well, for Mr.
Briscoe learned who the growlers were and they got their fill
of similar "soft billets." We were overrun with visitors.
Seventeen men went ashore on liberty this morning.

Tuesday, April 10, 1866. It was so rainy that our hammocks were triced up to the beams overhead till 10 o'clock
before stowing in the nettings and we were allowed to stay
below after all hands had done washing clothes in the fresh
water caught in the awnings. While below we discussed the
weight of our guns and the solid round shot thrown by the
different calibers of our navy smoothbore guns, many questions having been asked by our visitors concerning other gun
calibers than we carry. I made calculations for the boys and
gave them the following list, taking our old VI-inch 32 pdr.
as a basis, that being a standard gun in European navies :-
IX-inch acutal 108, nominal 100. weight of gun 4 1-2 tons.

X-inch	148,	150.	
XI-inch	197,	200.	8
XV-inch	499,	500.	25
XX-inch	1277,	1125.	50

The 32-pound shot is made on an allowance for windage,
or inequalities in casting, consequently the larger calibers,
requiring no more windage the actual weights would overrun
these figures probably. Our present VI-inch gun is a rifle,
throwing a 100 pound conical shot or shell quite effectively.

Wednesday, April 11. It is fair again. We are painting

the ship's bulwarks and other parts on the spar deck. I had
a small brush to paint the blocks about the rigging through
which the ropes led, Mr. Allyn watching me until he saw I
was doing it without daubing the ropes. I expected to hear
at supper time "Another soft billet for Stuart," but Kane,
the boss growler was dumb. He had been given a bucket
of coal tar with a brush to paint the anchors, manger, and
the range of cable that was on deck. Boatswain Briscoe at
his elbow to *encourage* him as only an old boatswain can.
We notice a change in the rig of the small fishing boats, lug
sails being used here in place of lateen. I went to the landing place in the 1st cutter twice this afternoon. Several
men came on board trying to ship. The liberty men have
all come off in good order and well satisfied with their trip.
They report the streets clean, the houses orderly, the liquor
good and cheap, and the police very kind and indulgent.

Thursday, April 12, 1866. I was given liberty ashore
with $8 in my pocket out of my wages. I found many nice
residences with terraced gardens and shrubbery upon extensive lawns. Trieste covers a large space of hilly ground
around the sides of the bay. It is the principal seaport of
Austria and has a population of 108,000. Railroads con-
nect it with Vienna, Venice, and other places. Leaving my
mates to their own ideas of enjoyment I strolled about the
city streets and took a leisurely survey of the fine buildings,
the strange trees and flowers in the well kept gardens, the
fountains with their artistically arranged masses of rock-
work, the statues and empty square which was crowded with
market tents when I came ashore in the morning. All of
the shopkeepers were very obliging, and some ladies were of
great assistance to me, understanding what I wanted by my
signs and putting my signs into German words. I bought a
number of articles not procurable on board the ship at any

price and others that would have cost twice the money if I got them out of the Paymaster's stores. There were sights very curious to me. At one time we saw two women hauling and two others pushing a long, low wagon loaded with new unpainted firkins or tubs, while a man (?) walked at the side of the load, one hand resting on the load as if he were steadying it, exerting no force in getting the wagon on. We longed to shake him. The women had rosy cheeks, bare arms, legs and feet, the full round skirts coming only a little below the knee, and they looked fully as strong and more self-reliant than the man. At another time we saw a single ox in a complete horse's harness except headstall and reins, between the thills of a small wickerwork frame on four little wheebarrow-sized wheels, the driver sitting on the front of the body of the wagon guiding the ox much as ox teamsters of New England would. A woman was driving to market a donkey loaded with quite an assortment of country produce and his own dinner, the woman balancing a large, flat basket upon her head and having a smaller basket in each of her hands. I returned to the ship at sun-

Going to Market.

set, the only one to do so. I was well pleased with my tramp and purchases, though very tired. Mr. Allyn was at the gangway as I reported and asked what I had in my hand—a small dressing case with spaces for writing materials. The marine didn't search me for concealed liquor, for "That will do, go forward," was my order. He had at last tested me. Some others came off at 9 P. M.

Friday, April 13, 1866. Another lot of men were sent on liberty although the time of the others had not expired. Mr. Allyn told them that reports of the actions of those yet ashore was so good he let them go, but he wanted all hands aboard the ship early Sunday morning. Our mess cook was one to go and I gave up my second day ashore to take his work that he might go, as this was to be the last chance at this port.

Saturday, April 14. I gave the boys one of *my* skouses this morning, adding a can of fresh beef to the usual pork, potatoes, and onions in the mixture. The men have a distaste for the canned beef as usually presented them, but the empty kettle showed the fault lay not in the beef. I had no part in holystoning the spar deck, but instead had my mess chest lid to holystone and inside of chest to scrub on that deck while it was wet and to help holystone the berth deck after breakfast. In the midst of the latter I was called to retouch the brightwork of my fellow handspikeman, who was ashore on liberty. I, and no one else, must do that brightwork when he is absent or sick, as he must do for me under like circumstances, an l the system of stationing men about a man-o'-war seems to be so perfect that it rarely happens that both are absent at the same time. Work on the armament of the ship takes precedence, and unless a man is at the wheel or on lookout brightwork must be attended to at once. We took in water in the afternoon and bent the light sails, so I suppose we are to go to sea by Monday if the men are off from liberty. Some of the men have come off noisy, but only one has gotten into the lockup, his offense being "crazy drunk" and smashing things.

Sunday, April 15. The mess cook came off last night, relieving me to go to deck duty again. I was sent in the 3rd cutter to tow the water boat ashore to the little bay back of the fort at Light House Point We passed two Austrian fr gates that were being plated with iron I judge to be not over five inches thick They have the new plow-pointed bow for ramming other ships. The broadside ports are narrow, only half the width of the height, giving a very small arc of training requiring them to fight broadside to the enemy. The casemate on the forecastle pierced for two guns has a square, nearly vertical face on its three sides, with but one side-port for broadside firing, so that but half her guns can be used at a single enemy. They were about the size of an old style 44-gun frigate. We think one of our monitors would sink them in short order. A heavy squall came up at noon and forced us to pay out chain and let go an anchor. After it cleared up we found the mountains in the interior were all white with snow. Several sailing vessels took advantage of the favorable direction of the wind to put to sea.

Monday, April 16, 1866. The squall of yesterday continued as a decent gale that held on till this morning. The police brought off four of our men that had forgotten to return, two being petty officers. We got under weigh at 1 P. M., leaving Samuel Courtney, the Engineer's Steward on shore. He had brought to the boat a part of the stores for their mess and had returned for more, but could not be found by the police up to the time of our sailing. We had a fair wind and set all sail. While at supper the wind shifted and we had to rush on deck to furl everything at once.

Tuesday, April 17. At 11 A. M. while exercising at sending down topsail yards we were in sight of a group of small, rocky islands. One of them was a curious pyramidal-shaped rock rising boldly out of the water, quite regular in outline at a distance, but losing its regularity as we neared it, when it assumed a pear shape, giving it its name of " POMO."

THE ROCK POMO.

Our sending down topsail yards as an exercise lengthened to an all day's job, for when we got the fore topsail yard on deck we found it needed many repairs

and alterations to preserve the strength required for safety
and at the same time to enable us to do the work quickly at
exercising with the fleet.   At 4 P. M. the Italian coast was
in sight.   While we were at Trieste Old Ti concluded that
he was entitled to liberty as well as the rest, and not being
allowed to go into the boat with the men went to the open
port of the pivot gun and waited until the boats shoved off,
then jumped overboard and followed them to the landing.
He returned at sundown for his supper and bed.   Swimming
to the grating of the starboard gangway ladder he called for
some one to help him out of the water, walked up the steps
and reported himself to the officer of the deck by a single
sharp bark.   "All right, go forward, Ti," and he gravely
walked forward shaking the water from his shaggy coat with
a vigor that called for the use of a dry swab on the part of
the maintopman deck sweeper.   That official did the duty
gladly for Ti is a favorite with everybody.

Wednesday, April 18, 1866.   This morning we are running along a flat coast with towns and single houses in view
at intervals as we pass.   A lighthouse is on the extremity
of a long, narrow neck of land which I suppose to be the east
cape of the Gulf of Tarentum.   We exercised with topsail
and topgallant yards again today, this time more to the satisfaction of all hands.   We are following the sun. around,
crossing the Gulf of Tarentum.   After supper all hands had
musket or Sharp's rifle drill, the marines at the bayonet drill.
We have an idea that we are to meet the fleet shortly from
the amount of drill of all sorts we are getting.   We are doing
our best to perfect ourselves so as to make a good showing
whenever the trial with the fleet occurs.   A man-o'-war's
crew take pride in the smartness of their ship, and brag all
they can.   In order to be able to brag they will work hard,
and with such officers as we have on board the *Ticonderoga*

they will work cheerfully to accomplish the tasks set them. Though seemingly unnecessary at the time, these drills give the men confidence in themselves and the ability to meet any emergency or peril under the guidance of their officers.

Thursday, April 19, 1866. At 8 A. M. Mt. Etna was in sight with its mantle of snow. At noon we were in the best position for a good view and I spent my noon hour sketching it. I give below a home-made cut of it from my sketch.

MOUNT ETNA, FROM THE EAST.

We are passing scenes familiar from our former passage of the Straits of Messina. The then leafless trees have assumed a greener aspect and though the hills still look bare as then the slopes are beginning to show the green of young grass. We anchored at Messina at 1 : 30 P. M., but got up anchor at 5 : 30 for Palermo. The vicinity of Messina is green at all points with villas, groves, and terraced gardens upon the steep hillsides back of the city and extending high up on the mountain's side. We skirted the northern shore of Sicily during the night.

Friday, April 20. We dropped anchor in the harbor of Palermo at 8 o'clock this morning and found the *Colorado* with a broken shaft. Admiral Goldsborough's orders are that we sail to-morrow for Marseilles to secure a dry dock for her repairs. Very good ripe cherries are offered along-side at ten cents a quart. Our boat was at the landing place several times to-day but no one was allowed to step ashore. They are making extensive repairs at the landing and will have a fine, substantial thing when finished. We find here the same honey-combed, ruinous walls shutting out approach from the sea except at one or more landings guarded by a fort or forts and sentry at the landing. Palermo is enclosed by high, steep mountains except on the side next the sea. From our anchorage the peaks and tops of the ridges appear to be destitute of trees, though in the city and suburbs they are to be seen in all directions.

Saturday, April 21, 1866. Our holystonings have worn our decks down to the heads of the spikes and our gang of carpenters are driving them in farther and capping them again with round, wafer-shaped wooden plugs. We sailed this morning for Marseilles with orders to use all dispatch and secure a dry dock for the *Colorado.* Fortunately we are down to the anthracite coal put aboard at Philadelphia, worth much more than its weight of the soft English coal to be obtained here, much of it in a state of dust. It is nearly six months since I heard from home and I had hoped to get letters whenever we met the Admiral but am disappointed again. A fresh breeze hardly in our favor compels us to frequently set and furl sails at each slight veering of wind. The 75 revolutions ordered are reduced to 45, as the boilers leak so badly under the higher pressure that wooden spiles have to be used. Since leaving home we have been running from place to place with little rest, and probably the boilers had seen hard service in the South Atlantic Squadron during the war without much repairing when the ship was fitted out for this cruise. At any rate repairs seem to give the Engineer's crew nearly constant employment while in port.

Sunday, April 22. Coming on watch and on lookout at 4 A. M. I found a stiff head wind blowing and the spray dashing over the ship's bows, wetting me through at once. We made land on the east coast of Sardinia at 9 A. M. As the gale increased we sent down topgallant yards. At 1 : 30 we began to make sail again and brought the revolutions up to 50. At 6 P. M. we were heading for the Straits of Bonfacio, between Sardinia and Corsica. We entered them at 7 and at 8 P. M. were through and heading our course. At sundown the wind went down and when we came out of the straits we were in a smooth sea under the lee of Corsica. We did some tall rolling as we entered the straits and I saw Lt. Snell, our Navigation Officer, (died in 1876) "settling accounts with Neptune," therefore I am not the only one on board habitually running in debt to his ungracious majesty. Capt. Steadman was on the to'gallant forecastle taking the measurements with him for guiding our course, and getting no answer to a question glanced at him and proceeded in the sighting alone. On getting a clean bill Mr. Snell straightened up and went to sighting again. The *Ticonderoga* has a habit of plunging deeply into an incoming sea and of then rising swiftly to a great height and bringing to view several feet of her forefoot. This gives to a susceptible person an unconquerable desire to bend low over the bow *to see how it looks* down there.

Monday, April 23, 1866. We are having a fine, warm day. We exercised at general quarters an hour in the forenoon, then all hands scrubbed blankets, mattress covers and clothes, at the same time tricing our mattresses to the rigging to air them. We washed down the decks in the afternoon. I have had a severe headache all day.

Tuesday, April 24. I went to the doctor and had my ears stuffed with laudanum last night to little perceptible benefit, and walked the deck all night with the pain in my head. At 8 A. M. we moored ship in the rain at Marseilles.

Wednesday, April 25, 1866. The Frenchmen are filling us with coal. From our anchorage near the coal houses we can see scarcely anything of the city, we being in a small inlet to the left of the main entrance to the harbor. What has been a rare sight with us heretofore is the use of horses and of carriages like our own at home. We have been busy with repairs on our rigging while the Frenchmen were coaling, and as they did not finish till after dark we were ordered to give the decks a sweeping and to turn in.

Thursday, April 26. We cleaned ship in the forenoon and put to sea at noon. A mail came aboard but still not a thing for me. On looking around as we came out of the Bay of Marseilles I could not help remarking how great the convulsions of nature were that formed the bay. The dip of the strata on the main land as shown in exposed places appeared to be *from* the shore, while the strata of the many rocky islands have dips as various as themselves. Many of these islands are fortified, and at the water's edge are worn into bluffs with many gullies and caves.

Friday, April 27. We sighted Corsica on the port bow at 3:30 A. M. At noon we were heading in for the straits with snow visible upon the Corsican ridges while the hills of Sardinia, less high at this point, were free from the white mantle of winter. We came out from the straits at 4 P. M.

Sunday, April 29. We dropped anchor in Palermo this morning at half-past four, a full moon enabling us to run in. We mustered in white frocks and white cap-covers for the first time this spring. Whenever white is worn during the day a change to blue flannel frocks and blue cloth trousers is ordered at the supper hour. A large number of visitors were on board during the afternoon.

Monday, April 30. I hear that an American ship lying in port is ready to sail and will carry a mail for us; also that the *Kearsarge* has returned to Lisbon from the African coast with the loss of four officers and ten men by the fever. I finished turning a pair of cloth trousers that had become threadbare; for increased prices for Paymaster's clothing compels us to economize in order not to run in debt to the Government, especially those of us who have assigned half-pay to our families at home.

Tuesday, May 1, 1866. Palermo is said to have 186,000 inhabitants. One can hardly imagine where they all live. It is true the city is built upon a series of hypothenuses to a sea level of the earth's surface and I am told that in the lower portions of the city they are packed like sardines, but in the more elevated portions much space is given to gardens and terraced lawns. The city has considerable commerce in fruits. I understand that much of the brimstone we have burnt during the past four years has come from their Etna furnace. Small, apparently wild strawberries were aboard for sale this morning. To-day we have hauled the sheet-anchor chain on deck in order to clean and whitewash the chain locker. The fore passage was given me with another man to clean and whitewash. In the afternoon we rove studding-sail gear and got ready for sea after supper.

Wednesday, May 2. We got up anchor with the *Colorado* and *Frolic* at 7 A. M., making sail at once, though the sails were of little account until we gained an offing where a stiff breeze and a heavy swell were found, making me seasick but driving us along at a fine rate. Steam was shut off at 10 A. M. We have on board a pair of Wallachian sheep, and a flock of turkeys, chickens, and even doves. The gobblers cannot even agree to disagree; either of them giving challenge a general rumpus occurs at once. The sheep stand on their dignity at all times and woe befalls either quadruped or biped presuming to venture within the circuit of the ropes

by which they were fastened under the topgallant forecastle.
When they first came aboard Ti was delighted. He thought
they would make him pretty playmates and commenced to
caper and bark in front of them, evidently thinking from the
close attention they gave that they appreciated his effort to
please them.   Getting a sidelong butt he incontinently left,
ki-yi-ing in most earnest fashion.   Ever since then he has
passed them with a growl and set teeth.   A stamp of a foot
and bowed head is an effective warning to him.   The little
Frolic has to use steam to keep her station although we are
making only 7 1-2 knots.   The *Colorado* is almost as steady
on the water as in port, but we are showing off with some
of our usual "ground and lofty tumbling," taking occasional
seas over either gangway.

Thursday, May 3, 1866.   A light wind, a smoother sea,
and a pleasant day greet us.   It is really cheering to be so
near to the other vessels of a fleet as to be able to exchange
greeting even by signal.   The Admiral salutes the Captain's
guests, the officers each other by waving handkerchiefs, and
the men recognize acquaintances by a stealthy swing of the
cap.   But there are other signals flying.   Little flags from
the *Colorado's* mizzen topsail yardarm tell us to prepare to
"shift topsails."   The tussle with the flagship's topmen is on
again.   Of course the *Ticonderoga's* foretop beat as usual,
but the maintopmen, although beating their opponent's tops
by a few seconds were so far behind their usual record as to
be booked for extra drill.   The foretopsail was shifted, the
sail set and the topgallantsail set above it in 9 1-2 minutes.
We had musket drill after supper.

Friday, May 4.   It was so nearly calm this morning that
the bows of the fleet pointed in different directions.   There
was a slight sprinkle of rain at 9 A. M., after which the sun
came out hot.   We broke out the hold (hoisted everything

upon deck) in order to thoroughly clean and whitewash it.
While washing decks this morning we caught a small land
bird about the size of a robin and the color of a partridge.
It had been flying about the ship all day yesterday. There
is a flock of another kind visiting us this afternoon, making
themselves at home everywhere, but particularly about the
quarter deck amusing themselves and catching flies. Kitty
amused himself forward watching and catching them, but Ti
took to the quarter deck for some sport with them. A kind
hand from the cabin had scattered bread crumbs and stood
watching them. Ti would follow a bunch of them and put
his nose or one of his great paws suddenly upon the spot
where they had been, but were not, for they would use their
wings to get just without his reach. A handful of crumbs
had attracted a busy bunch of birds. Ti lay down there
with his fore paws outstretched upon each side of the heap
and remained motionless except for the hairs upon the tip
of his bushy tail. They would sidle up to him turning their
little heads saucily to examine him as to his intentions, and
finding no harm came to the one lighting upon the top of his
head gathered in to renew their feast. Then came the time
for which he had waited. One great paw would swing over
and lightly touch the spot. Ti's tail would then thrash the
deck at a lively tattoo and lifting his head he would look at
the watchers with mouth open and tongue hanging at one
side in a jolly dog-laugh at the success of his joke. These
birds were yellow breasted, with blue heads, slate-colored
backs and wings, three white stripes on wings when open,
and the outer tail feathers also white. The tail was three
inches long, legs nearly the same, body slim and not over
one-and-a-half inches long when picked. They appeared to
be half starved. A schooner has been heading most of the
time as if her course should be across our bows, but with us

has been heading every way during the day. The *Frolic* is practicing at a target with poor success notwithstanding the dead calm. One of our ladders gave way to-day with a marine on it, his head striking upon a bundle of canvas in the hold, wrenching his back and otherwise injuring him; the canvas being under the open hatch at that moment probably saved his life, it breaking the force of his fall. A boat was sent to the Admiral after supper.

Saturday, May 5, 1866. Last night I had to call for help in my watch below, my ear paining me so excessively. The doctor found my head bathed in cold perspiration and quivering with the pain which was "clear inside," I told him. He ordered a flaxseed poultice outside with a morphine and aconite mixture internally. By midnight it began to feel easier and at 12 : 30, my watch being on deck, I was getting unconscious when a shipmate shook me and made me turn out not knowing that I was on the sick list. At the time it seemed to me that I was composed of two persons, and not knowing which of the two he wanted or which of them was me I turned out, giving some curious answers to him. He somehow found I was on the sick list and left me after he had helped me into my hammock again. Had I been over-sleeping and not excused his persistence in thoroughly waking me would have been thankfuly received; it was kindly meant though untimely. Land was in sight this morning, also several vessels. The *Frolic* is towing the *Colorado,* We had target practice with our battery after supper, and Robert Jordan of our IX-inch broadside gun keeps his name of best shot with the big guns, splintering the target into fragments with his first shell at 1400 yards. John Smith, Boatswain's Mate and captain of the XI-inch after pivot gun knocked off the upper barrel of six in the target at the first discharge, so that only those two shots could be fired until

barrels for another target can be saved. It is still calm and
the *Frolic* towing the *Colorado*. We are passing Elba and
a group of other small islands lying between the northern
point of Corsica and Italy.

Sunday, May 6, 1866. We have passed around the finger of Corsica and at sunset it shows in the distance on our
port quarter while the mountains of the mainland loom up on
our starboard beam. I had another night of pain and laudanum though doing duty.

Monday, May 7. We shackled to moorings at Toulon
about 9 A. M. My ear pained me badly this forenoon and
as I preferred to remain on deck and keep busy to being on
the sick list and staying below with nothing but the ache to
think of Woods told me to take the steady sweeping of our
part of the deck and he would get me excused from other
duty. That is about as heavy work as I feel like doing.

Tuesday, May 8. The Frenchmen brought off some very
good looking beef for our fresh soup but it was "blowed"
to make it look better and was refused by the doctor. Salt
beef was served out and the vegetables weighed out to the
messes to boil instead of a fresh soup. The French Admiral
visited both the *Colorado* and the *Ticonderoga*, receiving our
salutes and returning each.

Wednesday, May 9. While washing decks this morning
Ensign Dichman called us aft and read from the New York
Herald of April 14 and succeeding issues an account of the
Fenian move against Canada. Before reading he told us
to make no noisy demonstration, but it was hard work for
the men to obey. They put their feelings into the scrubbing
brooms as if the deck represented the nation that helped to
man the *Alabama* in her fight with the *Kearsarge*, and the
deck got an exceedingly thorough scouring. It looks as if
England might be paid in her own coin for her treatment of

us during the rebellion. We hoisted everything out of the hold to-day for another general cleaning.

Thursday, May 10, 1866. In the forenoon we cleaned and whitewashed all the barrels that were on deck. In the afternoon I was sent into the hold to help re-stow it, the capt.-o'-the hold with a gang on one side and I with another gang on the other side of the hold raced. We stowed the things as fast as those on deck could give them to us, and we of course had to come out even. It is rather curious that as steady sweeper I am excused from such details yet am at once called upon for any work in the hold, fore passage, or spirit room, but it happens so.

Friday, May 11. I am about sick with another intolerable pain in my head but doing duty for I dislike the after effects of the opiates given me. We are overhauling all the running rigging and stowing spare rigging in the hold. Of course I am sent into the hold at the stowing, the boatswain telling me that Mr. Allyn wants me to know where everything is in the hold. The capt.-o'-the-hold and I are good friends and he understands that I would not willingly take the billet from any one who desires to remain in the service, for the disrating of a man before he leaves a ship tells against him ever after, while the "C. H." that will follow his name to his next ship if he holds the billet at his transfer or discharge will benefit him greatly. I prefer to remain general-utility-man till discharged.

Saturday, May 12. I was ordered into the 1st cutter with the information that the first lieutenant knew nothing about the steady sweeper business. Either our Executive Officer is very forgetful or the petty officer over me a big—well—wishes to make me useful at such times as he can have me. The 1st cutter went to the navy yard and I was well paid for the row between these petty officers over me. Inside the

TOULON.

sea wall are moored the bulks of dozens of old, useless 120
and 74-gun ships, uncouth in form and bearing the signs of
decrepit age, yet for past services honored with a place for
safe repose until decay renders them unable to float. The
new vessels are a great departure from these old models and
are apparently the result of a study of our war experience.
It remains to be proved whether they are an improvement
upon our monitors for fighting purposes. The wind rose in
the afternoon and while going ashore the 1st cutter's mast
was broken just before we reached the landing. Half-an-
hour after our return to the ship it had been replaced by our
carpenters. The Captain's Clerk has brought on board a
new pet, a monkey. Ti and the monkey were friends at once
and no work could proceed for a long time, for men deserted
and the officer would stop to laugh at each new trick of dog
or monkey upon the other. We received water during the
dinner hour and sand at supper time. The sand had such a
share of loam that I had no doubt it would grow good potatoes, though it is intended for scrubbing decks with.

Monday, May 14, 1866. The Admiral hoisted his pennant on board the *Frolic* yesterday and this noon went to
sea bound for Gibraltar. The *Colorado* is discharging her
powder and shells preparatory to going into the dry dock.
At cutlass drill after quarters this forenoon I was sent away
by Mr. Wadleigh; I could not hear well enough to give my
opponent the cuts till he had come to his guard, though he
could not catch me napping in parrying his blows. While I
was at the landing I ran up to a store and got me a French
atlas which is not only of present use but will be a curiosity
at home for the small space given to American countries.

Tuesday, May 15, 1866. It is quite cold to-day. Samuel
Courtney, the Engineer's Steward left at Trieste April 16th
came aboard to-day. He had a last drink when he sent his

second lot of stores to the boat and remembered nothing more
till the police found him two days after in an old boat at the
wharf.   He was taken in charge by the American Consul
and forwarded from one consul to another in chase of us till
the expense amounted to $94 which will come out of his pay.

Thursday, May 17, 1866.   A gale that had been blowing
for some days abated yesterday.   Last night I was forced
to use the laudanum mixture in my ear again, lying awake
till 1 o'clock and waking again after three hours of troubled
dreams.   I can hear very little distinctly.   It seems harder
to bear from its being the result of a drunken shipmate's
target practice.   There is evidence enough recorded in these
pages of the injury done by intoxicating liquors to stamp
alcohol as one of the greatest curses to mankind.   Could
the injury be confined to those guilty of using it or tempting
others to use it there might be some limit to the curse ; but
the injury extends to all connected with the drunkard and to
the whole community.   The *Colorad)* has gone into the dry
dock at the navy yard.   While at the bookstore to-day for
some paper I caught sight of two views of Toulon which I
was very glad to secure at a franc each.   Opposite to our
anchorage is the residence and mercantile section of the city,
backed by a long, steep ridge ending at the right in a high
bluff.   All the rest of the harbor is devoted to use as a naval
station and to forts to protect it.   This ridge is bare as if
it were entirely devoid of soil, and the less steep slope at its
foot is only sparsely dotted with low-growing shrubs.   The
whole business seems to be connected with Naval matters.
I have seen no carriage or beast of draft or burden.   The
streets near the landing do not much exceed a rod in width.
At the edge of some of the narrow sidewalks are streams of
running water and the ladies' rotund skirts fill the walks so
completely that gentlemen have to jump across or into the

water to avoid a collision when they meet one. At least we sailors do for we wish to be polite. We have seen the chain gangs and galley convicts at work at the yard dressed in red blouses and yellow pants with chains from their ankles to their waists and thence connecting the two "yoke-fellows." The *Louis XIV*, a steam line-of-battle-ship of 120 guns, came in this forenoon. We bent light sails and got ready for sea this afternoon. After supper our division had cutlass drill. Mr. Allyn asked Mr. Wadleigh if Stuart didn't belong to his division. On being told that he had excused me because I could not hear but seemed to understand the use of the weapon, Mr. Allyn ordered me up to be drilled with the rest. I could make no cuts or thrusts ordered till my opponent came to that guard, but could defend myself without being able to hear. When I found they were exercising at will I "pitched into" my opponent in a way that set the officers gathered on the poop to laughing heartily as I sent my man's wooden cutlass flying out of his hand at their feet. Using an old swinging parry to a low body thrust, I was told by Mr. Wadleigh that it was old-fashioned and that it left me exposed to a smashing head-cut should the thrust prove a feint. He tried me several times on the new parry. I could take it when he thrust slowly, but when he put vigor into his thrust my weapon instinctively took the old swing taught me twenty-five years before on board the old *Columbus*. He at last feigned a thrust and made a blow at my head. I was there to meet him in spite of having swung around the circle. Capt. Steadman laughingly exclaimed, "It's hard teaching an old dog new tricks!" Mr. Allyn then excused me from further cutlass drill, being satisfied I could take care of myself. This morning our potato skouse reminded me of the question of the boy whose mother could afford only salt with their potatoes:—"What do poor folks do that havn't any salt for their potatoes?" We were in that predicament this morning, the cook giving us mashed boiled potatoes without the least seasoning whatever, although three pounds of mess pork per man are served out each week and four pounds of salt beef or its equivalent in fresh or canned beef. Pork put into the coppers to boil is punched by the ship's cook to get out all fat possible and the mess cooks are entitled to what they want of this fat, yet some are too lazy to call for it. Cans of fresh beef were behind the mess chest but last night in preparing his morning's skouse he neglected to even salt his potatoes. All hands growled and each one salted to suit himself.

Sunday, May 20, 1866. Yesterday we carried away our foremast again while going ashore in the boat. The wind came in heavy gusts. Early this morning we went to the dry dock basin where the *Colorado* is in dock. Her shaft is badly worn in the journal and it is thought she will have to get a new one made. The Frenchmen had measurements of her lines before she had been in dock twenty-four hours. We went to sea at 9 A. M.

Monday, May 21. We thought when we came aboard this ship from the *Princeton* that we were coming where we would have room to turn around, but our range has been gradually restricted till now we are reduced to the port side between the fore and mainmasts. We are debarred the use of under the topgallant forecastle because some of the *Colorado's* liberty men threw a bottle of liquor into one of the bow ports there while at Toulon. At quarters I could not hear the drum roll nor the fire bell ring on account of the roaring in my ears. We set the fore-and-aft sails at noon and at 3 P. M. added topsails and topgallantsails, being at the time off Majorca. The wind came dead ahead and we furled all sail at half-past-five. Musket drill came after

supper, the marines at the bayonet drill. My wallet with
silver coins of the different ports we have visited has gone
into the possesssion of some one not entitled to it. They
are marked and spending them at the bumboats alongside
the ship may result in detection.

Tuesday, May 22, 1866. We passed Ivica early this
morning and at nine o'clock were abreast of Cape St. Martin,
half way to Gibraltar. We had a good stiff breeze with all
sail set till 5 P. M. when we furled everything and exercised
at shifting topsails. The maintopmen beat us handsomely.
At 7 P. M. we passed Palos.

Wednesday, May 23. As I came off lookout at 4 A. M.
we were abreast of Cape de Gata. Small patches of snow
are still visible on the tops of the mountains back of the
cape. We are continually meeting vessels coming from the
straits with a fair wind to them.

Thursday, May 24. We came to anchor at Gibraltar at
eight o'clock this morning. Another dispute between the
capt.-o'-the-top and coxswain of the 1st cutter as to which
should have me resulted in my going to the Executive Officer
to know which I should obey. His words were to the point:
"You belong to the 1st cutter and will go in her." That
settles it for all time. A lighter that came alongside this
forenoon with coal had shipped so much water that it was
nearly in a sinking condition when it reached us and continued to take in water faster than coal could be passed out. I
thought that a few bags of sand or coal laid along the bow
would have stopped any more water coming in and save the
lighter and its load, but a sailor is not supposed to express
his idea of what should be done and I kept silent. The
men were ordered out and the lighter cast loose for it to drift
astern and return to the shore. It sank close under our
stern. The Spaniard in charge was frantic and prayed to

the Saints and the Virgin instead of throwing overboard coal or returning to the shore when he first found his boat was too heavily loaded for such weather. We picked up the crew and landed them at The Rock. At the landing we found the water very smooth under the lee of the mole which extends out from the town a long way and forms a platform with embrazures for guns protecting the landing and used for saluting. The Rock really did look impregnable with its numerous guns thrust from ports cut in the precipitous side of the solid rock high above the reach of an enemy's shells. Lines of tunnels have been cut within the rock along the northern half of the western side overlooking the Bay of Gibraltar and extended around the northern end facing the Spanish coast, and from these tunnels the ports were cut. These galleries were begun a hundred years ago and work has continued upon them ever since, so that at the present time (1866) they extend two miles along the northwesterly face of the rock. The circuit of The Rock is about seven miles, and the southern and western sides are completely encircled by a sea wall and fortified the whole distance, so it would be impossible to effect a landing unexposed to a heavy fire. The eastern side is precipitous and the northern point is one thousand feet above sea level. The town lies at the southerly half of the western side along a strip of more gradual slope at the foot of the steeper grade. Part way up this slope is an old Moorish castle built during the occupancy of the Moors. It has stood upon the shoulder of the hill for nearly twelve centuries. At the extreme highest point of the peak at the northern face a gun is stationed for firing signals. At sunrise and at sunset a puff of smoke is seen to issue from out of the rock at that point, followed some little time after by the sound of the discharge of this gun a thousand feet high, suggesting a lofty desire to show off before the world and be a warning to Spain. One fails to perceive the utility of packing the charges of powder all those miles of climbing to fire it off for mere show. It seems boyish.

Friday, May 25, 1866. The sun rose apparently fair but a dense mist clung to the side of The Rock. Soon after a stiff breeze from the Atlantic brought piles of clouds that came rushing on like successive squadrons of cavalry to the charge, changing to stratus, then to nimbus, and before the first coal lighter had been discharged we received a volley from these hosts of the air accompanied by a heavy sea. It cleared a little in the afternoon and I got a chance to sew. A man fell overboard from the whaleboat while it was being hoisted to the davits at sunset. A rope's end was thrown to him and he came aboard by it, reporting himself as "Come aboard, sir!"

Saturday, May 26. Another night of acute pain, leaving me weak and unnerved. These spells seem to follow damp weather. It is the Queen's birthday and ships of the several nations in port are trimmed with flags and the usual salutes were fired at noon. It was interesting to watch the puffs of smoke and fire issuing in succession from the black points high up the northern crag as the salute was being fired. I saw ripe apricots on board to-day. The colliers finished at 2 P. M.; we then spent the usual three hours cleaning ship. Two men were thrown overboard at quarters this evening by attempting to raise the after pivot port-rail to withdraw a wedge without first lowering the ports, as that would have been visible from the outside. The ports being hooked to the rail above them swung outward and downward, and by their weight carried the rail and men with them, sending the latter forcibly several feet from the ship in their dive. A few strokes brought them to the ship's side and hands helped them to the deck. The instant call for the 1st cutter's when

Mr. Allyn saw the men go was " belayed" when he saw the
men could swim.   It is said that we go to Lisbon from here
to meet the fleet.   Our officers are very particular about the
appearance of the ship and drills are constant.   The men are
just as anxious to keep our name as the crack ship, and the
drills are put through with a will.   The probabilities of our
success are a matter for frequent discussion, and the work
of individuals is criticised or praised freely.   One of the first
objects to strike the eye at Gibraltar is the Signal Station

THE PEAK OF THE ROCK.

upon the southerly peak, its flags immediately signaling the
character of sails as they appear in sight from either way.
The view presented is from a photograph taken at a point on
the peak a little south of the station.   The town extends
along the shore of the bay at the left some 800 or 900 feet
below, the Mediterranean is to the right and back or north
of the peak, and the Spanish coast in the distance.   The gun
that is fired at sunset is on the top of the farther peak.   All
approaches to the Straits of Gibraltar are in sight from this

signal station, and a detail is constantly on duty sweeping the horizon with a powerful glass. The weather must be very unfavorable for distinct vision to permit a vessel to slip by unobserved or with her character undetermined.

Sunday, May 27, 1866. We up anchor at midnight for Tangier, Morocco, and came to anchor at 6 A. M. Tangier is at the northwestern point of Africa. The Spanish coast is in sight to Trafalgar. The contrast between the scenery here and at the European ports opposite is quite marked. I expected to see only barren sand hills in northern Africa, but found the low hills crowned with verdure, while upon the opposite coast the towns are nearly always built upon narrow strips at the base of high, bare, rocky ridges or in little valleys between them. We have had several Moors aboard to visit us turbaned and cloaked in white, the richness of their robes denoting rank or wealth. They were shown over the ship and sat upon the quarter deck some time chatting with our officers through an interpreter. Our consul was on board early this morning. We think our coming is for some definite purpose in connection with the consul, but whatever it was we did not have to show our teeth.

Monday, May 28. Other visitors have been coming on board—large yellow grasshoppers or locusts. They have been very destructive this season—even eating the vines of potatoes. A stiff breeze from the land blows many on our decks and the water is almost covered with them nearer the land. A caravan camped near the beach last night, and at sunrise this morning they prostrated themselves upon knees and hands facing the rising sun. We got under weigh at 6 P. M. for Lisbon.

Tuesday, May 30. We got moored at Lisbon at 5 P. M. I have at last gotten a letter dated December 7th, stating among other things that the money letter from Fort Mifflin had not reached home.   It was in answer to mine from the Delaware breakwater.   (A few years after the war a trusted clerk in the Lowell Post Office was detected in purloining money from letters. Perhaps that may account for my loss.)

Thursday, May 31, 1866.   Another night of extreme pain. I got nicely asleep by one o'clock and at two was called to go on anchor watch. I went to the doctor in the forenoon and a chloroform mixture was applied within and behind my ear. After a long consultation between the three doctors I was given a letter to copy, apparently as a specimen of my handwriting. I was excused from duty.

Friday, June 1.   The Storeship *National Guard* is going home and will take some of our men discarded for various reasons. Rumor says that this ship is to sail directly for Trieste to protect our interests during the war that is liable to be declared at any day by Italy and Prussia against Austria. It was quite rainy yesterday and all last night. I got quiet about 2 : 30 and all hands were called at 4 A. M. to wash clothes. I washed only one piece that I must have for Sunday if we muster in white. I did not feel able to do even that but I disliked to put it upon my messmates, which they are required to do for a sick messmate. To-day the doctors are syringing my left ear preparatory to examining it with an instrument. Still excused from duty.

Saturday, June 2.   There was a consultation of Surgeons of the fleet on board this forenoon. I understand that the doctors proposed to send me home, but that Mr. Allyn objected so strenuously that they deferred to his wish. The quartermaster on duty aft had overheard their talk and told us that five were to go but I was to stay because I was so useful to Mr. Allyn when any of his petty officers are sick. I begin to think I have been almost too useful for my benefit, yet I could not help doing to the best of my ability whatever was required of me. A gang of caulkers from ashore are caulking our decks.

Sunday, June 3, 1866. I went on duty again. I am to apply to the Surgeon's Steward whenever the pain becomes severe and he will administer morphine tr. and aconite tr. to subdue it. I went ashore in the boat, landing at a square tastefully paved in Mosaic with small, round, smooth stones in two colors, white and blue. There was a fountain in the center of the square.

Monday, June 4. I had to call upon the steward for his mixture but it had no perceptible effect. We are busy at · setting up rigging. The caulkers finished their job at night.

Tuesday, June 5. We holystoned the decks after the caulkers in the forenoon and after dinner coaled ship. We lost a man from our boat while at the landing and in consequence our boat's crew are quarantined for two days from leaving the boat. We are thus punished for the act of our boatmate. I wonder if it ever occurred to our Executive that the desire to desert in this case could possibly have been on account of restrictions imposed upon all hands for the act of men from another ship. Even the best of men do not relish being punished for others' faults.

Wednesday, June 6. The report is that the Kearsarge is to go home from this port, and that we sail to-morrow for Trieste to protect our interests there in case of war.

Thursday, June 7. We commenced to get up anchor at 5 A. M. but found the mooring chains so foul with both anchors and each other that we had to "back" the capstan with two deck-tackles, one as a luff upon the other. The swivel to the mooring shackle had not turned and the ship in swinging with the tide hand wound the cables around the anchors and each other in all sorts of tangles, taking till 5 P. M. to clear so as to get the second anchor up. We then steamed down the river till 7 : 30 and anchored, there still being several turns of its own chain around the port anchor that took till 9 o'clock to clear; an anchor watch was then set and hammocks piped down.

Friday, June 8, 1866. We got under weigh at 5 A. M. and went to sea. We showed colors with the English mail steamer bound in to Lisbon.

Saturday, June 9. I missed my muster in the morning watch but the captain-o'-the-top learned that I was walking the deck till after 3 o'clock in my watch below and reported it. Mr. Wadleigh said I had probably lain down and gotten asleep and to let me sleep if I could. I waked at the noise of washing decks after daylight and hurried on deck to report myself as having overslept, expecting to be in trouble. "All right, we learned that you were sick," was the answer. This was but one of many acts of kindness to me from that officer, who, as my division officer had more direct control over me than the others, and to whom my infirmity was most troublesome on that account. At noon we were abreast of Cape Trafalgar, with the African coast in the dim distance and a stiff breeze sending the spray over our decks wetting our clothesbags that had been piped up while scraping and whitewashing the berth deck was going on. A large steamer is in toward the land keeping abreast of us.

Sunday, June 10. We passed Gibraltar at midnight last night and at 4 P. M. Nevada's peaks show their patches of white still unmelted by the heat of June. Yet more stringent rules are enforced and priviliges further abridged. We now have a space of about 1 × 6 feet per man to stay in during the day when no work is going on, and out of this is reserved at times room for a carpenter's bench with four men at work, also a blacksmith forge and anvil with two men at work. The combings of the hatches and the waterways are

scraped clean from any trace of the black paint given them
at the navy yard and are now to be scrubbed with sand and
canvass, the bitts and the pinrails about the masts have been
varnished with shellac and must be used with extreme care
as if made for ornament rather than the rough use originally
intended, the inner sides of the hatches that had first been
painted a clean white upon a lead color and afterward a sky
blue are now daubed with an extremely dirty shade of yellow. The men are proud of the name of being a crack ship's
crew, but they growl over the restrictions and unnecessary
work of a *fancy* ship. We are allowed to sit upon nothing,
to lean upon nothing, and touch nothing but the bare deck
of the port side between the foremast and a respectful distance forward of the gangway. Some threaten to desert at
the first chance but no one believes them to have more serious
desire than to have their growl out. They forget that part
of this is for punishment and may be only temporary. At
sunset the sea was smooth and the slight heaving motion ever
in force caused changeable glints of red, bronze, gold, green,
and blue reflections upon its surface rarely seen. The sun
set cloudy behind the snowy peaks at Cape de Gata while the
loom of the African coast is again visible in the southern
horizon. A glance at the map shows that it will remain in
sightable distance (by daylight) till near Cape Bon it trends
to the south of a direct course to the Island of Sicily. We
are to stop first at Messina.

Monday, June 11, 1866. Last night I took chloroform
mixture and had laudanum applied freely, then went on deck
to my watch again. We had target practice with muskets this
forenoon at which they said I made three hits out of four,
although my nerves were too unsteady and my eyes felt too
fishy to strike a bead. The officers used opera glasses to
score us. A very severe headache follows my night of pain

and narcotics. Did you ever see a nice large house, so splendidly furnished and decorated that no one was allowed to go into it, but an ell had been added to live in? I think the Government will have to build an ell to the *Ticonderoga* before long for the sailors to live in. The Sailmaker's gang are to have room to work in the port gangway, leaving us hardly room to swing a cat around by the whiskers, let alone by the tail.

Tuesday, June 12, 1866. A light is ahead at 4 A. M. We are varnishing the berth deck with shellac, an acceptable innovation as any grease dropped is easily removed, though it may be slippery during a heavy roll when wet. We had pistol practice in both forenoon and afternoon. One man let his pistol go off and the ball after glancing from the port-sill hit a darkie in the pit of the stomach, grazing the skin and dropping down his trousers leg when his waistband was loosened to search for it. Cæsar, a Portugese wardroom waiter, tried his hand at it. Pulling upon the trigger while cocking his piece it of course went off when he let go the hammer. It took a piece out of the halliard rack, glanced the broadside gun abaft the to'gallant-forecastle, then put out the light in the lantern at which Mr. Clark was lighting his cigar. Mr. Clark came aft and laughingly desired us to use some other target as he wished to finish his smoke. Cæsar was then made to stand at the port-sill after being told how to use his piece. This time he put the ball close to the side of the ship instead of the bottle some sixty feet away. The pistol was then taken from him.

Wednesday, June 13. Target practice with Sharp's rifles occupied the forenoon. The target was hung below the fore yardarm and we stood aft on the poop to fire. The ship was quite steady, giving an easy mark. I was also in good condition physically for quick and steady aiming. After firing

GIBRALTAR.

my sixth shot I was about to step aside as had the others, but Capt. Steadman said, "Try him again!" On the ninth shot I took deliberate aim and put the ball half in the bull's-eye, when he said, "That will do, he can't miss!" Going forward I found that I had hit the six inch target every time by catching sight as I raised my piece; eight being within the circle of three inches diameter. I had made the greatest number of running off-hand hits in the ship, though I could not brag much as more than half of the men had not hit the target at all. We lost sight of the African coast this morning.

Thursday, June 14, 1866. Exercise at general quarters and hauling both cables on deck to clean out the chain lockers kept us busy till dinner time. No land in sight all day. We made sail at 5 P. M. and shut off steam. Word was then passed for coxswains to see their boats well secured, so we may expect a rolling night if the wind continues to rise.

Friday, June 15. Sicily is in sight this morning all the way forward of our starboard beam. At quarters exercise this forenoon John Simpson, one of my launchmates of the *Metacomet* got a foot jammed in pivoting the forward XI-inch gun. The weight of these guns is such that they are apt to get away from the men if the ship is rolling while one is being pivoted. The gun at firing has its forward pivot pin inserted at either of the side pivots, s P, the weight of the gun resting mainly upon it, the training trucks of the rear end at some point of the training circle of that side. After the recoil the gun is run out to bring the weight upon that end of the carriage and enable the gun's crew to pivot the rear end to the center pivot, c P, and insert that pivot pin. The gun

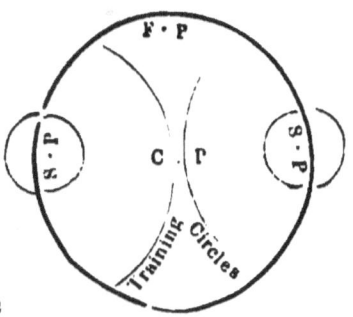

PIVOT CIRCLES.

is run in, the pin withdrawn from the side pivot and the gun
can then be pivoted on c p to the forward pivot and that pin
inserted. While being pivoted it receives its powder charge
and at this point meets its shell just at its muzzle, coming
from below. To fire from the opposite side the forward pin
is drawn, the gun continues to pivot while the loaders ride
and send the shell home, the pin is dropped into the side-pivot
socket, the gun run out, the center pivot-pin drawn, the gun
trained to the object and fired. In exercising without the
actual loading the maneuvers for pivoting and firing four
times must be performed in three minutes or the gun's crew
may expect more than the hour of daily drill until they can
accomplish it. Every move must be made with the precision
of clockwork, and the rolling of the ship interferes greatly,
so that at times the pivot pin cannot catch in season or the
gun races during pivoting, and some one suffers. Simpson
is the second man to be hurt in the same manner. Young
Parker, of the after pivot, had his foot badly hurt the day
after we left Lisbon the first time. We were off Palermo
at noon.

Saturday, June 16, 1866. We came to anchor at Messina early this morning and got ready to coal ship *as soon as
the decks were scrubbed.* At the same time all boat's crews
were ordered into clean white frocks and blue trousers. Figs
were offered for sale alongside. Squads of white habited
conscripts are drilling in every available level spot and a
steamer loaded with them is getting up steam for going to
sea. I was ashore in Sicily this morning for the first time.
Being boatkeeper I had none of the dirty work of coaling,
and sat in the boat all day mending stockings when the boat
was not called away. After supper the boats were hoisted
and the two watches were told that each watch was to fill a
side of the bunkers, then on an even keel, and when a watch

had filled its bunkers it would be piped down. Our watch got the port bunkers filled at 10 : 30 and got our hammocks. *Sunday, June 17, 1866.* The starboard watch did not get their hammocks till 2 : 30 this morning. They lost heart when they found they were beaten and at last sulked. A fireman, named Andrews, succeeded in stowing his bag and hammock on board a lighter and got away with them, going to a barque bound to The States, "where he can have room." We got under weigh at 7 A. M. Back of Rhegghium on the Italian shore is a singular spur of rock rising vertically from the surface of the ridge, jagged and split, with huge square boulders scattered at its base in positions to very strongly resemble a village. I have longed to visit it each time we have passed. Studdlingsails were set after dinner and at once a play at the braces and studdingsail tacks commenced that continued all the afternoon, the ship going two knots or less. A fishing smack came alongside and sold us some fish. At 5 o'clock we were reduced to reefed topsails, and later we furled everything.

Tuesday, June 19. We crossed the Gulf of Tarentum yesterday and sighted the east shore of the Adriatic last evening. This morning land was in sight all along to the east. Mr. DeLong had charge of our division at general quarters this forenoon, Mr. Wadleigh being sick. Word was passed at 6 P. M. for coxswains to see their boats well secured, a small gale blowing and the ship taking water over her sides.

Thursday, June 21. Immediately after dinner we began to send down light sails and gear, steaming our best with an Austrian frigate in chase. We were running them out of sight when we lay to for them to overhaul and examine us. We counted twenty-eight guns of a side as she ranged up beside us with her men at quarters and tompions out, near enough to toss a biscuit on board. Being satisfied with our appearance, and satisfied also that we really could show them a clean pair of heels, the officers saluted ours, their ship swung about and returned to her station at Polo. We were told to show ourselves anywhere except at our guns as she came up. We soon after started steam and at 5 P. M. made fast to moorings at Trieste. War had been declared against Italy and Prussia by Austria a few days ago.

Friday, June 22, 1866. A little before noon some fire was discovered in the coal stowed over the starboard boilers. The main force pumps were under repair, but the smaller ones were started upon the hot, smoking mass though with very little visible effect. Gas continued to rise and after dinner the Engineer's crew were set at work to overhaul the whole lot. They shoveled it forward and found it such stifling work in the confined space of the bunkers that no one could work there many minutes at a time. Volunteers were sent from the deck under a promise of a mug of beer for each shift of ten minutes. This brought out eager volunteers to get a drink, and an eight gallon keg procured from ashore was expended thus to quench the fire of their ardor before the fire in the coal was subdued. All the coal over the starboard boilers had to be hoisted on deck and the heated pieces thrown overboard or placed ready for use in the furnaces. The fire was supposed to have been caused by the ardor of the firemen in raising steam during the chase yesterday.

Monday, June 25. Martial law has been proclaimed, the lighthouse is unlighted and every precaution is taken to prevent the enemy's vessels entering unseen. To-day a first lot of liberty men went ashore. All day yesterday and to-day troops have been marching to take the cars for Venice, or rather Peschiera, near Verona on the western boundary of Venetia, some 125 miles from here by railroad, where a fierce battle is going on with the Italians, who are intent on

regaining that province and its city of Venice. An Austrian
side-wheel steamer of six 80pdr. rifles came in this morning
and her captain visited us at noon. Salutes were exchanged
between us. The Austrians claim a complete victory over
the Italians, driving them across the Po and taking 2000
prisoners. Yesterday we re-painted the inside of the bulwarks and to-day the outside of the ship. We saluted an
Austrian official visiting us in the afternoon. Every salute
brings the inhabitants to the housetops and wharves thinking
it may possibly mean a descent upon the city by the enemy's
fleet. Quite a number of army officers visited us and saw
the after pivot gun's crew go through with the drill of firing
from one side, loading while pivoting, and firing from the
other side in 39 seconds, astonishing them beyond measure.

Wednesday, June 27, 1866. This afternoon the last of
our liberty men were brought aboard by the police, a day
over their time. Some of them were petty officers. This
evening an Austrian steamer towed a fleet of small craft to
sea bound for Venice with government stores.

Thursday, June 28. I went on liberty with a half-month's
pay. Charlie Williams concluded to take a quiet stroll with
me and we first went up to the fort crowning a steep knoll
overlooking the center of the city. Finding an extensive
view from a square between the fort gates and a cathedral
we sat down under the shade of some trees awhile and took
a good look around to determine what we wanted to visit.
Around the Lighthouse Point was another bay into which
flows the Formio, with the extensive works of the Lloyds
stretching along its shore a long distance. It attracted our
attention most forcibly, so we struck down a flight of stone
steps at the cathedral front and through some steep paved
streets and then kept to the southward and eastward along
a seaside carriageway under the shade of a double row of

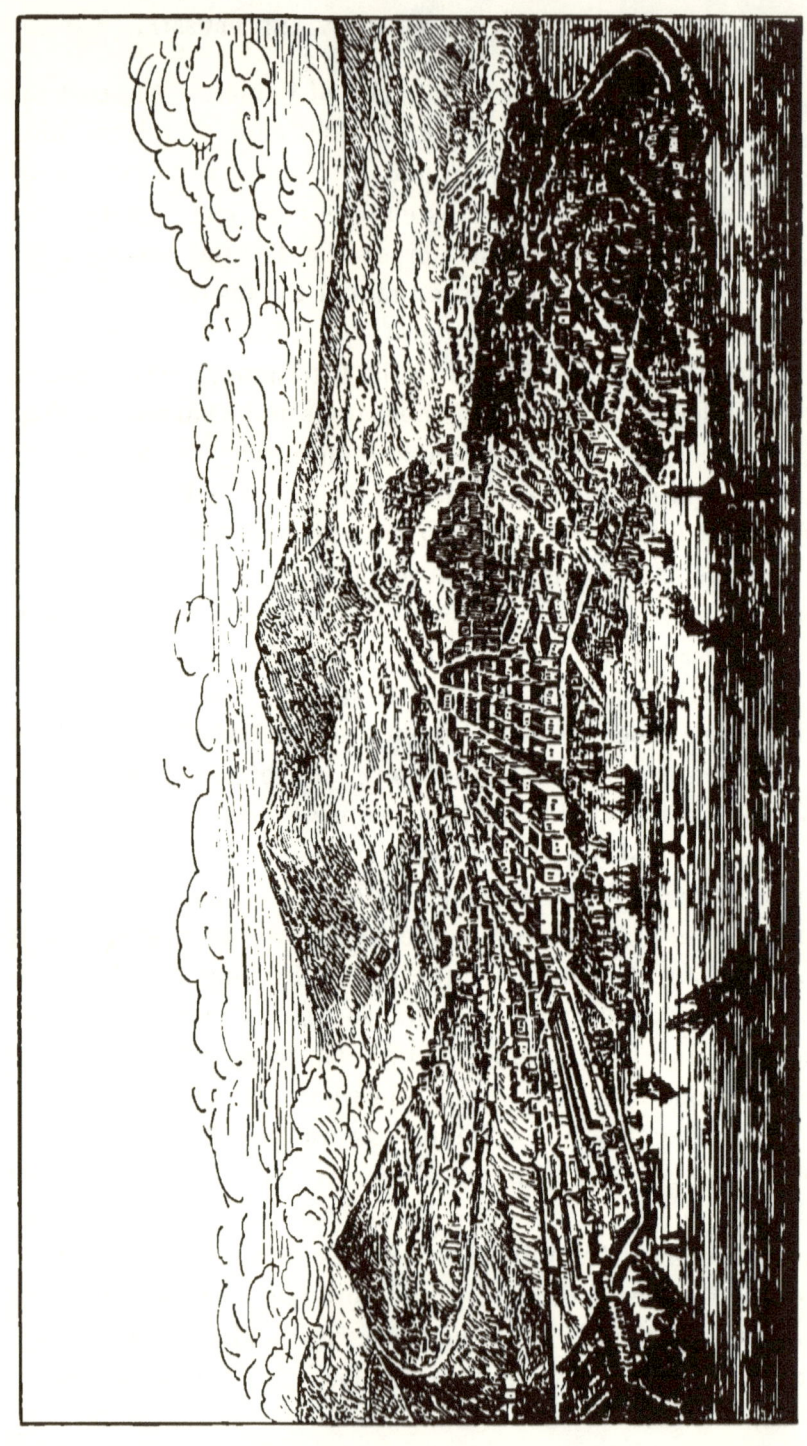

sycamore trees (*Kastagne salvatico*) that shaded the drive for a long distance. We found that the works of these Lloyd Brothers extend for a full mile along the shore and contain several dry docks, at least one of them large enough to take in our ship of 1800 tons. They also have several ways. Their machine shop is extensive and well equipped. Like the docks they and every thing about the establishment are of most solid construction. Their seventy odd steamers carry mail and passengers east from here, enough of them being in port at any time to form quite a feature in all views of the harbor. Their private office is one of the largest and finest business buildings in the city, the extensive lawn in front nicely kept and embelished with ornamental plants and statues. Their workmen occupy a tract between the works and the city, with fine residences for the overseers, while a grand mansion crowns the hill and commands a full view of the works, the bays, the city, and many miles beyond them. Past this establishment we took a road to the left leading to the gas works. Here the same care had been taken to beautify the grounds fronting their office and works. The road from here began to run through a cultivated valley, the soil a blue clay with a trace of sand and apparently a hard-pan subsoil, drained by open ditches and wherever recently worked was very lumpy. Corn was very weak in the stalk and the leaves were curled from drought. Returning to the city by another valley in the rear of the fort we started from we strolled to the railroad station at the other extremity, meeting many women of all classes, most of them showing traces of having been weeping bitterly. A train of wounded had just arrived from the field of battle and they had been to meet their suffering friends and relatives. Returning to the rear of the city again we saw a long baggage train being hitched up at one of the many barrack yards. We then took

a walk through one of their public beer gardens and reached
the business part of the city at 5 P. M.   Leaving Williams
here to remain ashore I made several purchases of clothing
and photographs of the city and its buildings, then returned
to the ship on the sundown boat, reporting with a desire to
finish my leave tomorrow.   Mr. Wadleigh had the deck and
the usual search for liquor was not required although I had
several packages in my arms that might have concealed it.

  Friday, June 29, 1866.   I went ashore in the market
boat early in the morning and first visited the market places

A MARKET-PLACE, TRIESTE.

with the ship's stewards, being greatly amused during the
progress of trading.   These market places are a curiosity.
I had seen something like them at Rio Janeiro with its lazy
venders of fruits, but here was activity personified by the
peasant women striving for the custom of the American blue-
jackets.   These peasant women come in troops early in the

morning with their donkeys and themselves loaded with all
sorts of articles for sale, and on entering certain squares in
the city raise a shelter and arrange their wares beneath it in
tempting display anywhere upon the cobblestone pavement,
leaving scarcely room for passing freely between the several
arrays. Placing themselves within their circles of goods they
wait for customers. The crooked lanes left about them are
crowded with housekeepers, basket in hand, seeking their
day's supplies. At a certain hour in the forenoon the square
must be vacated and by noon every vestige of a market has
disappeared and only the cleanly swept pavement remains.
Just outside the city I interviewed a gardener and his son,
named Antonio and Santo Diot who cultivated a small patch
of vegetables and weeds beneath the shade of fruit trees and
grapevines. There were at least ten persons in these two
families that somehow subsisted from the crops of about an
acre of land. I presumed that this must be supplemented
by day's work for others, for though their diminutive donkey
lived upon the weeds that thrived among the lumps of clay,
their cabbages were pierced in every leaf by smooth-skinned
green caterpillars (*Pieris rapæ,*) their plums and prunes
were blighted and falling from the trees, their grapes were
mildewed, their sorry specimens of corn were curled in the
leaf while just in the silk, still they were confident of being
able to support themselves in what was comfort to them. I
glanced within their shed-roofed cottages. Everything was
neat and clean within; still these mortar-laid rubblestone
shelters, with their earthen floors sunk two feet below the
surface, would convey a poor idea of comfort to the average
American day laborer. On climbing up a steep and narrow
way between high walls laid in mortar I got at last to the end
of habitation and of cultivation. I found that this lane led
to an old quarry in what appeared to be a goat pasture with

no fences of any kind in sight.   From here, I obtained a fine
view of the city and bay, and what pleased me as much—wild
flowers—single pinks growing wild, a little running vine,
white-flowered like a morning glory, very sweet and already
seeded, and a sort of moss in full bright yellow bloom that
covered patches two or three yards square.   Crowning the
acclivity was a high and solid wall with the Austrian ensign
floating from its flagstaff.   I followed a path around to the
front and found a shooting gallery in the basement of what
I judged to be a club house.   Several well dressed natives
were firing at a target about four or five rods distant, using
the window sill as a rest, though not hitting anywhere near
the center.   One of them noticed that I smiled at their lack
of success and offered me his loaded rifle.   I stepped back
enough to clear the muzzle of the piece from the window and
covering the center as I raised my piece fired almost before
the rifle touched my shoulder.   What appeared to be a man
with a bush in his hand sprang up from behind the target,
like a toy Jack in the box, proof of an absolute center shot.
A roar of laughter greeted the man when he offered me the
loaded piece again and I made signs for him to stand back
as I had and hit it himself.   I left them to continue their
sharp shooting and returning by the other side of the ridge
found myself in a grove of small oaks with their tops cut or
twisted off at a certain height as if for effect and having a
light sward beneath them.   On my way down the ridge I
obtained quite a bouquet of wild flowers, some of them old
garden friends at home.   I found everybody returning from
church and all of the shops closed.   I thus lost the chance
to buy some things for myself and others, but I saw the
ladies and peasant women in their best attire.   It was past
eleven o'clock and I took dinner at a restaurant and returned
to the ship somewhat tired but pleased with my trip.   Of

all my pleasant experiences none gave me greater pleasure
than to witness the lighting up of the countenances of the
little boys and girls as I gave them each a flower or a part
of whatever I might have in my hand at the time, and to hear
the invariable *"Ringrazio!"* (Thanks) returned as if they
appreciated the attention from the American sailor as much as
for the value of the gift of confectionery or flower received.
I had wanted to visit Maxamillian's Castle at the northwestern point of the bay of Trieste but the fifteen miles was too

MIRAMAR, MAXAMILLIAN'S CASTLE.

far to enable me to return on time.   I was the more anxious
to visit it from seeing the Mexican flag flying from its tower
and from the beauty of the place as described to me in partly
understood phrases by the photographer yesterday.   It has
seemed to me very strange that the owner of such a beautiful
home, moreover, that a person of Maximillian's taste could
consent to leave all these beautiful things, the associations

by which he was surrounded and the affection of these people
here, to become the puppet of so inferior a being as Louis
Napoleon.

Saturday, June 30, 1866. The men are not all off from
liberty yet. Our boat landed Mr. Hitchcock and the consul
at the railway station at sunset to go to Venice. Boatswain Briscoe came aboard to-day with a story of a Yankee
sailor who had astonished the natives yesterday by raising a
rifle and hitting the bull's-eye without taking any aim at all,
and had said "You hit it!" when offered the piece again.
He had made some very good hits himself at a rest and they
had about concluded that Americans were brought up with
rifles in their hands and could not miss. Acknowledging
that I was probably the one they spoke of he asked why I
didn't shoot again. I told him I thought I couldn't better
my first shot and was not sure of doing so well again, so I
preferred to give them a good opinion of Yankee marksmanship. "Bully for you!" he shouted. Rain and wind prevented an exercise at "Away all boats, armed and equipped."

Sunday, July 1. Our mess went in a body to the mast
with a request that I might be detailed as their steady cook
with the usual free ration as pay for the extra duty. They
liked my way of fixing up extras when I have taken their
cook's place. They were told they could have me, but that
I would be sent to do the duty of sick or absent men when
needed. They accepted the condition. From 7 A. M. to
to 5 P. M. I am excused from ordinary deck duty. News
from Austrian sources speak of a four days' fight between
Austrians and Prussians resulting in favor of the Austrians.
(Nevertheless I believe they lost a part of a province as a
result of their "victory.")

Monday, July 2. "Away all boats, armed and equipped!"
rang out just after 5 P. M. A stranger standing upon our

deck over the Captain's cabin would have thought we were
suffering a panic as he saw the ship's company rushing in all
directions, no one regarding another's doings, until as if by
magic they are seen clustered at the sides of the boats that
hang at the davits, one man at each boat with his arms full
of Sharp's rifles, another with Colt's revolvers, a third loaded
with belts having cutlasses and filled cartridge boxes for the
rifle and revolver of each man of his boat, a fourth with a bag
of hardbread, another one having seen that the boat's breaker
(water-keg) was filled, the coxswain with the boat's compass,
and marines with fixed bayonets stand beside the men at the
boat's falls.   The midshipman of each boat sees that every
man has provided the articles allotted him, and the officer of
the boat has his sidearms, perspective glass, and signal book.
When everything is ready he reports his boat ready for being
lowered.   In the meantime others who are to remain on the
ship are preparing to lower the howitzers into the bows of
the two largest boats.   All being reported ready the order
comes to "Lower away!"   Down go the boats, the men and
marines are in them with their officers, the rowers have the
oars in hand, and before a person a few rods distant could
recover from surprise at the sudden exhibition of life the
smaller boats are in line waiting for the adjustment of the
howitzers in the bows of the launches.   That required but
a few moments, when they joined our line and we rowed in
line about the harbor in compliance with signals from the
1st launch; occasionally those not rowing would be required
to use howitzers and rifles upon the imaginary foe we were
attacking.   An American merchantman was boarded by us.
They met us in fine style with cold water from their force-
pump as we appeared over the side of the ship.   We had a
merry time before the pump was captured.   Elated with our
success we then turned our attention to the small fort at the

the lighthouse. We formed in line a short distance from the fort and opened fire. The sentry gave the alarm, the garrison rushed to their guns and returned our fire by going through the evolutions as we were doing. It was a drill to them, and probably arrangements had been made with them and with our merchant ship previous to our starting. We were recalled from the attack by signal from the ship and retreated in confusion.—raced for the ship. The launches being encumbered with their guns per force "covered our retreat." We had enjoyed the exercise greatly. The mens' liberty is stopped because the others are not all off yet. A part of the marines are expecting to go ashore to-morrow.

Wednesday, July 4, 1866. We hoisted ensigns at each masthead and at the peak with the jack at the bowsprit at sunrise, and crossed to'gallant yards at the same time. At eight o'clock the English ram *Enterprise*, (built by the Laird's for the rebels) hoisted our ensign at the main and trimmed with a gauntline of signal flags from the bowsprit over the mastheads to the spanker boom end. Not having a set of small guns they recognized our natal day thus instead of by firing a salute with us at noon. We did not trim with a gauntline probably because we wanted to use our bunting to decorate the quarter deck for a ballroom under its awning. In order to give a clear space for dancing the after pivot was run forward out of the way, the two big guns pivoted to the forward gun's firing sockets. Trained sharply forward they gave to that part of our deck an extremely formidable appearance and impressed visitors forcibly with our power. Flags of all nations were hung from the edges of the awning as side screens, with a border of festooned signal flags; our own ensigns formed looped entrance curtains from the gangways; chandeliers were made of hoops with bayonets fastened to them for candlesticks, the bright blades glistening with reflecting light ; and cutlasses, pistols and muskets were arranged in various ornamental designs about the quarter deck. A band from ashore made the music, and Austrian belles with English and American ladies were the attractive features of the entertainment. As the dancing went on the screens at the gangways were removed to give fresh air and we before the mast could get a good view of the performers. We thought we could pick out the American ladies by the refined features and carriage common to all native American women, and even our Irish American shipmates bragged of the beauty of *our* countrywomen. The officers of the *Enterprise* seemed by their selection of partners to have the same preference over even their own countrywomen, and after we had seen these types together we did not wonder that many titled foreigners select American wives to grace their ancestral homes. There is a history connected with this ship *Enterprise* that ought to be an object lesson to all our future Diplomats and Administrations having to deal with England. This *Enterprise* was built for the Rebels, having armor for a short distance each side of the water line and armed with two 100-pdr. rifles and four broadside guns. She was all ready to go to sea as a rebel cruiser to prey upon our commerce. Our Minister, Charles Francis Adams, protested against her being allowed to go to sea and was coolly told in diplomatic language that there was no law in their statutes to interfere with her doing so. At the commencement of the rebellion Secretary Seward had felt that we were in no condition to accept a war with England, but at this time we were able to say " *You Must!*" Mr. Adams' short answer : " *This means war, Gentlemen!*" was very effective. Orders to stop her were issued within an hour and she was bought by the British Government. The two occurrences should be object lessons showing that the United States should have a

navy of sufficient power to enable us to say "You must"
at any time.   For dinner to-day we had nothing better than
the bean soup from the ship's coppers, but for supper I got
another kettleful of the soup of what would have been thrown
away by the ship's cook and adding some of the canned beef
lying behind the mess chest made for them our forefathers'
national dish of bean porridge.   Many of them had "never
tasted the likes" and pushed their two-quart pans up for a
second dose.   Some of the men paired off and utilized the
dancing music aft for a ball of their own under the to'gallant
forecastle, but the port watch of foretopmen were more of a
mind to look on and "ruminate."

Thursday, July 5, 1866.   News comes that the Italians
are concentrating a large naval force to attack Pola, a naval
station of the Austrians 100 miles south of Trieste.   We
expect to go down to witness the fight.

Sunday, July 8.   Several of our liberty men are still on
shore a week over their time.   E. J. Phillips, our Ship's
Writer is one of them.   He is English born and intensely
rebel in his sympathies.   Being also a college graduate it
has seemed strange that he should have entered the service
at all.   It is blowing a gale from the northeast, a fair wind
for going to sea, and we did so at 1 P. M. without starting
fires.   It calmed down to a light breeze before sunset.   The
men left ashore at Trieste number five desertions since the
restrictions and fancy business commenced, though the desertion of the ship's writer could not be for these reasons as
they did not affect him.

Monday, July 9.   An Austrian ram in fighting trim came
out from Pola this morning to investigate our character.
They know the ship well enough as far as they can see us,
but they must come close to us so as to make sure.   Her
officers saluted with ours by mutually touching caps and at

once returned to her station. We soon after set squaresails and started steam, heading across to the Italian coast. At 5 P. M. all hands were called to bring ship to anchor at Ancona and at 10 P. M. we had her safely tied up close to the shore with several hawsers astern and two anchors out with 105 fathoms of chain to each, all in eighteen feet of water.

Wednesday, July 11, 1866. The ship's writer's berth is given to a man named Berry, an English coalheaver and a rabid rebel sympathizer. It is a noticeable fact that our petty officers are foreigners as a body, yet the cry is raised that native Americans refuse to enter or remain in our naval service. Let all commands and executive offices on board our naval vessels be given to foreigners in preference to our native born officers and see how quickly the naval service will become distasteful to our Annapolis graduates. Men of American birth abhor foreign rule fully as strongly as an officer can. Three ironclads and a wooden frigate came in for coal and went to sea again when coaled. At 5:30 P. M. we commenced to heave in on our cables and got under weigh soon after 7 o'clock. Just outside we met a dispatch boat towing into port a disabled gunboat and found the fleet of eleven Italian rams, five wooden frigates, and six smaller gunboats under steam. One of them returned our salute. We were given new fire quarters this afternoon. While we were mustered under Mr. Wadleigh Mr. Allyn read to us our new stations in a tone too low for me to hear and this was repeated by Mr. W. to each in the same tone. As Mr. Allyn was walking away I turned my left ear to the man next to me and asked what my station was. He shouted, "*Pumps!*" loud enough to be heard over the ship, causing the 1st Luff to turn to see who had committed such a breach of discipline, but taking in the situation he went aft with a broad grin on. We were soon called to our stations by the rapid strokes of the bell and exercised a short time to see if each man understood his separate duty. We then exercised at shifting topsails, the new topsails being set with topgallant sails above them in six minutes. Both foremastmen were badly hurt by the topsail coming down upon them with a rush as they stood beneath. We fastened to moorings at Trieste about 6 : 30 P. M.

Friday, July 13, 1866. I got the barber to trim my whiskers after supper, but he trimmed them so short that I had him shave them clean, and they are all laughing at my lantern jaws, and at evening quarters even the officers, with suppressed smiles, call each others' attention to my changed, though not improved, appearance. I could draw my whiskers over my eyes before removing them. They were hot and troublesome about my mess work. The papers ashore say that Capt. Steadman has been promoted to Commodore.

Sunday, July 15. The sentence of a court martial was read in the case of a man named Smith for absence without leave. (Overstaying his liberty.) He is to have 30 days of confinement in double irons on bread and water, and to lose all pay due him. Being in debt, though a petty officer, that part of the sentence was remitted. He is a Virginian.* It is reported that Austria has given to France the Province of Venetia, hoping by the move to appease Italy, to whom the French are to transfer it, and thus enable Austria to throw her whole force against Prussia. The Italians accepted the gift but adhere to their treaty with Prussia, and it is even

---

* I think this was Chi f Boatswain's Mate Smith, who was disrated about this time for overstaying his liberty till the police brought him aboard in citizen's rig. He at one time told me his real name was Stuart and he was a nephew of General J. E. B Stuart, of the rebel cavalry, and a son of Judge Stuart, of Fauquier County. He was a quiet man and attended to his duty without being overbearing. He said he had no intention of overstaying or of getting into citizen's rig. Rum did it. Mr. Allyn was severely strict in his discipline as regards drunkenness and especially so with his petty officers, requiring them to set a good example before the rest of the men.

rumored that the Italian fleet is hovering outside of Trieste and may soon attack the place. It has been a very warm day indeed.

Monday, July 16, 1866. Last evening was very sultry and though my hammock was close to the hatchway I could not sleep. I went on deck at eleven o'clock and joined the "caulkers" trying to get some sleep on the bare deck. The air was very heavy even on deck. A thunder storm was in full blast out at sea. On its reaching us we found it to be wind and lightning with very little rain. Mr. Clark had the deck and gave orders to pay out fifteen fathoms of the mooring chain and to clear away the starboard anchor for letting go. Instantly there was a rush to get below away from the work that would require but a few men for a few minutes. After the anchor was dropped these men started to return to the deck but found a marine at each ladder with a bayonet in his hand. They couldn't come up. Mr. Clark took a good look at those who stayed on deck to do their duty, to know on whom he could depend. He found them almost to a man native born Americans, and *we* found that the three launchmates of the *Metacomet's* old crew were among the number. After the marines were withdrawn those below came skulking up, but we were in possession of the best places.

Tuesday, July 17. We exercised at all boats' armed and equipped, at this time providing everything required for an extended trip :—a tool box containing an ax, hatchet, saw, hammer, nails, tacks, sheet lead, marlinspike, spun yarn, a palm, needles and twine, lead line, lantern, candles, tinder box, flint and steel, fishhooks and lines, trailing lines and muffling mats for oars, chisels, bitts and brace. This box fitted under the thwarts. For provisions we had hardbread, canned beef, and cans representing coffee and sugar packed in a mess kettle with pans and spoons. In one of the boats was a medicine chest, and each boat had its grapnels and lines for anchoring, besides the arms and ammunition. In passing a bag of revolvers into the 1st launch boatswain's mate Jack Williams and quartermaster Bishop lost the bag of fifteen pistols overboard, from Bishop's not being on hand when the order was given to "Down boats and man them."

Wednesday, July 18, 1866. Submarine divers have been at work to recover the bag of revolvers lost yesterday. On one of the ridges to the north of the city and in sight from our anchorage is a monument said to be upon the spot where Napoleon Bonaparte brought his forces to a stand and after his army had suffered from sickness to a great extent withdrew without making any attempt to take the city.

Napoleon Monument.

Tuesday, July 24. Yesterday afternoon we were warping the ship around a few points at a time while the officers tested the accuracy of the compasses. To-day all our boats were armed and equipped again. Rumor reaches us of the loss of the *Shamrock* and the safety of her crew at Messina.

Saturday, July 28. We slipped our moorings at 8 P. M. last night bound for Venice and anchored at nine o'clock this morning some distance below the city. At 1 P. M. we up anchor and felt our way up to the city. We took a berth nearly abreast of the Doge's palace and quite near the landing. Our boat landed the consul at his door. These canal streets seem very odd to us.

Sunday, July 29. Our decks are crowded with visitors, gondolas plying to and from the ship with full loads. We wonder at the accuracy with which these gondolas are steered about in a crowd with so little room to spare that one could step from boat to boat while the oar is still in action. The rower stands upon a platform near the stern of the gondola and rows with a pushing motion, keeping the blade under water while bringing it forward nicely feathered for a new stroke. Old Ti was given to our consul at Trieste and the monkey is disconsolate. He will not allow any strangers to come near him.

Monday, July 30, 1866. Our decks have been crowded with visitors again since ten o'clock. I counted seventy-five gondolas around us at one time, and as each gondola would average ten passengers to a trip and made two trips an hour some idea of the number visiting us during the day may be formed. I stood at the foot of one of the berth deck (step) ladders for a long time taking the hands of ladies to assist them down, another man being at the other ladder and we were kept busy by a continual stream of them. Others of the mess cooks relieved us when we were tired, and steadied the guests in the most polite manner, to the evident delight of our officers, pleased that a good impression of the character of the ship's crew as well as the ship would go abroad.

Tuesday, July 31. One would think that the whole surrounding country had turned out to do us honor. Our ship is more densely crowded than yesterday. The visitors are first class and they include many Americans. An estimate of 20,000 visitors since our arrival would be clearly within bounds. Tourists must have flocked to Venice to see us.

Wednesday, Aug. 1. Several of us were on a four hours' leave ashore to-day. Four of us secured a guide and telling him how short our time was put ourselves under his care to show us the most noted objects. We first visited the Ducal Palace. The outside of this building is highly ornamented with carved work at all parts that could possibly allow its use. Entering by an arched gateway from the Riva Schiavoni, a broad, street-like landing, we found ourselves in a large courtyard with a fountain in the center and several fine

statues. We were led to the right up a flight of steps to a verandah that extended around the three sides of the building looking upon the courtyard, an angle of the Church of St. Mark forming the fourth side. From this verandah doors led into rooms and halls of the building. Here artists were copying some of the famous paintings that covered the walls and ceilings. We were shown into the Hall of Judgment. None dared disobey a summons to appear before the dread Secret Tribunal within this gloomy chamber, from which the condemned crossed The Bridge of Sighs to be seen no more.

THE BRIDGE OF SIGHS.

And We "stood upon the Bridge of Sighs" made famous by Byron's verse, and from its windows overlooking a canal

ST. MARK'S CHURCH and CAMPANILE TOWER.

saw a palace or a prison on either hand. The small bridge in the foreground with its stone steps and railing is similar to all that we saw in the city. The Bridge of Sighs is the one connecting the second story of the palace at the left with the upper story of the prison at the right. Retracing our steps we saw in one room portraits of the long line of Doges, but that of the traitor at the head of the stairs leading down to the Ducal Library has been effaced by a coat of black paint. At the foot of these stairs we entered a long gallery lighted by lamps and leading into the library. Shelves, and counter cases filled this large space. I noticed many manuscripts in Greek characters within these cases and among works on the shelves in various other languages were Reports printed by our own Government. Returning by the same way, which I think must be an underground passage as the Ducal Library is a separate building opposite the palace, we re-entered the palace and emerged by the hall of paintings first seen. In the courtyard our attention was directed to the angle of St. Mark's Church that forms the fourth side of the court-yard. The statues and carved or chiseled work were very fine, though some were too true to nature to pass muster in our New England clime. Passing through a small gate we entered a street parallel to the Riva Schiavoni. There was no need to call our attention to the angle of St. Mark's upon this street, for it was of a character to rivet the attention of the most indifferent observer. Only by a photograph can an idea of it be gained. A view of the front of the church on the opposite page will show its character. Our guide hurried us on to see this Grand Front of St. Mark's and the Campanile Tower in the Grand Square. The five great arches are profusely ornamented in the stone by the chisel. On the level, pebble-paved square stands the lofty Campanile Tower, the breeding place for innumerable doves that are daily fed

with grain scattered on the pavement. Between the palace
and library are seen the two columns of St. Theodore and
the Winged Lion of Venice near the edge of the landing
(seen on page 170) from which the old Venetian naval ar-
maments embarked upon their expeditions and the Doges
annually took their barge to go in procession to wed the sea.
The finest objects to be seen are the four Bronze Horses

THE BRONZE HORSES.

standing upon a gallery above the central grand arch, and
said to be trophies from Jerusalem. Within the church we
found the floor paved with small smooth pebbles of various
hues laid in mosaic patterns, and many arches upheld the
three great domes. These domes are conspicuous objects

from any point of view. From the inside of the church we see glass panels around their bases giving a dim light to the interior of the great building. Upon these panels are painted representations of all the Saints in the calender. Judging by their features some of them might be anything but saintly. Our attention was called to several noted relics, among them the stone upon which John the Baptist's head was cut off. I grieved our guide by remarking that they took some pains to provide such a hard stone instead of a wooden chopping block which would not have dulled the ax so badly. The stone looked just like a piece of white quartz with broad red streaks, and there was no avoiding the conclusion that it was selected to deceive the credulous. He shewed us no more relics. We next visited the Church of Sts. Stephen and Paul. Its great attraction consisted in its exquisite marble statuettes representing The Three Wise Men bringing gifts to the Babe in the Manger, and Christ Disputing with the Doctors. In the first servants were unloading the camels, one camel being in the act of nibbling the top of a cactus, while the ox in the next stall was turning his head sidewise to look over the partition at the babe in its mother's arms. In the other the boy Christ was standing in an elevated pulpit evidently holding his auditors spellbound at his words, their countenances showing consternation as well as wonder. One of the doctors was about to turn over a leaf of an open book upon his knee while looking up at the boy with a very puzzled brow, his left elbow crumpling the lower corners of several leaves in his confusion. Two others were looking intently over his shoulders, the one at the right arresting the turning of the leaf with one hand and pointing to a passage on the printed page with the other; and the little boy, Christ in the pulpit was calmly confounding them by his superior knowledge of the Scriptures, paying no heed to the advance

of his mother and members of the family in the distance ; for
He was about His Father's business.   The figures were not
over eighteen inches in height, but the attitudes were very
"speaking" and the work exquisite.   The building had less
pretentions to spendor than that of St. Mark, but these two
works of the devout sculptor hold more influence for a true
knowledge of the Savior than all the splendors of the other.
Connected with this church is a hospital, while with the first,
through the palace, is a connection with a dismal dungeon.
The one was for show, the other seems to have been devised
to promote the welfare of man.   Taking another course by
way of the narrow paved alleys instead of the canals we
came to the Grand Canal at its famous bridge, Rialto that

GRAND CANAL AND RIALTO.

spans the width of about thirty yards by a single flat arch.
The roadway of this bridge is a series of stone steps about
eight or ten feet in width with a covered arched stall at the
sides of each step of a single stone.   As no vehicles are in

use on land in this city of canals and alleys they have no need
to provide sidewalks.   This space on the bridge is occupied
by stalls for sale of curios or trifles that are eagerly sought by
tourists as souvenirs of their visit.   I got a bead-work bag
and white and mixed-colored shell-and-bead-work ornaments
to coil about the heads of the loved ones at home, not for-
getting to lay in a set of twentyfive photographs of noted
points from which I have selected those copied to illustrate
this, my diary.   We returned to the ship at sundown highly
pleased with our four hours in Venice, every man on time,
"clean and sober."   We were a talkative crew that evening.

Thursday, Aug. 2, 1866.   We returned to Trieste.   The
war with Prussia is said to be ended, but that with Italy is
to go on.

Wednesday, Aug. 8.   News comes of the successful operation of the Atlantic Cable.   Our monkey has received a
complete sailor suit.   He seemed pleased at first.   At our·
quarters this morning he was sitting upon the lever of the
pumps abreast of our gun and becoming dissatisfied with its
restraint upon the free use of his finger nails upon his back
he attempted to pull his frock over his head without first
loosening the necktie, resulting in his " bagging his head."
At this he became belligerant, lost his balance and fell over
backward but clung by his feet and hung chattering with
rage, none daring to leave their quarters to assist him, or to
even smile at his ludicrous predicament.   At retreat from
quarters he got help to replace the frock upon his back, the
men then getting away quickly.   Last night the Captain
gave a supper to some civilians, and the crews of the 1st and
3rd cutters were kept up till eleven o'clock to put the guests
ashore.   The boats' crews were allowed five minutes to go
with the guests but they stayed a half-hour to "go with each
other," dodging the midshipman from one saloon to another.

The guests must have been liberal for the crews of both the boats came off in a state that caused them to be blacklisted and their spending money stopped.

Thursday, Aug. 9, 1866. When Mr. Clark was showing some ladies the berth deck he pointed out our mess chests as belonging to a certain number of men called a mess, and we who were standing beside the chests were called mess cooks. "We *call* them cooks but they do no cooking; they draw the day's rations, prepare them for cooking by the ship' cook, and wash the dishes." I think he must have had Brennick in his mind's eye at the time. Brennick is acting as cook of the mess next ours. He wanted to borrow our mill, saying "I have to grind some coffee; but I don't know how it will grind, for it seems rather damp." I looked and found it was *raw* coffee. I told him it would have to be roasted first. He exclaimed "The Old Harry take the stuff; they have bought a dozen pounds of it and I will have to pitch it overboard, for I can't roast it." (He comes from the blue-nose country where coffee doesn't grow.) I had just roasted a lot of it for him to grind as Mr. Clark came along.

Saturday, Aug. 11. The Austrian fleet came in to-day in the teeth of a norther after a great battle with the Italian fleet at Lissa off the Dalmatian coast about 150 miles south of here. There were twelve sidewheel vessels of various sizes, five armored ram frigates, seven wooden frigates, and a line-of-battle ship. They have received severe damages. One of them has lost her prow and all masts but the mizzen. They were forced to run every heavy weight aft to keep her afloat. This is the first battle with the new plow-pointed bows for ramming and the effects produced, and injury to an assailant will probably be studied from this actual test. If the Italians lost the day they did not lose their honor.

Monday, Aug. 13. We commenced to coal ship before

breakfast. We hoisted the American ensign at the fore and mizzen mastheads with the Austrian ensign at the main and saluted the Emperor of Austria as he passed us in his steam yacht on his way to inspect his fleet, which was anchored in the bay south of Lighthouse Point. Rain commenced to pour in torrents at noon, interfering with our coaling. At tattoo this evening we succeeded in getting up a band from among the ship's crew. We have had two fifes and two tenor drums for some time. To-night we added a bass drum and cymbals, making the ship quite noisical if not musical.

Wednesday, Aug. 15, 1866. Our ship's company were drawn up by divisions on the port side of the deck, with eight sideboys at the gangway, and the marines drawn up on the quarter deck to receive some high naval official and his suite. The after pivot gun's crew were called to quarters to show them the working of that gun. They showed great interest in its working and pivoting. We learn that Lt. Snell and Lt. Terry have been promoted to Lt. Commanders. A while ago Ensigns Wadleigh and Dichman received their promotions to Masters, and now Ensigns Clark and Wright are made Masters. Among our Line officers we have :—

1 Commodore,	Steadman,	7-stripes on cuffs, formerly	6	
3 Lt. Commanders,	Allyn,	4-stripes,	"	4
	Snell,	" "	"	3
	Terry.	" "	"	3
4 Masters,	Wadleigh,	2 "	"	1
	Dichman,	2 "	"	1
	Clark,	2 "	"	1
	Wright.	2 "	"	1
2 Midshipmen,	DeLong,	*	"	*
	Hitchcock.*		"	*

We thus have among our line officers neither Captain, Commander, Lieutenant, nor Ensign. In the Staff we have a full

Commander, in Surg. Gunnel, 5-stripes, and other grades in the Engineer's department. We on deck have no connection with the last or the Lieutenant of Marines. A coalheaver, named Deets, finds that an Engineer officer has some power over him, for he has just been put in double irons on bread and water for "disregarding the order of the officer of the watch in the engine room until a third time ordered to resume his work, and then insolently saying ' he would be done as soon as any of them.'" He will be court-martialed.

Friday, Aug. 17, 1866. The *Minerva, No. 52*, of the Lloyd Bros.' mail line came in from Constantinople and was quarantined on account of cholera at that place. The English steamer from Alexandria a few days ago received the same treatment, a yellow flag at the fore-mast-head.

Saturday, Aug. 18. It is the birthday of the Emperor of Austria and we were called at 4 A. M. to trim the ship with a guantline of flags from the bowsprit over the mast-heads to the end of the spanker boom. We run it up at sunrise and fired a national salute at noon. The Austrian fleet fired a grand salute at sunrise and each hour of the day a single ship saluted. While we were hoisting the catamaran float used in washing the outside of the ship this morning the falls parted and Schofield fell with it to the water. His arm was broken and he was hurt otherwise so that he would have sunk had not Trainor jumped overboard and rescued him. We took in water.

Monday, Aug. 20, 1866. The twenty-fifth anniversary of my first entering the navy. What a contrast between my present grade in the navy and what it might have been had I waited a few weeks and filled the midshipman vacancy by the promotion of my brother's chum and our schoolmate who became Assistant Secretary of the Navy during the war and is now a captain. In that case I might have outranked all

but one officer in this ship. Boys in their impatience to do
"something big" rarely adopt the best method for attaining
the desired result. Their choice more often destroys their
opportunities for advancement through life. Let every boy
who reads this ponder well before making his choice. We
sailed for Candia late this afternoon, making a circuit of the
Austrian fleet lying in the other bay, saluting by three dips
of our ensigns. The band on the Admiral's ship also gave
us their version of "Hail Columbia" as we passed.

Thursday, Aug. 23, 1866. I was excused from duty last
night on account of the pain in my ear. I took laudanum
but got no sleep. My restless turnings caused my hammock
lanyard to part, but a man lying upon the deck beneath me
broke the force of my fall so that I was not hurt. The im-
pact woke him from his sleep with a yell. Corporal Hooper,
of the marines, had been dreaming of trying to fire one of
our IX-inch guns at an approaching enemy but it hung fire.
He had pulled the lanyard a second time and after hanging
fire a moment it went off rather unexpectedly to him. The
noise of its supposed explosion was the yell of the man that
I fell upon. It awoke him as he sprang out of his hammock
to avoid the supposed recoil of the gun. Hearing some one
say, "Are you hurt much?" and also hurried trampling of
the watch on deck taking in sail he fitted the whole into his
dream and thought some one was hurt by the recoil of the
gun he had fired. It was quite a while before others could
convince him he had been dreaming. This morning we were
opposite Brindisi, (Brundusium,) running along the Italian
coast upon the long flat tongue of land which forms the heel
of the Italian "boot." Keeping on the same southeasterly
course, at 4 P. M. the Grecian highlands were in sight on
our port beam, with fine weather and all studdingsails set.

Friday, Aug. 24. At midnight last night the long roll

called us to quarters for powder drill. The watch on deck
cast loose and provided everything required for a fight with
the guns so that when the watch below had hurriedly dressed
and had lashed up and stowed their hammocks they had only
to take their places beside us for the officers to report their
respective guns ready for action.   (I think that the big guns
were loaded, then run out and secured.)   We passed Cape
Matapan at 4 A. M.

 Sunday, Aug. 26, 1866.   The wind began to rise this
morning and the sea responded quickly.   We had supposed
we were to go into the harbor of Candia, but instead we ran
into the little bay of Suda just beyond, the head of which is
within two miles of the city of Candia.   We passed the fort
at the entrance long before sundown and steamed silently in
without a pilot.   As we neared two Turkish men-o'-war, one
a frigate of 50 guns, the other a 100-gun ship, we dropped
a kedge astern and then anchored between the two without
recognition of any kind, and kept our ensign flying all night.
A boat from one of the ships came alongside to learn our
business and how long we intended to remain in our present
position, and why we did not salute.   We heard the Captain
say "According to the regulations of the United States Navy
we are not allowed to use our big guns in salute."   These
unusual occurrences led us to conclude that we might have
a sudden call to use the contents of those big guns and our
gun captains had agreed upon certain spots in each ship for
targets, sure that our close range would enable us to smash
in their wooden sides at the first discharge.   We realized the
advantage of our position in that not all their guns could be
depressed to injure us without also hitting their own consort.
The Turkish officer had remained in his boat and must have
seen our saluting guns just over the heads of his men.   A
short time after this the *Arethusa*, an English frigate lying

in port fired a salute of seven guns with the American flag
flying at the foremast head. That meant that our consul had
just left her side and we at once understood that our business
here related to our consul who had evidently been compelled
to take refuge on board the British frigate with his wife and
child. The British Consul came to our ship with them in one
of the *Arethusa's* boats. We found our consul to be Colonel
Maggi, of one of our Massachusetts regiments. Late in the
evening the 1st cutter, armed and equipped, under command
of Mr. Dichman, accompanied by Dr. Gunnel took the consul and his family ashore and remained over night to guard
them, the British consul going with them. We noticed that
the *Arethusa* lay in a good position to rake the Turks, and
her boat's crew assured us they were all ready to help. The
cause of the trouble we did not know. We knew we had a
duty to perform and trusted to the guidance of our officers
that we would be required to meet no *unnecessary* danger.

Tuesday, Aug. 28, 1866. We lay all the day yesterday
between the two Turkish vessels, with no work going on and
the men almost spoiling for a fight, ready to spring to their
guns at the first tap of the drum. This morning, however,
we noticed that our officers had relaxed their watchfulness
and concluded that the Turks had complied with our demand,
whatever it was. When Capt. Steadman went on board the
two ships and received their salutes this forenoon we knew
the trouble was settled. In return the Turkish Admiral and
quite a number of his officers visited us at noon. The yards
were manned to receive him and a salute fired. Our Consul
had come on board with the 1st cutter's crew and when the
Turks left us they took him with them and the frigate gave
him a consul's salute. We then shifted our moorings from
between them.

Wednesday, Aug. 29. We up anchor at 10 P. M. last

night. The moon shone full and bright as we went out so
that we got quite a good view of the bay. The wind rose to
a gale before morning'and continued all day. My ears got
up steam about sundown and I had to get stoppers of cotton
saturated with laudanum in them before going on watch.

Thursday, Aug. 30, 1866. Another blow set in last
night and we make slow progress against the gale. We did
not reach Syra until 7 : 30 this morning. Several barrels of
both flour and dried apples were condemned as unfit for use
as food and thrown overboard. Some of the dried apples
were marked as purchased in September, 1863, and all were
infested by small flies and their maggots. Some of the flour
required only the addition of soda and water to effervesce,
and had plenty of weevils and grubs to stock the whole of
the ship's stores. Our provisions received from the storeship at Lisbon were evidently gleanings from the vessels of
the returned blockading squadrons. I have achieved an un-
enviable notoriety with the Paymaster and his Steward, the
latter laying to my account the request of the mess cooks to
have their bread weighed out to them in the light of day in
stead of in the bread-room where they could not see the
weights. He says there was no complaint until I went to
the berth deck to cook, and then within a fortnight my beef
was taken to the mast as short in weight. (It was proved
short.) His statement was made at the mast in answer to
our request, implying that I was the unreasonable instigator
of all the complaints. The Master-at-arms, however, told
Mr. Allyn that it was the general desire of the men as well
as of all the cooks to see the weights. Mr. Allyn decided
that our request was reasonable, and that the bread barrels
be hoisted upon deck and the net weights upon their heads
be taken down by a petty-officer for comparison with the
amount to which the rations entitled us. We were perfectly

satisfied and answered Mr. Allyn to that effect. At 3 P.
M. the gale is blowing with unabated fury, but we go to sea
to-night. I have had little chance to see the city, which is
built upon the sheltered side of the hill farther within the
bay than our anchorage. Upon a contiguous spur beyond is
another portion or suburb of the city. Upon the point of a
bench jutting out seaward are several windmills flying round
furiously in the gale. The little inner bay is crammed full
of vessels of all classes. The mailboat from Constantinople
is flying the yellow flag of quarantine. The boats' crews
find hard, wet pulling against the gale when coming from the
city, for the protection is but partial at our anchorage. We
went to sea at 4 P. M.

Friday, Aug. 31, 1866. The ship made good speed all
day and at 7 P. M, we dropped our anchor close in to the
Asiatic shore below the mouth of the Hellespont between the
shore and the Island of Tenedos, having passed the fort on
the island and the lighthouse in mid channel. The site of
ancient Troy is somewhere abreast of us, above is Abydos,
and opposite is Imbrios and the Peninsula of Chersonessus.
There is a pleasure tinged with sadness in looking at shores
that have seen so many vicissitudes and become so famous
in history now lying desolate and groaning under the heel of
a despotic and barely civilized government.

Saturday, Sept. 1. We got under weigh at 4 A. M. in
hopes to reach Constantinople before dark and steamed up
the swift current past fort after fort until we reached the
town of Dardanelles, where every vessel is required to stop
and obtain leave of the Sultan before going farther. We
shackled to moorings on finding no telegraphic answer to our
request by telegraph. We are daily hoisting up provisions
to serve out and finding them unfit for use. The pork that
we received yesterday under protest had scented the whole

ship so this morning that our officers ordered it to be thrown overboard and good served in its stead.

Sunday, Sept. 2, 1866. I judge that we have already come higher than allowed, for we slipped our moorings and dropped down a mile below the fort and came to anchor in the stream. It may be that they are paying us off for our late disrespectful actions at Sudi. (Some years after this I learned from an officer of the ship that the fort at the entrance to the harbor of Sudi fired across the bow of the ship as she was about to enter just after sundown.) They did not seem to have the best of feeling toward the *Ticonderoga*.

Tuesday, Sept. 4. We are still waiting for the telegram. It commenced to blow again this afternoon. Our consul came off at 5 P. M. with three ladies and several children in the 1st cutter and after looking about the ship were put on shore again, the spray dashing over the boat all the way and the men having hard work against the wind and tide in their heavily loaded boat. The dingey got adrift while being hooked on for hoisting and the 1st cutter was sent after it.

Wednesday, Sept. 5. Word came at sunset that we may come to the city as soon as we are ready. We did not give them time to get word to us to the contrary but as soon as everything was quiet ashore we up anchor and started at 10 o'clock. Twelve miles above the point where we had been lying four-and-a-half days waiting for a telegram of the one little word, "yes," we passed the reputed spot where Leander's famous swimming feat came off, and where his little less famed imitator of the almost present generation boldly plunged into the sweeping current and breasted the stream to the other side, apparrently from no other motive than to show to the world that it was not such a very great feat after all that had been said about it. The same stream still flows steadily and sweeps everything upon its current swiftly and remorselessly onward and downward, testifying to the great boldness and power of endurance of those two mortals.

Thursday, Sept. 6, 1866. At seven o'clock this morning we were in the Sea of Marmora, where no telegrams could reach us or forts enforce any farther delay in our reaching Constantinople. At 3 P. M. we anchored before the city, in plain sight of the Golden Horn, St. Sophia's dome and Moslem minarets, and directly abreast of the Sultan's Palace at Galata. In the view given of a part of Constantinople,

CONSTANTINOPLE.

Galata occupies the whole foreground, the Golden Horn is in the center, and a part of Seraglio Point in the background, extending quite a distance to the left beyond the view given. The Sultan's workshops are in the extreme southern part of Seraglio Point not represented. The mosque at the extreme right of the background is St. Sophia. Pera, the European

or Christian quarter, is farther to the right of Galata than
the view extends.　Some of our officers who came up when
we were first stopped at the Dardanelles say that this is the
dirtiest place they ever visited and that no amount of money
would tempt them to remain in it.　They were glad to get
aboard again.

Sunday, Sept. 9, 1866.　We up anchor at 4 A. M. for
Bu-yuk-de-rah, the residence of Foreign Ministers.　It is
up the Bosphorus and within sight of the entrance to the
Black Sea.　After coming to anchor we found that we would
swing afoul of a Greek brig, and the Boatswain was sent on
board with a party of men to hoist her anchor and move her
to as good a berth out of our way.　All hands were called
to muster and Capt. Steadman read to us a letter he received
last night informing him officially of his promotion to the
rank of Commodore from July 25.

Monday, Sept. 11.　A day for visitors.　Several Foreign
Ministers came on board and witnessed our drill at the pivot
gun aft and received their proper salutes on leaving.　They
came in boats called kyeets that are unlike anything we have
seen.　The curve at the stern is broader than at the bow,
the flatly rounded bottom forward lies out of water for several
feet of the boat's length.　That of the American Minister
is a nicely appointed affair with its gilded stars upon a blue
ground, its red and white stripes, and golden eagle with wings
outstretched perched upon the bow just in front of the staff,
which bears the flag denoting the nationality and rank of the
occupant.　It has ten rowers using long sweeps.　They rise
to a stooping posture when bringing the sweep forward for
a stroke, then place one foot against the thwart abaft them
and straighten up for a pull, dropping upon their own seat
with a bump as their stroke finishes.　The Ministers' body-
guards are a study for an artist, with their curved scimiters,

curiously mounted single-barrel, flint-lock pistols and yata-
ghan stuck in a sash belt. They held their heads high.

Tuesday, Sept. 11, 1866. It is the birthday of the Russian Emperor and our ship is trimmed in honor of the day.
The Prussian and English Ambassadors visited us and we
saluted them on their leaving the ship.

Wednesday, Sept. 12. Word was passed yesterday that
all able to show a dollar might have liberty ashore till sunset.
Not hearing the word passed I missed going. Supposing
that others would be given liberty in like manner I asked Mr.
Allyn that I be allowed to go the next time as I did not hear
the word passed yesterday. He said, "The men behaved
so badly yesterday that I had concluded not to give any more
liberty here, but *you* can go."   I asked him when, and was
told "Just when you please." " For how long, sir?" "Just
as long as you please," then turning to Mr. Wadleigh, who
had the deck, he told him that when Stuart was ready to go
he might call away the 2nd cutter and put him ashore. It
created considerable surprise among the boys when those in
the gangway who heard the request and answer went forward
and reported it. Of course they understood that Mr. Allyn
did this partly to show them that soberness ashore and good
conduct generally is appreciated by him, and that they had
only themselves to blame for the stoppage of their liberty.
They all said they were glad I could go. I went ashore at 11
o'clock. Passing through the dirty, crooked lanes of the town
I climbed the northerly slope of the ridge at the foot of which
the town lies. The trail led part way up the slope from the
ravine to the north, and it was completely arched over by the
branches of scrubby oaks whose tops had been cut off at 8
feet or less from the ground and the suckers allowed to grow
and interlace over the trail, forming a deliciously cool arbor-
like path. Across the head of a small branch of the densely

wooded ravine to the right I noticed oak and chestnut were
the prevailing trees, the latter with burs green and prickly,
the nuts just forming.   On reaching the bare head of the
ridge at about the letter *k* in the word Buyukderah upon the
map given below I had an almost uninterrupted and compre-
hensive view of the Bosphorus, the Black Sea, and the ridges
adjoining.   Between me and the Black Sea was a low spur
of bare white rock, and I would
have crossed to it and followed
down it to the Black Sea shore
in spite of the deep gully to be
crossed to reach it, only that I had
little time for so extensive a trip.
I turned to the left along the top
of the ridge till I came to the hut
of a vineyard keeper.   Entering
the gateway to beg a drink of
water two large dogs at
once bounded out to dis-
pute my entrance, but the
keeper soon stopped their
music and taking a small
bucket went to a well to
draw some cool water for
me.   By my measure of
the well rope I found it
was 75 feet to the water
from the surface.   I then
inspected his vines.   I

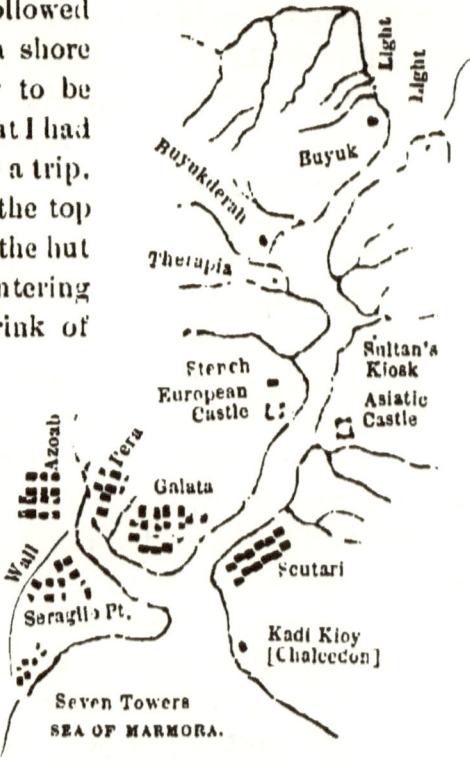

Constantinople and The Bosphorus.

saw that they had been trimmed annually to within six inches
of the ground and showed a stump of that diameter and only
that height, from which two or three small shoots not over
two feet long grew and bore two or three enormous bunches

of delicious grapes. He cut a bunch each of raisin, wine, and table grapes and would accept no pay for them, desiring instead my name upon his register of visitors. The three bunches filled my cap bagged out to its greatest dimensions and I was glad I did not stop on the way for anything to eat. The vines were set only 2 1-2 feet apart each way and the soil was kept loose and free from weeds. Growing upon a very steep hillside with no visible means for irrigating at all I wondered where the grapes could have gotten the moisture for the juice in them. The dogs soon became quite friendly after I had offered them my hand to smell and they seemed inclined to show their friendship by rubbing against me, one on either side. I continued my walk along the ridge in sight of the little cove, the shipping almost at my feet but so far below me that they looked like skiffs rigged for some fancy parade. Upon the side hill I came upon two Turks plowing with a yoke of oxen and a primitive plow. The plow was a fork of a tree, the main stem cut down to four inches broad on one side and three limbs left, the two lower ones started out quartering to each other from

A TURKISH PLOW.

the same height upon the tree and formed alternately the mould-board or land-side, their outer faces being flattened. Half-way between these limbs, a little higher up, a third limb had been left for a single handle. Into this handle and near its lower end a long pole for a beam was morticed and pinned. An ax, an augur, and a chisel were all the tools used so far in its manufacture. In making the point a thin triangular piece of iron of eight inch sides is used, with a deep cut on two sides, and holes punched in the position indicated in this figure. The parts with the holes in them are bent around the sole stick, apparently while the iron is hot, and fastened by nails driven through the four holes. The yoke is fastened to the plow-beam. Beneath it is a thin slat the length of the yoke. It has four sticks fastened into it to serve in place of our bows. These sticks are passed through the yoke and fastened very much as we fasten our bows. To drive the oxen a line is fastened to the inner horn of each ox and held in the hand holding the plow. To guide the team the driver would pull upon the line of one ox and punch the other with a long stick that he held in his free hand. The other man walked ahead and poked the bramble or blackberry roots out upon plowed ground for their roots to dry. The plowman walked some three furrows distant upon the plowed ground that the part then used as a land-side might have a vertical position. I suppose they called it plowing, though the furrows were not three inches deep. By following a spur and then a steep ravine, ending by plunging down a deep gully caused by rains that had cut through a series of old terraces, and had completely ruined them, I reached the broad valley of the creek south of the town. The only sign left of former cultivation of these terraces was a lone fig tree still bearing a bountiful crop amidst the surrounding desolation. In an opening into the valley as I entered it I came upon a man lying asleep under a tree, with his small flock of sheep and herd of young cattle grouped about him. He did not waken though the animals rose quietly and allowed me to stroke them and put my arms over their necks. They gathered about me to lick my clothing as if they knew that I was an Old Salt by my uniform. I concluded they had not been salted very recently and that I better get out of their reach while I had a uniform fit to go aboard the ship in. I soon crossed a road, one side of which was roughly paved with round stones, apparently for winter use, as all travel was on

the unpaved side.   I found the bed of the creek entirely dry.
At one place a mule was attached to the lever of a whim for
hoisting water from a deep hole close to the bed of the creek.
By gearing a great wheel was made to turn within this hole.
The fellies of the wheel being hollow, each with a hole at one
side, they filled as they entered the water at the bottom of
the hole and as each felly reached a certain height during the
rotation of the wheel its contents poured into a wide trough
beside the wheel till at the highest point that felly was empty.
This water was used in a field of corn where men were gath-
ering the crop from egg-plants set in each hill of corn.   In
crossing a dry level field on my way to the town I found
many delicate pink blossoms of a lily type that I thought
were colchicum blossoms from their springing up from the
ground with nothing but the flower and its stem to be seen.
I wondered whether it might not be "The lily of the field,"
that our Savior called attention to, and I tried to dig down
to the root but failed to find more than the dead remains of
an outer husk-like covering for the few inches I could dig
in the hard baked soil.   Nor could Dr. Hyde identify it for
me farther than liliaceous on reaching the ship.   Just outside the town and at the mouth of the little dry stream that
waters the valley—when it rains—is a rustic coffee and wine
garden, laid out in walks and flower beds, with shrubbery
and curious fences of honey-combed rock hooked together by
wires and hung upon chains between posts covered with the
same material bedded in cement.   A two-story octagonal
summer-house with a spiral staircase in the center, and all
covered with this material and rustic wood-work presented
one of the neatest attractions imaginable.   From the upper
platform a fine view of the whole grounds was obtained ; its
avenues and paths of washed gravel stones rolled hard and
bordered by beds of many shapes, filled with many colors of

geraniums, petunias, marigolds, asters, and other brilliant
flowering and foliage plants in masses showed as parts of
one great kaleidoscopic figure radiating in harmonious variety from this central point. Its many rustic arbors, ponds
with ducks, geese, and stately swans, with other attractive
features made me willing to pay my piaster (4 cents) for a
table-spoonful of a muddy beverage they called "Turkish
coffee." It was here I saw my first swan, here I took my
first look at really artistic rustic gardening, and here I had
my first experience in ridding myself of swarms of teasing
boy and girl beggars by at last offering them a stone in a
way they could not help understanding. Soon after leaving
this tastefully arranged place, which I judged was the resort
of the Europeans for an afternoon stroll, I came to a group
of sycamores whose gigantic trunks were crowded into an
irregular mass with a hollow in the center, and forming a
large area of shade beneath its branches. An enterprising
Turk had built a small shanty upon the loose sand in the
shade between these trees and the dry bed of the creek, and
had placed seats of rough boards around under the shade.
This seemed to be a place for meeting by Turkish men and
women, but I noticed that they all squatted upon the sand
instead of sitting upon the benches. A group of women
were seated together, some of them with their veils raised.
I made it convenient to pass them so as to see their faces.
Before they got sight of me I saw enough to convince me
the veil was worn more to hide uninteresting vacuity than to
prevent outsiders seeing the loveliness of the Moslem harem.
On reaching the town I saw the ship salute the Persian Am-
bassador to the Sultan as he left her side. The natives took
quite an interest in the American ship. I saw nothing in
town that I cared to buy and returned aboard at 5 P. M.

Thursday, Sept. 13, 1866. We up anchor at 8 A. M.

for Constantinople. We got a good view of the beautiful shores of the Bosphorus on the way down. On passing the residence of an American missionary upon the Asiatic shore we were saluted from the upper windows by ladies waving little American flags, and by the boys upon the piazza with the true Yankee "Hip! Hip! Hurrah!" We mounted the rigging quickly at the order, "All hands cheer ship!" and greeted them with three rousing cheers, while the officers returned the salute of the ladies with their handkerchiefs and three dips of the ensign. How their hearts must have leapt with joy at sight of their national flag borne by their Nation's ship, ever watchful to protect them in their extremely dangerous position. Only such as they can realize what that flag means to those tarrying amidst these Moslem fanatics.* Four lonesome years they had lived, knowing that flag alone, and the power to avenge that might possibly be represented by it, had secured their residence from the torch of the incendiary and themselves from immolation or the fury of fanatics. We had been deemed brave because under that flag with arms in our hands and comrades beside us we had risked our lives for our country. What must be due to these ladies who all this time had trusted their lives under the folds of that flag, (so far as earthly trust went,) unarmed and alone, laboring to improve the condition of those who hated them with an inveterate hatred! We gave them the meed of greater honor than ours. Men's eyes were moist when we reached the deck.

° The presence of forty-one of the men-o'-war of the European Powers and of the United States at Constantinople to protect the citizens and missionaries of their respective countries from the wholesale massacres of native Christians at the time of putting this page into type, December, 1895, shows what might have been the fate of foreign missionaries in the reign of Abdul Aziz but for the restraining presence of Christian fleets. My own Division-officer, Master G. H. Wadleigh of that time is now Capt. Wadleigh, in command of the MINNEAPOLIS. We may rest assured that his ship will protect or avenge as far inland as his guns can send a shell or men can go, for he was a sterling man, of a most kindly disposition. and an excellent officer.

Our sentiment was quickly changed to merriment. A short distance inland from our missionary was the residence of the Greek Consul. He probably supposed that the cheers and flag dipping were intended for him, for he hurriedly dipped his flag. He received the customary dips in return. These dips a Turkish steamer going up stream appropriated to her own account and deadened her way until she could hoist her flag in order to be able to dip it. The Turk got the return of the compliment. We begin to think we are creating some stir among them. None, however, show us the friendliness and consideration that the Russians observe toward us. A boat's crew going alongside one of their ships is invited on board and all they have in the way of sailor courtesy they offer heartily. They remember and always speak of our own attentions to the crews of their ships when wintering in our ports during the rebellion. The bad behavior of the men at Buyukderah resulted from the "treating" by the Russian sailors on their Emperor's birthday with money furnished by their officers for that purpose. We should never fail to get help in our need when Russian sailors or their officers were within call. At 9:30 we anchored at Constantinople and received the greetings of the Turkish men-o'-war. In the afternoon Mehemet Ali, Captain Pasha, visited us and we exchanged salutes.

Friday, Sept. 14, 1866. We received a visit from the Grand Vizier. We manned yards for him and gave him a salute of 19 guns. I bought a pair of white satin Turkish slippers on board for my better half, paying $1 for them. I also got several photographs of parts of the city and of the Sultan, his little son and his daughter, Mehemet Ali, and the Grand Vizier. (I had secured photographs of the sovereign of each country we had visited. The portraits obtained here were good, but the views faded so badly that cuts from them could not be made, except from the partial view of the city given on page 187.)

Tuesday, Sept. 18, 1866. We got under weigh at 6 : 30 A. M. for the Island of Cyprus, calling at Syra to leave our pilot.

Friday, Sept. 21. We passed the Island of Rhodes.— In the forenoon we attempted to exercise at quarters, but a few rolls of the ship of her own sweet will sent our pivot guns flying at a greater speed than we would have cared to show visitors. They did not wait for orders or stop to let the pivot bolt drop into the socket. We were glad to hear the order to secure our guns.

Monday, Sept. 24. We arrived at Larnaca at 8 A. M., finding the consular flags of several nations, but no war-vessels.

Tuesday, Sept. 25. There is a story floating about decks that the Turks have arrested the body servant of our Consul, Gen. Di Cesnola, and were keeping him in prison in spite of the Consul's protest. He had referred the matter to our Minister at Constantinople, E. Jay Morris, who sent us to settle it according to our idea of what should be right. On our appearance the Turks changed their mind about the man, but the consul, with our consul from Beiroot, who had come to assist, demanded not only the man, but an apology, and an indemnity of $20,000. This forenoon the Commodore came off from ashore and as soon as his head appeared over the gangway gave an order to " Beat to quarters for target drill, and set a target one mile out to sea!" After our second heavy gun had been fired at the target the Commodore's Clerk exclaimed "See them run! Oh, *see* them run!" The people were leaving the town at a double-quick, thinking we were about to knock their houses to pieces over their heads for the insult to our flag. The deep and prolonged b-o-o-m

of our heavy guns, so different from anything they had ever
heard, was a revelation to them that demands thus endorsed
better be obeyed without further parley.   These Turks seem
to have forgotten us as a nation worthy of consideration,
having seen none of our war-ships since the opening of the
rebellion ; but our little corvette is opening their eyes through
their ears.   When it came to our turn to fire on the second
round Mr. Wadleigh took the gun-lanyard from Jordan and
took a piece out of the staff of the target.   A boat came off
soon after and our quartermaster on duty at the time tells us
that after some conversation he heard the Commodore say
to the Turkish officer, " No, sir !   We must have the man,
the apology, and $20,000 indemnity."   The boat appeared
again within an hour and offered the man and an apology.
The answer was the same with the addition of " I go to sea
at sundown, and this thing must be settled before I sail ! "
When the boat appeared again it was accompanied by one
bearing the two consuls, showing that they had acceeded to
our demands.   It appears that the b-o-o-m of our big guns
was all they desired to hear of our argument.*

Wednesday, Sept. 26.   We got under weigh at ten o'clock
last night, the Beiroot consul still on board, and steamed
rapidly along the coast toward the east.   We anchored at
Latakia soon after noon.   Latakia is built upon and partly
with the ruins of the ancient Laodicea, which, with Collosse

---

near by, (where was one of the churches that Paul wrote to) was destroyed by an earthquake in 65 or 66. The ruins are visible, mixed with the houses of the present inhabitants. Those of Collosse do not appear to have been disturbed at all though eighteen centuries have elapsed since its overthrow.

Thursday, Sept. 27, 1866. We up anchor at eight o'clock last night with the Beiroot Consul still on board and arrived at Beiroot (or Beyrut as it is also spelt) at ten o'clock this morning. We found here the British corvette, Cossack, and a Turkish man-o'-war. Directly back of the town some 20 miles distant apparently, they look so distinct, we see the Mountains of Lebanon, their tops hidden at times by clouds and seemingly destitute of vegetation. The decayed aspect of the town is relieved in a measure by trees and gardens. At various points are seen the ruins of ancient buildings or fortifications. It is a dreary looking place.

Friday, Sept. 28. We sailed to-day for Joppa. We ran along the land all day and passed Sidon and Tyre; also close to Mount Carmel, "dipping its feet in the western sea," the Mountains of Samaria in the distance visible from our deck.

Saturday, Sept. 29. We reached Joppa early this fore-noon. A stormy night gave our watch one hour for sleep. Before breakfast we holystoned the spar deck. During the forenoon we mess cooks were scraping the old coat of white-wash from overhead on the berth deck. After dinner Mr. Allyn sent for me to know if I would like to go to Jerusa-lem. Of course I would, and was told to take my place in line with eleven others in the starboard gangway. Commo-dore Steadman then came to us and said that "your conduct while on board this ship has been so unexceptionable that I allow you to go to Jerusalem at your own expense." Mr. Allyn then told us to get ready and report in the gangway, when a month's pay would be served to us, and that animals

and a guide would be ready for us when we got ashore.   The
boys jokingly called us the twelve apostles, and they wanted
to know which of us was Judas.   When I reminded them
that Judas was not one of the Apostles, Webster retorted
that I must be Paul, for I wrote most of the letters.   We
found the animals waiting, but they did not all have riding
saddles.   It fell to my lot to straddle what we call an apar-
ejo, (pronounced ap-ar-a'-ho,) the top of which is of the size

and shape of a hogshead.   I
had neither bridle nor halter to
guide the beast, and was thus
completely at her mercy.   The
accompanying home-made cut
shows the manner of my ride.
The mule would not allow me
to sit in any other way till we
began to climb the hills, when
I found she liked to have me
hang my feet in front of the
saddle and each side of her in
going up hill, but that I must
"fleet aft" on going down hill
or her head would go down and

On My Way to Jerusalem

heels go up, causing me to make faster time on the way to
Jerusalem than my mule did.   I walked over half the way
to relieve the strain upon my muscles and aching joints.
Several of our officers had started a short time before us.
For the first three or four hours of our route we crossed a
plain that reminded me of the Sacramento Valley at the same
time of the year.   The soil had the same baked and cracked
appearance.   The bed of a small stream we crossed was dry,
but a stone arched bridge gave token that at times it became
unsafe to ford.   Hardly a traveler was seen on the road.

THE DAMASCUS GATE, JERUSALEM.

At one place we saw a huge pile of grain with men throwing it into the air for the wind to blow away the chaff just as they did 2000 years ago. It was dark when we stopped at Ramleh for supper and to wait for the moon to rise. Soon after starting we commenced to enter the hills. Again was I reminded of California by the large olive trees scattered singly and of a rounded form, looking by moonlight like the live oaks of the foot hills of the Sierra Nevada. A second stop was made at a Bedouin camp in a deep hollow just after our animals had slid down an incline with all four feet close together. I got a cup of coffee here that was very refreshing, and my limbs and joints were greatly relieved by the rest. By alternately riding and walking I got along more easily. Surely no road in California could be much rougher than this one over the three mountain ridges between Ramleh and Jerusalem. In places flat layers of what I took to be limestone formed steps or terraces of naked rock too high for the animals to mount, and they would go a hundred or more feet to the right or left, where they knew was the easy place for going up or down. Had this zigzag course been by continuous gains upon the desired course they would have been welcome, but to have a mule with a Mexican pack-saddle carry one down hill awhile and then without warning to suddenly turn and almost jerk the saddle out from under a man by leaping or scrambling to the next rise is far from a pleasant experience, especially when a man is very sleepy, after thirty hours of continued action. Daylight of Sunday found us still climbing the desolate hills of Palestine, white with a honeycombed rock which covered the greater part of the surface in high steps or natural terraces. We passed a few cultivated terraces, the soil hidden (or held down) by stone chips, and grapevine stumps about six feet long lay prone upon them with bearing shoots springing in a green

mat from them in all directions. Every country seems to
have its own way of growing the grape. Each may be the
best for its own locality. As we were climbing the last of
the hills we began to see life stirring. A train of donkeys
laden with melons for Jerusalem struck into the road ahead
of us. At last, though too late to see the sun rise behind
the holy city we got a view of Jerusalem. The morning sun
was well up over the Mount of Olives beyond the city when
winding around the head of a ridge the city burst suddenly
into full view. Our fatigue was forgotten. We quenched
our thirst at the Upper Pool of Gihon as we passed and entered the city by the Jaffa (Joppa) gate, in the western wall.
We were led through narrow, crooked streets, sometimes
under arches, diagonally across the city to the Frank quarter
near the Damascus or northern gate. where the Meditterranean Hotel was kept by one Hornstein. We were all very
lame after our unusual exercise, and hungry also. After a
long time of waiting for breakfast we were served with a
few fried eggs and a cup of coffee. Finding the boys were
rather slow to start to see the city, most of them preferring
to sleep. I thought I would retrace our course to a photographer's place we passed before entering the city. Missing
my way to the Jaffa gate I tried to go out by two others in
succession that I supposed were city gates. At the last I
got hustled out for my persistence in trying to get out of the
city by the way of the Temple grounds. I had a glimpse of
them that paid for the rough usage. Failing to get out of
the city I made my way back to the hotel. Here I learned
that the boys had just started with a guide for the Mount of
Olives, and being shown the way they took I gave chase. A
few rods of start in this dirty city of crooked lanes and laby-
rinthine courts is sufficient to give a stranger the slip. I
saw nothing of them and strayed into a ruinous part of the

city in the northeast corner that appeared to have never been re-built. A pack of wolf-like dogs snarled at me for my disturbance of their feast. I thought of the fate of Jezebel when they surrounded me, and I was glad to find a broken place in the wall where I could climb up out of their reach. Here was a gate closed up with masonry, and a great space within the wall at the corner was entirely covered with large broken blocks of stone in heaps as if the ruins of overthrown buildings. Once upon the wall I did not regret missing my way. My only regret was that I did not have a revolver and a full box of ammunition for a little target practice. As I stood upon the battlement near the corner of the wall the Valley of Jehoshaphat opened out wide below me. Over against me to the north was a curiously shaped hill, its top but little higher than the road west of it leading to the north. Its southern face was very steep, with several cave-like holes that reminded one of a boy's pumpkin lantern without any light. It appeared to be a slight spur-ridge ending in a bluff.* To the east the Valley of Jehoshaphat narrows and deepens rapidly to the south, and beyond are the three round tops of the Mount of Olives, while far to the north and west the hills and mountains extend to dim blue outlines, all of them doubtless famed in Jewish history. I judged that the battlements on the wall where I stood were two feet thick, braced every ten or twelve feet by masonry extending about six feet toward the inner face of the wall, cutting the top of it into sections. Inside the braces was a passage of two to three feet giving a clear walk from gate to gate. The whole thickness of wall was about twelve feet. I followed this passage nearly to the Damascus gate and descended by a broken place in the inner face of the wall as I wished to go by that gate to find the photographer. In the center of the

---

c Since found to be Mount Calvary. Its summit is visible from the whole north wall.

arch of this gateway is a hole with rocks poised about it to drop and close the gateway in an assault. I asked the sentry if I could go out and in freely at this gate before going out. I found that the photographer was at church. While waiting for his return a gentleman called and I asked him the site of Calvary. Finding that I was a protestant he said: "We know not." (The hotel man had told me, "inside the Church of the Holy Sepulcher," and I concluded *that* was a mole-hill mountain.) I then asked him the way to the Mount of Olives, and he kindly offered to show me, saying he would like to go himself. We returned past the Damascus Gate. Near it he pointed out a garden belonging to the Russian-Greek Convent northwest of the city, which will become a beautiful place when the trees have attained more growth. What we call an orchard is a garden here. Just east of the Damascus gate I was shown a spot under the wall where a fold in the strata formed the roof of a tunnel-like cavity under the wall. I learn that the holes in the bluff to the north bear the names of "Tomb of the Kings," and "Grotto of Jeremiah." One branch of the Kidron starts from here, as also a branch of the Gihon, the Kidron win ling around the northeast corner of the city and the Gihon around the northwest, both being broad flats of but slight depression. The water from these join the main torrents east and west of the city to meet at the southeast of the city on their common way to the Dead Sea. Having the longer course to their junction the fall of the Gihon is more gradual, though both are torrents. The Kidron has a fall of six-hundred feet in a mile. As we passed around the northeast corner we found the road grade near the wall about five feet fall to the hundred until we came to the eastern gate just north of the Temple Area. Outside of this gate tradition says St. Stephen was stoned. There are two graves just outside the gate and perhaps his remains lie in both of them. From the wall at this gate the best view is obtained of the cliff on the opposite side of the lower half of the Valley of Jehoshaphat, where are tombs variously ascribed to different individuals according to the religious belief of the namers. That accorded to Absalom has no contestant to the honor, for Jew, Moslem, Catholic, and Protestant alike cast a stone into a hole broken through one side of its roof, in abhorrence of a son rebelling against his father. The two others are ascribed to Jehoshaphat and Zechariah, or St. James. From this gate the land slopes rapidly to the south and east. We crossed the dry bed of the Kidron by an arched bridge of stone that my guide said was undoubtedly the one over which David had fled before the forces of Absalom, his son. Near here was a small spot walled in and containing several large and very aged olive trees which the Franciscan monks in charge had propped up with heaps of stones and cared for as the ones under which Christ and his loyal disciples sat waiting for the traitor to appear and betray him. The eastern gate of the city and the road from it was in sight from this point and possibly these trees or others near by were the ones under which they sat. Close to this spot my Protestant guide, whom I found to be the Prussian vice-consul here, showed me a tree near the path by which we climbed the Mount, that he had no doubt was here in John the Baptist's time. It was very aged in appearance near the ground, but aloft it was still green and thrifty. At intervals I would stop to get a view of the city, but my guide seemed anxious to have me reach higher ground before looking. At the summit was the little Chapel of the Ascension with its "footprint left by our Savior on his ascent for the last time." We had passed many honey-combed ledges early this morning and did not care to spend time to look at this. The whole mountain was sacred as the favorite resort of our Lord through all his ministry. After going a few steps beyond the crown of the mount my guide bid me look. Who could gaze unmoved. Beyond a stretch of hills the eye rested upon what appeared an immense cauldron of molten lead that though only about fifteen or twenty miles distant was over 3900 feet beneath us. There lay the glistening grave of unrepentant cities, buried more than 1300 feet beneath the ocean's level. There too lay Jordan's silver ribbon in a waving course through its valley to the bitter Sea of Salt, whose precipitous shores looked as if the crust of the earth had suddenly dropped out. There were the Mountains of Moab beyond the sea, grimly desolate. The little village of Bethany was just around the point of the hill below us; Jericho on the other side of that hill to the east, with the Fords of the Jordan not far from it; far to the southeast Mt. Hor, the lonely burial place of Aaron, raised its dim blue head far above all intervening or surrounding peaks; and to the south of us, just hidden on the other side of the hill only eight miles distant, was our sacred Bethlehem. I gazed silently at the different objects as he pointed them out, but had to turn away to hide the emotions that welled up at sight of all these places spoken of in the Book of Books. Here we stood among tombstones of Hebrews of a former age upon the bare summit of Olivet and conversed upon the incidents called to mind by places pointed out to me. A community of feeling and thought, despite the difference in our positions, made us feel like old friends. On our return descent I was made happy by the receipt of sprigs of olive from Olivet for my wife and children, cut by Prussia's Representative, Fane' Geran, as souvenirs of our visit together. On the way down we had a fine view of the city from a point a little higher than the city wall, that might well might have been in the mind of our Savior (though then three days' walk

distant) when he uttered those sorrowing words recorded in
Luke, 13 : 34 :—"O, Jerusalem, Jerusalem, which killest the
prophets and stonest them that are sent unto thee ; how often
would I have gathered thy children together as a hen doth
gather her brood under her wings, *and ye would not.*" From
this point Jerusalem is still beautiful even in its imitation of
its former self. What must have been the pride of the Jew
as he stood upon this western slope of Olivet and looked
across the deep chasm of Jehoshaphat to the Temple and
many palaces overtopping the walls of the city, which were
of themselves a wonder. Some idea can be formed of these
walls from an outline of them ascertained by sheer digging :

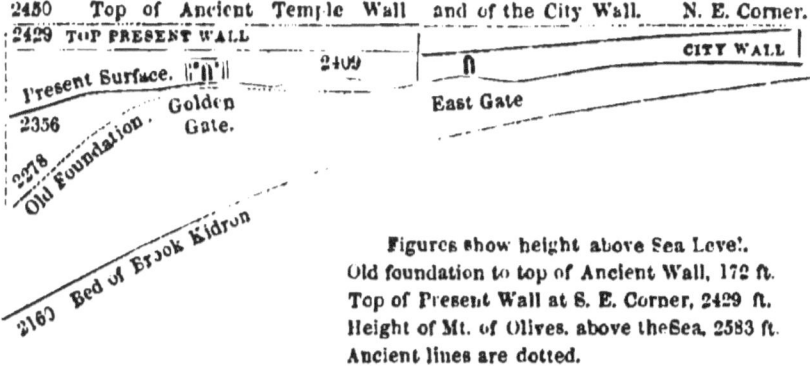

Figures show height above Sea Level.
Old foundation to top of Ancient Wall, 172 ft.
Top of Present Wall at S. E. Corner, 2429 ft.
Height of Mt. of Olives. above the Sea, 2583 ft.
Ancient lines are dotted.

Elevation of Ancient and Modern Eastern Wall above Sea Level.

Within the half-mile opposite the Eastern wall of the city
the Kidron has a fall of over 150 feet, and in the next half-
mile to its junction with the Gihon near En Rogel, or Joab's
well, it has an additional fall of nearly 350 feet. This long
face of wall was from 25 to 30 feet high at the northeast
angle. The present wall slopes 21 feet to the northeast angle of the Temple wall, from which point its top is level to
the southeast angle, where it has a height of 2429 feet, above
sea level, and a height from the present surface of 73 feet.
The old Temple wall was 21 feet higher, and its foundations

at the southeast angle are buried by the debris of its overthrow for 78 feet, giving its former height as 172 feet. The
Golden Gate is walled up, (Ez. 44 : 1, 2.) It is 2389 feet
above the sea, nearly on the level of the ancient Outer Court,
which was 2409 feet, while the Court of Gentiles was 2419
feet and the Court Israel was 2429 feet above the sea. The
highest figures given to parts of the Temple Area by Engineers surveying the ground was 2437 feet above sea-level.
As that was at the base of the Temple itself, and the Eastern wall was but 13 feet higher, the whole grand front of the
Temple was plainly visible from the Mount of Olives, which
was 133 feet higher, with an air-line distance of a-half-mile.
The most conspicuous object now to be seen is the octagonal
Mosque of Omar, built upon the site of Solomon's Temple.
We passed the miserable village of Siloam perched upon the
verge of the precipice overhanging Tophet. as that part of
Jehoshaphat is called, and crossing the Kidron bed climbed
to a tunnel part way up the steep hillside south of the Temple wall. Entering the tunnel we descended some thirty
steps cut in the rock to a pool of water. Coming from the
fierce glare of the sun I was glad to take the offered hands
of some Arab boys to lead me down to the brink. I found
an oblong tank cut in the rock about 6x15 feet in size partly
filled with slightly brackish water. We watched for its returning flow which occurred in a few minutes, showing that it
comes from its source through a syphon. The Catholics call
it the "Pool of The Virgin," which of course could not have
been its name at the time of Christ. My Protestant guide
thought it to be the fountain of the Pool Bethesda, which he
supposed was the one now called the Pool of Siloam, though
there was great uncertainty as to the true location of the Pool
Bethesda. It is 850 feet south of the southern Temple Area
wall. The water flowed away by a subterranean channel

cut in the rock 1100 feet long through the hill or spur called
Ophel, south of the Temple, and emerges as the Fountain
of Siloam at the southwestern face of the spur near its point.
From this small tank cut in the rock it flows into a larger
reservoir, 53 feet long, 18 feet wide at the top, and 19 feet
deep. The lower end is a vertical wall, but the other sides
are reduced in width by steps or terraces having drops of
about four feet, with quite narrow walks at the foot of the
drops around the three sides cut in the rock. This reservoir
is variously called the Pool of Siloam, King's Pool, and Old
Pool. My guide thought it might be the Pool Bethesda, as,
coming from an intermittent source it would also intermit.
(He probably reasoned that being the lower and larger of the
series it would be the only one in which bathing would be
allowed, the upper ones being reserved for drinking. For
the same sanitary reason the reservoir northeast of the Temple close to the East, or St. Stephen's Gate, called Birket
Israel by the Arabs, and Pool of Bethesda by Catholics, can
hardly be the true Pool of Bethesda. The Pool of the Virgin and the Fountain of Siloam are each too small for any
number of persons to find room for waiting about them.) A
hole near the bottom of the vertical wall lets the water out,
and probably once had a gate to control the outflow to use
it for irrigation. The pool was nearly empty and as my
guide pointed to the green and slimy surface he said, "But
the angel has ceased to trouble its waters." Not far from
here, at the junction of the Kidron and Gihon or Hinnom,
(Gehenna, as he called it,) we passed a well 125 feet deep,
called by the Arabs, Joab's Well. It is otherwise called
En Rogel, and Nehemiah's Well. It is walled up with hewn
stone in a square shaft, one side extending up above ground
and overhanging the well. Standing about and waiting their
turn to draw water was a motley crowd watering their camels

and washing clothes.   From this point the city appeared to
be built upon the edge of a cliff, with a deep gully in its face
near its eastern side, and from the western part a great land-
slide had nearly filled the gully, with a sloping mass of loose
rubbish.   The Tyropean Valley was originally a very deep
gulch passing close to the southwest corner of the wall of
the Temple and I was told that it was filled with 100 feet of
rubbish, and there were signs of there having been a bridge
with spans 150 feet in height crossing this gulch from the
Temple to Mount Zion.   On climbing up the steep slope of

Gihon Lower Pool.

MOUNT ZION.   From the Southwest.

Mount Zion we found the foothold very precarious.   We
slid back at nearly every step in the loose rubbish of the city
wreckage that still slipped freely down the slope more than
three centuries after it had been dumped here out of the way
of the re-builders.   A shaft sunk forty feet had not reached
bottom and was found too dangerous work to be continued.
On Mt. Zion is a large square building called David's Palace

that may be upon the site of the Palace of David. To the
west of it are the European and American cemeteries. The
present city wall does not take in Mount Zion. On entering
the city by the South or Zion gate I was shown the leper's
quarter, a cluster of low stone and concrete huts not
over ten feet square, with a small dome in the center of
the roof for standing room, and a door so low that
they must stoop to enter the hut. There was no sign of a
window or opening other than the door. The lepers were
seated upon the ground against their houses and about the
gate plying their trade of begging. Here we parted after

GEHENNA. and THE WESTERN WALL.

exchangimg addresses and good wishes, he advising me to
follow the wall on the outside on my way to the photographer's, as I would then have made a complete circuit of the
city wall. The view of the Western Wall of Jerusalem was
taken from the southwest, beyond the lower part of Gihon,
where it merges into Hinnom. It looks as if at different

times it had been used as a quarry for stones for building
the walls of the city.   I judged that the widest excavation,
if an excavation, was about fifty yards in width and some
twenty yards deep.   The Jaffa Gate is at the inner angle
at about the middle of this wall, and the road to Joppa runs
close to the farther half of the wall shown for nearly all its
length.   I was greatly disappointed at the photographer's
to find that though the man had a large view of the city in
four sections, each ten inches wide, taken from the Mount of
Olives, I could not have it because to-day was the Sabbath.
I was forced to return to the hotel to a very late dinner of
boiled rice and boiled mutton.   The boys had engaged an
Arab guide to show them the sacred sites and wonders of the
city.   While with him we were shown in David's Palace the
"Room in which Christ ate His Last Supper!"   It was also
"King David's Throne Room!"   "King David's Tomb is
beneath us!"   (Down cellar.)   Some of the boys wanted
to see it, but a guard with drawn scimetar stood on the first
step and they found that only the Faithful were allowed to
go.   At the Church of St. James he showed us the "Stone
upon which John the Baptist was beheaded!"   I said that I
saw the same stone at St. Mark's Church at Venice and I
thought it exceedingly miraculous that it should be in both
places at once.   He was somewhat surprised at it, but said
this was surely the true stone.   "No, they had not found the
ax, yet," he responded to my query.   One of my Catholic
shipmates came to his rescue by saying, "'This must be the
true stone anyhow—Don't you see the blood streaks?"   Of
course I admitted that both were true stones, and peace was
restored.   This stone was in a glass case just high enough
for the lips of devotees to meet it easily, and as the glass in
front had been conveniently broken the marks of the ax had
become effaced by kisses of worshipers.   At any rate there

was a smooth spot hollowed into that part of the rock. He took us around to a narrow court alike interesting to the Jew or Gentile, though the interest of the Jew is one of sadness. It is called "The Jew's Wailing Place." They gather here

THE JEW'S WAILING-PLACE.

on their sacred days by some huge stones twenty-seven feet long by nine feet high, at the base of the western wall of the Temple Area, the nearest they are ever allowed to approach their Holy of Holies. They have good reason to believe these stones form a part of the substructure of their ancient western wall, and they meet to weep and wail by them, taking up the lamentation of Jeremiah, (Lamentations, 5 : 2, 20.) praying for the coming of the Messiah, witnesses of God's Word being fulfilled in them. It was a sad sight. Their inheritance was held by the children of the bond-woman and they were thrust out from the house of their fathers. The entrance to the court was abreast of the wall between the Court of Gentiles and the Court of Israel at the southwest corner of that court, and the outer wall of the Court of Gentiles would cut it in two, he told me. The cut shows quite distinctly the line of demolition and renewal of the wall. He took the Catholics of our crowd into the Church of the Holy Sepulcher. I did not care to see the "Rock riven by the Earthquake !," "The Pillar to which Christ was bound when scourged !" "The stone upon which he sat when crowned with thorns !" "The Tomb !" (in the cellar,) or "Mount Calvary !" (in one of the attics.) They saw all these within the walls of that church and heard them announced in tones that challenged dispute, therefore they were there. I spent a couple of dollars in crosses of pearl and of olive which of course were claimed to be bits from the true cross, (what a big one it must have been unless it has been growing ever since.) These with the bits of flinty limestone from Mount Zion and chalky limestone from the Mount of Olives, also twigs of olive from Gethsemane and Olivet made about the sum of the souvenirs of my visit to Jerusalem. The son of our landlord told me that he had ridden to Joppa in three hours, which I set down as the most miraculous miracle yet recorded in this miraculous place. I was tired of the great number of miraculous nothings shown us. I could believe that cleansing this city of the horrible filth that fills it would be a miracle worthy of record, but such a thing does not seem to be given a thought. At 7 P. M. I had slipped a franc into the hand of the guide for the use of his horse on the return trip and with Master-at-arms Collins was sent ahead to the Jaffa gate with the complaint of some poor fellow ringing in my ears that he had a horse when he came up. We found the main gate closed for the night and had to wait for the guide to pass us through the side gate. We did not wait to see how the mules with pack saddles got through the needle but pushed on. I got several good naps in the saddle during the night, a trick of my crossing the Plains. It was broad daylight when our horses stopped at Ramleh for their breakfast as well as ours. A short distance out of Joppa we met a Dr. Smith, one of a company of emigrants from the United States lately arrived to settle in Palestine. He was having trouble with a camel driver who could not or would not understand him. The camel was loaded with a part of some machine to go out to the company's reservation. We stopped with our countryman until our guide came up.* He straightened things out very quickly. I sought the photographer at the camp of the emigrants on the beach and persuaded him to return to town with me for his set of views of places in Palestine. This made me too late to go off in the boat with the others. Quartermaster Bassett remained to look me up and we went aboard in a shore boat. On my reaching the ship's deck I began to feel so faint from my continued action for fifty-seven hours that I could hardly answer Mr. Allyn's question of how I liked Jerusalem. He was satisfied that I was sober and let me go forward. I lay on the berth deck all that afternoon and slept. Our party had returned clean and sober and another party of twenty-seven were started, with time extended to Thursday.

Tuesday, Oct. 2, 1866. The wind rose at sundown and the mountains are hidden by clouds. The ship rolls heavily.

---

* After many troublesome experiences from the ill will of the natives and lack of knowledge of climatic conditions required for successful farming here, this company broke up and most of them were sent home by our Consul.

Thursday, Oct. 4, 1866. The liberty men all returned early, and the officers were not far behind. They were all enthusiastic over their trip in spite of the rain and mud of the latter part of the time. Our officers had telegraphed to Constantinople for a firman permitting our party to visit the Mosque of Omar. They got the benefit of the permit. I give a photographic print of it on the page opposite. They also visited Bethlehem and saw the spot where The Babe was born, marked by a silver star let into a block of white marble within a small chapel built over the spot. From the

BETHLEHEM.

descriptions they gave of what they saw I judge they were regaled with the same kind of miraculous nothings that we saw and heard while with the Arab guide at Jerusalem. The cut shows the remains of old terraces that were doubtless cultivated at the time of Christ. At the left is a convent, but whether Greek or Latin they did not know. Catholics and Protestants among us agreed that these monks would have rendered far more acceptable service to God and their fellow-men had they made these terraces blossom with roses

Mosque of Omar.

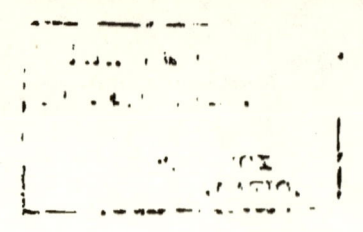

and bear fruits that would have relieved the locality of its
desolate barrenness instead of leading their present lazy life.
At 11 A. M. we got up steam and left for Alexandria.

Saturday, Oct. 6, 1866. We came to anchor at Alexandria. I find that my trip has exhausted me so greatly that
I am hardly able to keep about my work.

Thursday, Oct. 11. Last night Quartermaster Bassett
came to my hammock to tell me I was to be promoted to
Surgeon's Steward unless the present incumbent came off
from overstayed liberty this forenoon. I got the Stewards
and boat's crews to hunt him up and tell him he would be
disrated unless he came off at once. They found him and
brought him off in the market boat before breakfast. The
promotion would have kept me in the ship long after my term
of service had expired, and disrating for cause would have
been a permanent injury to him.

Saturday, Oct. 13. We sailed for Tripoli in the evening.

Friday, Oct. 19. We anchored outside of Tripoli late in
the afternoon of yesterday, and to-day we came inside and
hoisted the yellow flag for four days of quarantine.

Thursday, Oct. 25. We went to sea at 10 A. M. bound
for Malta.

Friday, Oct. 26. We arrived at Malta at noon and were
ordered to make fast to moorings off the Navy Hospital for
fourteen days quarantine. An English mail steamer direct
from Alexandria coming in at the same time was allowed to
enter without quarantine. The Commodore objected, and
threatened to go to sea tomorrow if this discrimination was
persisted in. They offered to allow boats to come alongside
to trade, but he refused to have any communication with the
people of Malta under such circumstances.

Saturday, Oct. 27. We went to sea at 1 P. M. The
people of Malta lose the profits on from $2000 to $3000 of

trade on account of general liberty that was to be given. I went to the doctor this morning for a sore throat that had troubled me ever since my trip to Jerusalem. He found an ulcer on one of the tonsils. I had to give up work entirely.

Sunday, Oct. 28, 1866. I was very feverish this morning. During inspection after quarters, while standing in line with the other sick waiting for the Commodore to come down to inspect the sick bay, I began to feel very faint and would have fallen had not Dr. Hyde caught me and held me up. The Commodore was just coming down the ladder, but Dr. Gunnell met him and pressed him back with the remark that there was no serious illness on board, only Stuart was having a bilious turn, to which he is subject. The Commodore took the hint and backed out. They evidently could not account for my utter collapse and did not want the Commodore to be obliged to report any suspicious illness at the next port. I had my hammock at once and Dr. Gunnell came to feel my pulse several times during the day as I lay dozing. The Surgeon's Steward came to me and confessed that he had made a great mistake in giving me podophyllin with other ingredients in powder instead of in more than one dose in the form of pills. Though rather heroic his dosing was effective in removing my feverish symptoms. He begged me not to report him. I set his mind at rest on that score, for he had hardly been himself since his spree at Alexandria..

Monday, Oct. 29. We arrived at Tunis after breakfast. Dr. Gunnell was down to see me early this morning and he appeared greatly pleased to find that I had lashed up my own hammock and had it stowed in the nettings. It enabled him to report a clean bill to the Health Officer, and no quarantine was required of us.

Monday, Nov. 5. I came off the sick list to-day, though still weak. We left Tunis for Gibraltar Thursday, and are running in sight of the Spanish coast. Our tea was spoiled at supper through some derangement in the condenser that caused it to give out brackish water. There was some sputtering, considerable laughter, and very little tea drank. I asked the boys what they thought we did before the Mexican war when we had no tea and sugar ration in the navy. They gave it up. I told them we "touched the pen" for tea and sugar every three months, and it came out of our wages. They wanted to know how we came to have it now. I told them it was given us in place of part of our old grog ration. After supper the scuttlebutt was soon emptied. It was filled again with the brackish water just from the condenser. It made the men even more thirsty. They thought I must have some cold coffee in my mess chest as I did not haunt the scuttlebutt. I reminded them that I was on the sick list at breakfast and no coffee had been saved, then showed them the silver franc that I had been sucking to overcome thirst, a plainsman's trick on a long, waterless drive. At first they accepted the brackishness as a joke and spat it out with a grimmace,—then a growl,—and finished by blasting it in most approved man-o'-war's-man's style until the condenser gave out pure water. Then we *drank!*

Tuesday, Nov., 6, 1866. Approaching "The Rock" this forenoon we got a view of its eastern face and could also see the western face of Ceuta, on the African coast, fifteen miles distant. We could not see the strata at Ceuta distinctly, but it is said to coincide so closely with the eastern cliff of The Rock as to lead to the belief that they were separated by some great convulsion of nature, giving rise to the name "Pillars of Hercules." At the foot of the cliff of The Rock is the little Spanish fishing village of Catalan, lying along an extremely narrow beach, with buildings crowding each other close up to the overhanging cliff and down to a line of beach

surf-washed during easterly storms.   Fishing boats were
drawn up on the sandy beach close to the houses.   As one
of our Hibernian shipmates put it, "The whole products of
the land must come from the sea."   As we rounded the south
point of The Rock, where it was possible to effect a landing
under the most favorable circumstances we saw fortifications
close to the bluff shore line.   At the extreme south point a
lighthouse stood upon a slightly overhanging low bluff, with
barrack buildings and a smooth sloping parade ground near,
the smoothest and about the nearest level spot on The Rock.
This is Europa Point.   The shore here trends to the north,
and we skirted the entrance points of the little Rosia Bay,
its steep shores lined with fortified walls.   We got sight of
more powerful works as we neared the entrance to the Bay of
Gibraltar, where the shores are less steep.   We anchored at
noon in the bay and went into quarantine.

Wednesday, Nov. 7, 1866.   We steamed alongside a coal
hulk and took on 230 tons of coal.   An Italian steamer was
taking coal from the other side.   She was loaded with emigrants bound to The Platte.

Friday, Nov. 9.   We went out of quarantine at 8 A. M.
and trimmed ship in honor of the Prince of Wales' birthday.

Saturday, Nov. 10.   We sailed for Lisbon at 4 P. M.

Monday, Nov. 12.   We moored at Lisbon without any
quarantine being required.   I got six letters from home, the
latest being seven months old.   Their numbers show that
three are missing.

Sunday, Nov. 25.   The *Colorado* came in this afternoon.
She brought me a letter dated Nov 17, 1865, one year and
eight days old, forwarded from the receiving ship *Princeton.*

Tuesday, Nov. 27.   I have been troubled with frequent
bilious spells since my visit to Jerusalem.   While furling
topsails to-day I became suddenly dizzy and lost my hold,

so completely that I would have fallen had not young Parker given my elbow a cant over the yard that enabled me to get a grip. Capt.-o'-the-top Woods reported it to Mr. Allyn, and I am not to go aloft again while in the ship.

Friday, Nov. 30, 1866. I was transferred to the Storeship *Ino,* homeward bound. The Surgeons had reported my condition to the Commodore and he to the Admiral. Mr. Allyn had opposed my being sent home until Woods' report of my dizziness while aloft. He had said that I was "as useful to him as any seaman in the ship, for he could put me anywhere." He now agreed with them in helping me off and at the same time took care to secure a seaman in my place. In transferring me he said it was by the Admiral's order. I signed accounts with my second installment of bounty and $62.63 of wages due me.

Tuesday, Dec. 4. The ship was cleared of cargo yesterday, and we have been stowing heavy shot from the *Stonewall* for ballast, to-day. My old messmates, Norwood and Webster came aboard this afternoon, being transferred on account of having but a short time to serve. All of the invalids of the fleet were also sent on board.

Wednesday, Dec. 5. The *Miantonomah, Augusta,* and *Frolic* went to sea at 4 P. M.

Thursday, Dec. 6. The *Colorado* and *Ticonderoga* went to sea at 7 A. M.

Saturday, Dec. 8. We took in coal for cabin and wardroom fires on the coast. In the afternoon I was sent in a boat down the river to Belem for sand for scrubbing decks. We landed at the ruins of the old fortifications destroyed by the great earthquake of 1755. We could trace the line of the walls for a long distance along the river's bank. These Catholic countries seem to desert localities where the "Visitation of God" has been of destructive effect. Here as was seen by me when a boy in the navy at Callao, Peru, the walls remain nearly buried in sand just as left by the shock. At Callao there were some rooms only partially buried that we could enter. (Vol. I, pp. 19-20.) We had no time to examine these ruins, but the general appearance of this bank to the sandy point of old Callao was as of two peas from the same pod. While on liberty in the city of Lisbon I saw a ruined church whose roof was gone and grass was growing upon the top of its walls. A sentry was at one corner of its walls close to the street, where a portion at the ground had been thrown out, leaving a cracked and overhanging wall of concrete eight feet thick. A sentry has stood there for over a century through rain and shine by day and by night instead of demolishing or repairing the building. On our way down stream we had kept to the middle of the current, but were glad to hug the shore upon our return with our loaded boat in order to avoid that same swift current as much as we possibly could. We passed close to the beautiful church at Belem, one of the few buildings not demolished at that "*tremblor granda*," also the fine tower of Belem Castle, from whose highly ornamental walls a shot was thrown just over the head of the *Niagara's* seaman in the waist-boat of that ship who was heaving the lead when chasing the Rebel ram *Stonewall* out of Lisbon.

Tuesday, Dec. 11. The Queen of Spain arrived at sunset in a Portugese man-o'-war and received a general salute. The show was fine, and those who saw both were reminded of the reception of Victor Emanuel's daughter when she came to marry the King of Portugal. The flashes of the guns in salute showed with fine effect against the dark background of mist to seaward and lighted up the King's Palace, abreast of which they lay.

Wednesday, Dec. 12. We got under weigh at 11 A. M.

with a fair wind and favorable tide to sail down the Tagus,
bound for Boston. The breeze died away as we reached the
mouth of the river and the tide turning we drifted back two
miles and had to anchor.

Thursday, Dec. 13, 1866. At noon we were safely outside the bar at the mouth of the Tagus. One of our officers
from the *Ticonderoga* invalided home is Mr. Moore, of the
Engineers, a son of my old captain on the *Apprentice*. He
reported to our Executive, Mr. Mallard, that I had been sent
home on account of liability to dizziness during frequent
bilious attacks that had troubled me lately, and that I had
nearly fallen from aloft a few days ago. I was told not to
go aloft hereafter, and they would find work for me on deck.

Tuesday, Dec. 18. I was sent to cook for the petty officers mess yesterday. To-day they filled themselves with a
big baked apple pie that I made for their supper, and voted
it "bully." The apples, though fresh and good, had accumulated in the mess chest waiting for some one to come that
could make use of them.

Wednesday, Dec. 19. Yesterday's fresh breeze that was
setting us along finely on our course has increased so that
we were under topsails all last night. All hands were called
at 5 A. M. to reef topsails. We found that a maintopsail
sheet had parted, and the watch were vainly trying to secure
the flapping sail. The Carpenter's Mate had a shoulder put
out of joint by the thrashing of the sail before it was brought
under control.

Thursday, Dec. 20. The Captain's Cook blew up his
coffee pot this morning and got badly scalded. An English
steamer ran down under our stern just at noon to ask our
latitude and longitude. We gave them Lat. 32 ° 20′ N.,
Long. 30 ° 22′ W. She was from Pernambuco, bound for
Lisbon, and asked for our name. We gave *Ino* for answer.

After a moment's hesitation her captain shouted "I suppose you do, but *I* would like to know, that I may report speaking with you." Capt. Garfield responded, "We spell the name *I-N-O,—Ino.*" "*Oh!*" came back as an echo, and they forged ahead and turned upon their course. At 8 P. M. we passed a brig from Oporto for Rio.

Tuesday, Dec. 25, 1866. Gideon's band is not quite so noisieal under the topgallant forecastle, for its numbers were sadly depleted by slaughter yesterday. By the generosity of Captain Garfield and our wardroom officers we dined on sea pie made in the coppers with geese and ducks that have had the run of that deck. Their leader is still alive and all last night strove to make up by alertness and the force of his clarion notes for all losses sustained.

Thursday, Dec. 27. This noon we were in Lat. 31° 08' N., Long. 34° 13' W., with the ship rolling along at the rate of eight knots, everything lashed securely and we all elated at the prospect of reaching the Bermudas within two weeks.

Sunday, Dec. 30. We are over half way to Bermuda, being in Lat. 31° 11' N., Long. 43° 21' W. We have on board 27 days rations of water.

Tuesday, Jan. 1, 1867. The course was changed last night to direct for Boston. This morning I caught a piece of seaweed on the logline while hauling it in, showing that we are getting into the influence of the Gulf Stream. The bit of weed was sent into the cabin, and about every person in the ship came on deck to look at the sea from whence the welcome visitor came. We will probably be just as glad to be well out of this stream. We shifted topsails yesterday, bending our new winter sails ready for the rough weather we must expect soon. We are 1400 miles from Boston.

Friday, Jan. 4. A northwest gale commenced yesterday.

This noon we had reached Lat. 34 ° 20′ N., Long. 50 ° 59′ W., 1000 miles from Boston, but we are unable to lay our course and we may have a tedious passage yet unless the wind changes.

Saturday, Jan. 5, 1867. At midnight last night we were reeling off eight knots with a fair wind, making all hands feel jolly over our prospects. Our watch was about to be relieved when a heavy squall came on, setting all hands to furling and reefing for two hours before we could go below. When we came on watch again at four o'clock it was blowing with great force and had just taken our new foretopmast-staysail clear out of the bolt-ropes, and a fierce squall with thunder and lightning was raging. It was pitch dark except when the flashes revealed the flying scud. The hatches were battened down and all hands remained on deck. A short exposure to the pelting rain sent the water in streams down our necks, even filling our boots. The storm raged with great fury until noon, when it subsided rapidly. It left us with the ship rolling heavily and going only 3 1-2 knots toward the west at 7 P. M. Among the *Stonewall's* sails we found a staysail that replaced our lost one.

Sunday, Jan. 6. We have fair weather again, with a leading breeze. Our longitude this noon was 53 ° 20′ and at 8 P. M. we were only 900 miles from Boston, plowing merrily along at the rate of 12 1-2 knots.

Wednesday, Jan. 9. A heavy squall came up soon after 8 P. M., Sunday, and we were soon under close reefed fore and main topsails, steering north. To-day we were forced to furl the foretopsail and lie to. At 1 P. M. a barque was discovered through the scud close aboard and bearing down upon us under bare poles. We had to keep away to prevent a collision. She soon after came round and lay to, heading with us. At noon the barometer stood at 28.98, but at 7 P.

M. it had stood for an hour at 29.32.   At noon the boys were
glad to crawl up to the open mess chest and get a slice of
half-boiled pork and some hardbread.   The ship has tumbled
about so that the galley cooks have been unable to cook the
officers' dinner.   At breakfast we had rather exciting times.
The ship was decidedly lively in her motions.   I did not try
to spread any mess cloth, but wedged the coffee and skouse
kettles into the chest and each man made his way up to me
where I had lashed myself to be able to use both hands, and
I filled for him a pot of coffee and a pan of skouse.   An
unusually lively jump of the ship would take a man off his
feet and he would land on top of the mess to leeward, or a
vicious roll would send everybody and everything not lashed
or braced sliding to leeward in a heap together, laughing or
cursing according to their experiences or dispositions.   We
were only four day's sail to Boston three days ago, but we
have lost 100 miles since then.

Friday, Jan. 11.   Yesterday we were able to set a little
sail and were recovering some of the loss, when the gale set
in with its old vigor and we were reduced to close reefed
fore and main topsails.   To-day we are again plunging our
bows into the seas with all the sail the ship can bear, 800
miles from our port at noon and going our course.

Saturday, Jan. 12.   We have been under close reefed
topsails since January 4th except for a few hours.   To-day
the wind shifted more to the northward and brought with it
frequent squalls of rain and hail.   At noon we were in Lat.
37 ° 23′ N. Long. 57 ° W., 620 miles from our port, but
with little prospect of reaching it for some time yet.

Monday, Jan. 14.   One of the Captain's servants died
last night and was buried to-day.   He was a mulatto named
James Culbertson, from Philadelphia.

Tuesday, Jan. 15.   The reefs were shaken out of the

topsails and topgallantsails set. All battens were removed from the hatches for the first time in ten days. We were put upon short allowance of water to-day. It was calm in the afternoon, but a stiff breeze sprung up in the evening that sent us along on our course finely.

Wednesday, Jan. 16, 1867. At 10 o'clock last night all hands were called to shorten sail to close-reefed fore and main topsails again, the ship heading her course till midnight, when we had to lie-to under a close-reefed maintopsail, the barometer falling to 28.92. To-day is a little less stormy, we setting the foretopsail close-reefed at 3 P. M.

Thursday, Jan. 17. To-day we have a fair wind that is not too strong for carrying sail, so we are doing something toward getting home. The main topgallant yard has to be fished before we can set that sail. At noon we were in Lat. 37 ° 03′ N. Long. 59 ° 05′ W., having gained twenty miles in the past five days.

Friday, Jan. 18. A gale set in last night that has set us back into the Gulf Stream.

Saturday, Jan. 19. We have been going north all day. The breeze calmed down in the afternoon so that the sails flapped against the masts as we went to supper at 4 o'clock. A little before 5 o'clock the barometer began to drop rapidly. All hands were called to shorten sail in tones that meant an urgency. We rushed on deck and found the ship was being encircled by a dense bank of black clouds, rising to nearly overhead, their edges in rapid motion. We were in the center of a circle of calm with only the low waves from the commotion about us reaching the ship. (See frontispiece.) The yards were braced to receive the wind from any quarter, and the men lay aloft promptly to furl and reef. Very few orders were given by the officers and those were in low tones. The hatches were closed and battened down. Life-lines were stretched along the deck and every precaution taken to meet—we knew not what. The clouds did not meet overhead. There was something weird in the hushed calm about our ship with the ripple of the waves against the side plainly heard as if at anchor, and our masts pointing into the bit of clear sky, while great commotion was evidently all about us. (The half-tone frontispiece is from a photograph of my crayon copy of a pencil sketch I had taken that evening. The photograph was fading.) The squall passed around us and at six o'clock gave us a breeze that enabled us to lay our course. It has been very cold all day with occasional hail. Our position at noon was Lat. 40 ° 30′ N. Long. 61 ° 05′ W., 420 miles from Cape Cod, or 470 from Boston.

Sunday, Jan. 20, 1867. A stiff breeze is pushing us along to the westward and southward. We had a slight fall of snow during the morning watch, and had hail, rain, and reefing of topsails during the day.

Monday, Jan. 21. A warm southeast wind sprung up this morning. At 9 A. M. we were 240 miles from George's Banks, and going on our course at 12 knots. A heavy rain squall set us to furling and reefing, but it did no worse than to wet us through. We caught two days' rations of fresh water in the awnings, putting us upon full rations again.

Tuesday, Jan. 22. Our breeze of yesterday left us in the mid watch with a heavy squall of wind and rain. We had to shorten sail for it. At noon we were in Lat. 40 ° 35′ N. Long. 64 ° 49′ W.

Wednesday, Jan. 23. We reached soundings at 65 fathoms on George's Banks at 4 A. M., 90 miles from Cape Cod. This evening we passed a large vessel with main and mizzen masts gone, and the men were still at work clearing the wreck. Some miles astern we had passed some floating wreckage and had previously passed an abandoned ship, the foremast alone standing, its yard swaying and a few shreds of canvas and bolt-rope whipping in the wind. It was very heavy weather all night, but the gale coming from the east we made good progress. We got up chain and shackled to the anchors.

Saturday, Jan. 26, 1867. We made Cape Cod Light at nine o'clock last night. At daylight to-day we took a pilot and beat in to the entrance of Boston harbor. Two tugs made fast to us at 2. P. M., and we ate supper at anchor off Charlestown Navy Yard. The pilot told us that over 140 vessels had been lost or dismasted in the gales of the past fortnight and that the *Ino* was the first sailing vessel to arrive at Boston since Christmas.

Tuesday, Apr. 2. We were all transferred to the *Ohio*, when the *Ino* went out of commission, and in order to avoid being drafted to go to the World's Fair in the *Franklin* I was advised by Lieut. Sumner to apply for my discharge on account of my deafness. An examinatin was ordered, and to-day the order for my discharge came. Being discharged upon my own application I have to forfeit my final bounty of $100. I received the $100 second installment of bounty due fourteen months ago and $62.02 of pay due, of which 71 cents was prize money for two captured blockade runners during January, 1865. At supper time I was at home in Dracut, Mass., with my wife and children. An account of other parts of my life is given in my book on THE DUNCAN STUART FAMILY IN AMERICA. I am now a FREE MAN, and having roamed to satiety, am fully determined to make this

THE END OF

MY ROVING LIFE.

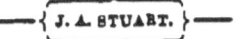